I0640037

Take a journey into the unknown:

"Monique said her *guardian* has reached out, the thing's got to go, it's him or me. If the devil wins this fight, I'll carry it inside me the rest of my borne days, but hell or high-water Willem, the girl will be free of it tonight."

"I don't understand?"

Binford's steel-gray eyes burn into mine. "I ain't no damn priest, I'm a soldier, this here's the only way I know how to do this sort of thing."

"Do what?"

"Hit the devil with all I got, when it ain't ready, put this here knife into it. Kill it." He withdraws the long silver blade from its sheath glinting under the kerosene lamplight. It's razor-sharp and carries strange meandering inscriptions forged into the metal.

"Kill…the demon?"

"*Pure-Silver* is this knife's name in Choctaw, it's a demon killer. It belonged to my pap and his pap a'fore him and is a'gonna kill this devil that's haunted this woman since she was a girl." Our conversation comes to an abrupt halt when we hear Morgan and Georgiana approach. "Quiet now, take the other side of Jerome."

I'm at complete odds to whether I'm about to take part in an exorcism or a murder.

-Excerpt from The Lower Passions

The Wicker Woman

c. M. E. Nyberg 2018

www.menyberg.com

The Wicker Woman published 2018
By M. E. Nyberg. All rights reserved.

No part of this book either text or illustration,
may be used or reproduced in any form without
prior permission of the author or publisher.

All names are fictitious. Any resemblance
to persons living or dead is purely coincidental.

Book design by Don Mangione

Cover photography by M. E. Nyberg

ISBN 13: 978-0-9970986-2-4
eISBN 13: 978-0-9970986-3-1

Registered with Library of Congress
Copyright #TXu-2-076-182
November 16, 2017

Other books by M E Nyberg

...

The Profound Art of Omens
The Man Who Would Be Coyote
The Wicker Woman

For Vance and Val

Table of Contents

~.~

Chapter *1*: *Girl on the ledge*

I've no idea where I am. I'm expecting the afterlife, those diaphanous realms of either angels or devils. This looks like the ceiling of a warehouse.

Night? Or the dreaded underworld; the dense lower plane of perpetual darkness? Music–*heavy metal*–is vibrating the air molecules around me. Where the hell? I recall being shot...shot in the head...*the Hollowman*. Fuck. If I'm dead, then this could be the lower realm Lucien spoke of, dark...and apparently very loud.

It's excruciating but I manage to sit-up, gather my thoughts. Like cold water in the face, I realize I'm in Morgan's warehouse; her apartment in NYC. But...how can I be here? No connection. Horror floods my memory...shot in the head at my flat in Soho, London, by the hideous man without eyes. My body actually convulses with the memory. But this isn't London this is New York.

Getting to my feet, like a walker on a wire, I wait for the vertigo to subside. The music is so incredibly loud it pounds on my eardrums, shaking my skull. The moment I switch off the stereo, the silence is so absolute it's like a vacuum pulling me in the opposite direction and I nearly blackout.

The apartment gazes back, listless, neglected. I sense its loneliness. I'm amazed by the sheer chaos of the place; beer and liquor bottles steep the tables that once possessed art and photography. There's an army of over-stuffed ashtrays, dozens of discarded packs of cigarettes.

—

I stare at the place; the place stares back. Is this actually Morgan's apartment, or a carefully designed doppelganger? Have I been shot down dead and this is an interim between worlds, another plane of existence?

There's a small antique mirror that hangs on the wall above her desk. It takes everything I possess to look. For some reason I'm surprised. Willem Furey, calmly gazing back from the other side of the glass. Nothing seems to have changed, no bullet hole in the head, no blood. I've also no money, credit card or identification, only the dark indigo suit I'm wearing, an older one from the rack in London I've no recollection putting on.

"Hello? Is anybody here?" The place is silent, only the sounds of the city pulsating outside. I go to the front of the apartment and rip back the large black curtain that hides the wall of glass overlooking the street, New York, people teeming about the sidewalks below, under a soft rainfall, cars honking as they press to get through.

Opening one of the panes, I *breathe in* New York. The smell instantly grounds me. No other city in the world smells like this one. New York? Morgan's apartment…how? A tension permeates the moment, as if the image might crack and shatter into a myriad of pieces.

The kitchen is in shambles. I know she's not been here since she left. *Since she left*…like another lifetime.

"Morgan? Is anybody here?" My voice sounds like gravel beneath leather soles. I then spy the front door left ajar and my anticipation races. However, the hallway outside proves lonelier than the warehouse. Perhaps they've stepped out? No, the elevator is sitting open, locked.

Closing the door, I study the vacant rooms. Absolute stillness. "What's going on?" I shout aloud as if the place itself could answer. It responds with an indifferent shrug, as if at odds with its state of neglect; mourning the loss of its beloved master.

Everywhere is chaos. There is no longer *the feel* I experienced earlier, the creativity and light. Now, the place seems on-edge, like a pet thrown into the street loses trust, its innocence.

Wandering the derelict rooms, I realize someone has been living here, their clothes and things strewn about helter-skelter. Morgan's bedroom is in ruin, the artwork and photography fallen or tilted oddly, clothing and junk everywhere, as if a cyclone had swept through. I notice the clothing and jewelry has a familiar look; leather pants, t-shirts advertising musical concerts and equipment, skull rings and crucifixes scattered like rice across the dresser...boots; Georgiana Snipes. I then find Babe, her bass guitar, on the floor next to an Ampeg speaker cabinet with the cone kicked-in.

"Georgiana?" I call as I pick up the bass and set *her* back upright against the amp. "Georgiana!"

After another fruitless search, I discover rainfall dripping from the ceiling in the very back of the apartment. Upon closer inspection, I see it's not coming from a leak in the roof but an open trap door at the top of a narrow metal ladder leading up into the night.

"Georgiana!" I call into the darkness, drops of rain finding my face but there's no answer, merely the hum of New York outside. Reluctantly, I pull myself to the roof.

When I emerge above the trapdoor jamb, my eyes lock on a lean black shadow standing atop the precipice of the building overlooking the street. The image is bizarre. At first, I'm not even certain it's a person. When I realize it is, I tighten my collar, extract myself from the portal and carefully weave my way across the rooftop to the girl on the ledge.

She looks taller than her normal six-foot frame, standing on the ledge, her normally wild black hair hanging straight from the rain. Yes, it's her, Georgiana Snipes, the songwriter for *Concrete and Steel*. She's oblivious of me, strangely transfixed upon the street below, her beaten leather jacket drenched; left open to the wind despite the whip of the rain. She stares into the space below as if into an abyss.

In the dim light, she looks like a shadow cast by an invisible person, standing on the very edge of the precipice, like an enormous ebony bird, about to set to flight.

"Georgiana…" It's as if she's been turned to stone. I repeat her name. She turns and looks at me with bicolored eyes–the blue iris oddly iridescent, the brown iris black as night-and glares at me like a wolf in the dark. I look over the edge of the building. Four stories straight down and my head spins. "What are you doing?" I inquire, the rain falling on our shoulders.

"*You*," she whispers like a drowning man gasping for breath. "How can you be here?" I don't have an answer to this question. How can I tell her I've no idea how I got to this place?

"I was in the neighborhood," I mumble.

She stares at me unrelentingly, her pupils like two shards of obsidian. "How?" she asks again, her voice cracking.

"Why are you on the roof?" I ask and her answer is long in coming. She glances at her boots, mere inches from the extreme edge of the building and something comes alive inside her.

"I live here. What are you doing here, Witchboy?"

"*Witchboy?*" I echo, total confusion; however, the question softens her mood.

"Sorry man. Tiny came up with that name for you, after your little speech at the club. It sort of stuck." My mind returns to the last time I saw her band perform at Klub Netherworld, a New York nightclub; the moment I told them about the changes happening in Morgan and her moving back to her familial home in New Orleans.

Thankfully, she retracts from the edge and pulls a cigarette from inside her jacket. She seems thinner, paler–if such a thing were possible-than the last time I saw her.

"How's it going?" The expression in her eyes concerns me. "What's wrong?"

"*Wrong?*" She laughs; a searing, scathing laugh. "Where do I start? Let's see, oh yeah, when I was born, then it sorta heads south from there."

"I thought things were looking up for you and the band?"

"You'da thought right?"

"Did you make it to Europe?"

"Oh yeah, we made it alright."

"What happened?"

"What didn't?"

She goes catatonic. I take the cigarette from her fingers, cup it in my fist against the rain. "Tell me about it?"

"What's to tell man, we fucked up."

"Who did what?" The question puts a strange expression on her face.

I study her, sitting on the very edge of the building like a gargoyle hunched against the rain, the lights of the city framing her in silhouette.

"Well, Bambi was too drunk to get through the performance at Shepard's Crossing...that didn't go over so well. And Tiny went on a binge in Belgium and disappeared for two days cancelling a gig there." She pulls another bent cigarette from her jacket and lights it, the glow from the butane coating her features in an ephemeral glow.

"So? You cancelled a couple gigs, that happens."

"It gets better."

"Oh?"

"Victoria gets stage-fright. It just comes on her sometimes, when she's high, which is most of the time. Sometimes we get through it...sometimes we don't. So, that happened, twice. Then I collapsed on stage in France...that's when Nyle pulled the tour. We got to sit around New York for awhile and think about it."

"You collapsed on stage?" The question ignites her.

"Sorry, is there an echo around here?"

"What's wrong?"

"Nothing's *wrong*, who says anything's *wrong*?" she snaps. "It's happened before. No big deal."

"Did you see a doctor about it?" She glares at me and returns to smoking in silence. "What about the US leg you guys were talking about, you're not doing it?"

"Oh, *that?* We start tomorrow."

"Really? That's great." Her expression says otherwise. "It's not?" She stares into the mist, the rain looking blood red under the neon lights. "What's happened?" I ask and she instantly grows fiery.

"You know what? You ask a lot of fucking questions Sherlock."

Her phone rings–a Sex Pistols tune; she curses at the name on the screen. "Yeah?! What's it to ya asshole?" she shouts. I've no choice but to eavesdrop on her conversation as the rain slowly begins to subside. "I'm still at Morgan's. I can't go back there, you ass. Why do you think Nyle?" she says acerbically, lighting another cigarette with the one she's already smoking. "Quit threatening me. Well it feels like it." She gazes up into the night, pain cutting into her face like a black and white intaglio print.

I drop the cigarette over the ledge watch as it seeks the shadows of the street below

"I'm just the lousy *bass player,* remember? You're as much to blame for that as her. Don't deny it. I'm through playing games with you and her. I know what the two of you are doing." She realizes I'm listening. "Change the subject. Yes, I'm ready. I said I'm ready, so I'm ready. Well I'm saying it big-shot I'm ready! Yeah, well, screw you." She's about to throw the phone into the street when something said catches her ear. "What did you say? When? You're saying we won't have video for the east coast shows? That's bullshit Nyle! Video was the one thing we had going right. Well get a new director, *mister rock and roll.*"

As they banter on and on, she begins looking me over in the weirdest manner, as if sizing me up and a strange feeling encapsulates the moment, like the stillness before a storm.

"Oh, so it's *impossible* huh? *Mister rock and roll*, the guy who *knows everybody in the business.* Well it just so happens I got a video director right here…sitting in front of me. What, you think I'm making this up?" She covers the mouthpiece. "Hey, what's your name again?"

"Willem…Willem Furey."

"His name is William Furey. William Furey. Yes, you've met him you ass, the gig at Klub Netherworld...right...how would I know?" She extends the phone in my direction. "Our big-shot Producer wants to blather at you."

I take the device. It's dented, the screen is spider-webbed with cracks. She punches the speaker button and listens in on our conversation. I immediately recognize the British accent.

"Hey mate, how's it going? We met a while back at one of the New York clubs, you're the cameraman I spoke with, right?"

"Well, yes, I'm-"

"I've got a little problem bucko, my video director is having a baby, his wife is going into labor as we speak. David's flying back to Vegas now. I need someone to keep it together until we make Vegas in a week." Georgiana gives the phone *the finger*. "We start in Baltimore tomorrow, then Atlantic City, Jones Beach, Atlanta, New Orleans, Houston, Vegas, then we're in LA for a week. Interested?"

"I'm not sure. I doubt I'm the right person."

"You told me you've directed before."

"Yes but-"

"Know how to op a fly-pack; *Grass Valley* switcher?"

"Yes, but-"

"Almost no content. Just a head-roll that loops for half an hour before every show, then it's a straight three camera cut to *I-mag* and out. What do you say chum?" I mull this over silently when Georgiana chimes in.

"You're blowing it Producer-man, better throw your cards on the table."

"Tell you what, I'll double the salary, just for the week, don't tell David." After a brief pause, he inquires, "What are you doing mate, are you working or what?"

"I'm on my way to New Orleans actually. I need to see someone there, right away." He jumps on the comment.

"We're in New Orleans in five days mate."

"Yeah, I heard you mention that."

"Tell you what. Jump in with us until New Orleans, I'll have David back by then anyway…or I'll get someone else. Free meals, four-star hotels, front-row to all the shows."

"I need to get to New Orleans right away."

"We'll be there in five days. Tell you what, you can break away after the show in Atlanta. Fuck it, I'll fly you out, deal?" I mull this over, enthralled by this strange, bizarre occurrence. "Well?" he presses while I force my mind to work. It's slower than taking a flight from New York but then again, I've no money, ID or even a credit card.

"Let me think it over."

"There's no time to think about it, the bus rolls at seven tomorrow morning." The phone goes silent. I look at Georgiana smoking in the rain. She gives the phone *the finger* again, the skull ring glittering in the blood red neon.

"I'll call you back in a little bit Nyle."

"Look mate, I don't have anybody else at the moment. If you can't do it say so, so I can cancel video on the coast."

"Can you give me an hour to think it over?"

"I've got a tour to run bud. Between you and me I could give a shit about fucking video. I need to know right now."

"He'll do it Nyle," Georgiana says.

"That's a *yes* then?"

"I'll call you back in a few minutes," I say. He grunts and hangs up. I look at her, trying to read the expression on her lean face. "I need to think about this."

"What's to think about? It's so obvious."

"What's obvious?" She ignores the question. "How long was I passed out on the floor?" I ask and she instantly focuses on the question.

"Hey, what about that? How in hell did you get in here? I locked the stairs *and* the elevator." I stare at her. There's no explanation I can give.

"I don't know." I can't read her face in shadow. "Georgiana, I've got to get to New Orleans right away. I need to see Morgan, it's crucial."

"So, do it then. What's hanging you up Romeo?" I stew over this last remark, how can I possibly tell her the truth, my sudden inexplicable appearance in this place? "What's *Plan B*, Einstein?" she asks, reading the confusion on my face.

"*Plan B?* There is no plan B."

"No plan B…" She sticks the phone in my face. "You better call him back right now or he'll cancel video on the leg." I take the phone.

"What a weird way to get to New Orleans."

"Watch, your rate will drop since you didn't say *yes* up front." I stare at her sitting in the darkness like an ebony scarecrow.

"What should I do?" There's a glow about the contours of her face before she flicks the cigarette across the rooftop.

"I could care less what you do," she says sardonically and leaves for below.

When I climb back downstairs after calling Nyle, she's in the shower. I use the opportunity to phone Villa Magenta, Morgan's home outside New Orleans but they've taken the phone off the hook yet again. When I try Morgan's mobile it too has been disconnected. I then call the ISO office back in London, knowing no one will be there. A recording of Beryl Collins' voice, the company's implacable financial controller, sounds in the earpiece:

14

'You have reached the offices of Karras and Corbeau, Investigators of the Strange and Occult. Please leave a brief, mind you brief, message including a return number and the country of origin from which you are calling, good day.'

I hang up and stew over my options. Last I knew, Lucien was at the Apache reservation in the American Southwest and his recalcitrant partner, Anton Corbeau, lost deep within the Sud-du-France. They both shunned telephones like the plague. Reluctantly, I decide to phone Beryl's flat in Knightsbridge, despite the late hour. The phone rings once then goes silent, except some strange incoherent whispering.

"Hello? Beryl?" Nothing, only the sound of what seems like fabric being brushed across the mouthpiece.

"Shhh…" is all I can hear from the other end of the line, then, "Why are you phoning the landline?" a young woman's voice whispers. "Mum's seriously pissed over your antics. You're trying to get me in trouble is what."

"Stella?"

"No, Teresa May."

"Stella, it's Willem." I then hear the phone clatter upon the table and the closing of a distant door before the phone is loudly taken back up.

"Willem? Is it really you?"

"Yes. Stella, I-"

"Where in fuck you been eh? Naughty boy. Everyone's in a snit over you Willem, buggering off for weeks at a time. They think you've gone on a binge. Have you? You can tell me love."

"Stella, listen to me. I need to talk with your mother, right away. It's urgent."

"At this hour? You're daft Willem. Got yourself into trouble 'ave you? Where are you? Tell me."

"New York."

"You dirty little liar. Don't think Mum's not run the machine on you. She knows you've not left the EU."

"Stella, I'm calling you from New York. I'm sorry but you'll have to wake her, it's imperative."

"Why?" *Why*. How do I even begin to explain? Shot down in cold blood in my flat in London only to awaken in Morgan's apartment in NYC.

"It's too difficult to explain. Stella, go wake Beryl, put her on the phone." She exhales loudly into the mouthpiece.

"Tell me your little hiding place or I'll hang up. I mean it Willem. I'll do it."

"Stella, I'm in New York. Listen to me, something very serious has happened. I need to speak with-" She hangs up and the line goes dead. "Dammit!" I shout aloud and re-dial, but she's left the phone off the hook.

Like all Karras and Corbeau employees, Beryl Collins doesn't keep a cell phone and I don't know Stella's. After a number of futile attempts to reconnect, I give up and collapse on the futon Morgan keeps in the *guest room*, a glorified name for a walled-off area she stores her photographic equipment.

Deep into the night I'm awakened by Georgiana's unexpected appearance at my side. My shocked reaction brings a dramatic response. "What?!" she shouts at me. "You think I'm trying to jump you?"

"No, you startled me, I was asleep." She just stares at me, a silent black silhouette in the dark. "What's the matter?"

"Nothing's *the matter*," she snaps, then after a few moments, "I have trouble sleeping alone sometimes...I get...nightmares, ever since I was a kid," she mumbles and just sits there.

"You can lay down, it's all right." She stews about this for a minute before she lays her head into my shoulder.

"Don't get any big ideas, you're just a warm body."

"I know Georgiana."

She jams her arm under my back and scissors my legs between hers, pulling my body tightly and I'm forced to sleep in this position, listening as she quietly hums herself to sleep.

Chapter 2: The Wicker Woman

Exactly six-thirty AM, we're standing on the sidewalk outside Madison Square Garden, 8th Avenue, the backside of the building, a misty ethereal morning, lazy, nearly quiet. We've taken a cab from the Tribeca warehouse. I've no possessions to speak of; Georgiana carries only Babe, in a soft-shell case, slung over her shoulder.

A muscular guy with lots of finely crafted tattoos on his neck and arms watches us exit the cab. "What's with you two?" he asks, and we look at each other.

"This is Vince, our stage manager. He's in the industry; a bunch of fricking tours already."

Waiting with us on the street are Giles and Waddles, the tour's *House* and *Monitor* sound mixers. Giles is lean and wiry, Waddles, the opposite. Dominic, the band's old sound guy, now the lighting designer for the tour, is cavorting about with Desi, a young woman with blue hair wearing cargo shorts and a pink tank-top that reads: *Bitch*. I notice a distinct iciness between her and Georgiana when they join us.

Dominic has no recollection of meeting me at Klub Netherworld, in fact I'm certain he's either seriously hung-over or on some kind of medication. Tiny, the band's 250 lbs. drummer, arrives accompanied by her significant other. *Tink* is bigger than Tiny and–amazingly-meaner.

Two silver Prevost tour buses pull up, hissing air as they lower themselves to the curb. The drivers open the doors to the lower luggage stow and beckon us to put our baggage into these bays.

Vince nudges Georgiana, nodding his chin toward a yellow cab pulling in. We watch Victoria, the band's ebony-haired guitar player, exit the cab with her suitcase and disappear into the band's tour-bus.

"Your girlfriend VD is here, don't you wanna go hug?" She glowers; he looks at me. "So, who's the new guy?"

"Willem. Nyle asked him to cover video while Dave has his baby."

"I know all that already Georgiana, that's not what I asked. I asked *who* is he?"

"Morgan's boy-toy. He's supposedly done some touring." They stare at me like a monkey at the zoo.

"You always wear a suit to a load-in?" he asks with aplomb. I've really no idea how to explain it.

"No. I thought I'd try something different." He stares at me placidly unmoving.

"Don't get in the way of my *load-out*, hot-shot," he says pointedly. "I cut through video cable like crap through a duck if your shit gets in my way." I assure him I know *the drill*. He prods Georgiana chain-smoking beside us, lighting one cigarette with the other. "You take time out between fags to breathe in oxygen?" She tries to ignore him; his stare relentless.

"What?"

"You ready?"

"Why's everybody keep asking me that? Yes. I'm ready!" she shouts, tossing the spent cigarette in the gutter.

"Excuse me," he says to those of us nearby. "Is somebody having issues?"

"Knock it off Vince," she grumbles.

"Things not going the way you hoped Princess?"

"I don't want to talk about it." She starts to leave but he grabs her arm.

"You better *talk about it* Georgiana. The way you chicks are getting on, this will be the shortest tour in rock history." She pulls her arm free, snarling below her breath.

"Like I said, I don't want to talk about it." One of the drivers approaches. "Change the subject."

"Oh, okay, uh, did you get the *pan-head* running?"

"*No*," she says like ice.

"Of course not, because you're a chick Georgiana and a chick has no business screwing around with a fifty-nine pan-head." Vince looks at the driver standing at his elbow.

"Who we waiting on Vince?"

"Who d'ya think Bob?"

"Bambi," the driver says.

Vince holds his arms straight in the air. "Goal."

"Has Nyle arrived yet?" Vince and Georgiana exchange *a look*; nearly a sneer.

"Nah, guess he's late too," he says as a yellow cab arrives and Bambi, the group's lead singer, gets out, being brusque with the cabbie, her long wavy hair, wild and disheveled.

"You think I was born in the Bronx! You took the long way buddy. I ain't paying you shit. Fuck you!"

Vince instantly joins her at the curb. "Not taking the private jet?" Nothing. "Hey, you're early," he says glancing at his watch. "Oh wait, I was looking at my watch upside down." Nothing. "Hey Bambi. At least you're doing something right, your clothes aren't inside out."

"Fuck off Vince," she says wrenching an enormously large suitcase from the backseat of the cab.

"That's the love I get for helping you out? *Fuck off Vince?*" He looks at the skinny *backline* tech standing next to him. "My baby sister Rick, the jewel of her mother's eye."

"Can't you fucking help?" she says gesturing at the multiple bags and suitcases inside the vehicle.

"Do I look like a backline guy to you Barbara?" he says, and Rickey immediately helps lug her stuff to the sidewalk.

"You're an ass," she shouts. He nods profusely.

"That's right Bambi. Nice. That's getting off on the right fucking foot. Guess what you'll be doing in two, maybe three hours? Asking me for favors. You just fucked yourself."

"Vince, either help or shut up."

"Buzz!" Rickey shouts at the heavy-set guy in a cannabis t-shirt drinking a *Monster* energy drink. "Little help please?"

Georgiana joins us at the curb to get a better look at all the baggage emerging from the cab; the cabbie demanding payment. Vince shakes his head crossing his arms, a Bushido katana tattooed across his right forearm.

"Jesus Bambi, did you bring enough shit?" he asks siding up to Georgiana. "You could learn *yet* another lesson from Georgiana, bring your ax and your toothbrush, the rest will sort itself out."

"Fuck off!" she shouts then orders Rickey and Buzz to remove another half dozen bags from the trunk of the cab. When the cabbie tries to intercede, Barnes, the security guard for the band, shoves him aside, then tosses a wadded-up twenty-dollar bill at him.

The arrival of a black limo grabs our attention and Vince again shares *that look* with Georgiana. "Hey, look who made it." He steps away to greet Nyle climbing out of the back of the automobile.

"Sorry I'm fucking late," Nyle shouts, emerging from the vehicle. "Everybody here?"

"Waiting on you," Vince says.

Nyle shouts to the bus driver, "Bobby, let's roll 'em!" We all quietly board the buses.

Our bus is immaculate, fully carpeted and clean, with a table and leather couches all around, everything polished and new. There's a large television screen behind the driver's station hooked into a wireless receiver playing Stanley Kubrick's *Full Metal Jacket*.

The front lounge also has a small kitchenette and sink with running water. Fletcher, third man in the Sound crew, is making a pot of coffee using Fiji bottled water. There's a toilet with a push button sliding door just like in Star Trek.

The lounge, at the back of the bus, has a video screen and stereo system already blasting rock. The rear lounge is also equipped with a built-in beer cooler stuffed with ice. Someone has stocked it with Heineken and Corona beers, two of the crewmembers already *testing the wares*.

Situated between the front and back lounges, within the very center of the bus, is a long narrow compartment with twelve bunks, six bunks on each side stacked three high. Each bunk has a curtain that can be drawn closed to separate it from the rest of the bus. Inside each bunk is a small drop-down television monitor routing signal from the satellite dome on the roof.

I'm on bus number two. My bus mates are Giles, lead sound mixer, Chuck 'Waddles' Waddell the band's monitor mixer and Fletcher, their audio assistant. Also, on our bus are Dominic and Desi covering the tour's lights and Rickey and Buzz, our *backline* techs, responsible for the musician's equipment, changing strings and tuning their instruments. There's also a young guy with a full red beard named Jody, the production assistant, and Phyllis the tour's publicist.

Our driver, a tall lean Texan named Robert already christened *Bob2*, tells us to '*Saddle up.*'

I take one of the center bunks on the right but end up moving to an upper when Florence, the tour's production coordinator, ambles onboard with her suitcase and soft bag in tow.

"Yolanda wants me on *number two* with you guys so Clive and Barnes can both ride with the band." She slumps onto the couch next to the table. "You guys got coffee?"

"Go for it," Giles says taking the bus manifest from her laptop bag.

"Who are Clive and Barnes?" I ask more to make conversation. She ignores me, searching for a cup, inquiring if there's cream in the bus refrigerator. She's young but looks careworn; her youthful brow, furrowed.

"Clive is our rigger, Barnes is the band's new security guy," Giles says looking over the sheet of paper in his hand. "Flo, who's on bus one? We're already at ten people." Florence stops what she's doing and starts counting on her fingers, decorated with elaborate flower pattern tattooing.

"Nyle, Vince, Clive, Barnes, the girls…the new keyboard guy, I forget his name…"

"Nigel."

"Whatever…and Yolanda, think that's it."

"Damn, ten people. Why does Nyle have a bunk? He'll never use it."

"Um, cuz he's the boss? Where's my bunk?"

"Willem's giving you his, you get center rear on the right."

"Thanks," she says to me pouring coffee. "I can't climb or crawl because of my back."

"Yeah, they told me, no problem."

She tosses her multi-hued hair and sniffs the air. "Who's smoking dope?"

Waddles, jumps on the question. "Dom and Dizzy…and *Backline*. It's seven in the morning," he expounds.

She gives him a droll look. "And your point is?"

"Certainly not their professionalism."

"Come off it dude, you smoke," she says and the remark ignites him.

"Not fucking seven thirty in the morning Flo!"

"What do you expect, they're *squints* man, and *backline*. Sort of comes with the territory doesn't it?"

His retort is cut short when a buxomly blonde woman, with heavy make-up, enters from the street and everyone is handed per-diem for the first week, an envelope with three-hundred-and-fifty dollars cash inside. For me, it's literally a Godsend. I realize I don't even have a wallet to hold the money.

"Is everybody in?"

"We're *a bus*," Giles answers.

"Did Flo get a middle bunk?" she asks, looking directly at me. "She's got a bad back."

"Willem gave her his," Giles says, "we're all good. When do we roll?"

"The drivers are scoping the route now."

"Baltimore's that way," he says pointing over his shoulder. She extends a heavily jeweled hand in my direction.

"We haven't met," she says eyeing my suit, collar to cuff.

"Willem," I say, shaking her hand.

"Yolanda, I'm the tour manager, thanks for helping out in a pinch."

"Sure. Did Nyle tell you I finish before New Orleans?"

"Yeah. We're supposed to have Dave back by then. You can't stay on until LA, just in case?"

"No, I'm sorry."

"Dave'll be back by then," Waddles interjects. "How long can it take to have a baby?"

"How would I know," she answers coolly. "We'll stock the buses in Baltimore gang, you'll have to rough it until then." She sniffs the air. "The boys are at it already?" Everyone exchanges *the look*.

"When are we loading in?" Giles asks.

"We pushed back to nine," she says pouring a coffee.

"We were supposed to roll at seven Yo. It's already seven-thirty."

"Bambi was late."

"No shit, what's new," Waddles exhales. "Why don't you guys just fly her so we can get our shows loaded-in on time? Why even drag the band around with us?"

"Nyle wants to save money. What difference does that make now Chuck?"

"You don't have to load-in three semi-trucks of gear Yolanda, we do."

"We're going straight to the venue. The stagehands are already prepping."

"What's to prep, until we get there with the gear?" This remark effectively concludes the discussion and she stalks off the bus. "Useless, completely useless," Waddles mumbles pocketing his per-diem and pouring another cup of coffee.

"Get used to it," Giles says, heading for the back lounge with the rest of the crew's per-diem.

We roll into Baltimore and there's a small army of black clad men and women on the dock watching our arrival. When we disembark, our group disperses with half the crew loitering about the loading dock, some on their cell phones, some smoking cigarettes. Vince emerges from the stagehand's office and glares at us.

"What are you standing around for? Get on the floor."

"What's the plan Stan?" Dominic asks and Vince looks like he'd like to cut out his tongue.

"I pitch you catch. Tell me you haven't forgotten how to do this numb-nuts?" Vince shouts over the banging of truck doors and aluminum loading ramps. "*Power* and *Lights* Dom, right? Your distro rolls with the motors, Clive's hanging your *points* now, split your *hands* and get your fucking truss together. Your shit needs to be in the air a-sap. Try'n pretend it's a *real* tour Dominic." He looks at Desi snuffing out her smoke. "Dizzy, *catch* stage-right. Don't fuck up my flow. Waddles, I'm sending all Giles gear *front-of-house*, your gear stage-left, any more stupid questions?" Everyone instantly breaks, like a huddle. He stares at me placidly. "Furey, why does the look on your ugly puss make me think you don't have the faintest idea what the fuck's going on?"

"I don't know where to set up my equipment."

"Because it hasn't been decided yet ding-dong. Check out a radio with Flo. I'll call you in an hour when we're ready to dick with it. Grab some chow…or go buy yourself a new frickin' suit Furey, that one's starting to look a little frazzled."

This last remark does not go unappreciated. I immediately hit the street and track down an apparel store.

Using well over half of my per-diem money I purchase a pair of black Levis, a couple t-shirts, some underwear, a toothbrush and toothpaste, a razor and shaving cream, a pair of Adidas, a jacket and some socks.

When I emerge from the fitting room wearing what I'm buying, the merchant seems suspect about my motives but is gracious enough to hang my suit and I stow it in the closet in the back of the bus.

Load-in is tight but we manage. I've a small fly-pack with a Macbook for driving *the show content* on playback software. The cameras and projectors are being sub-rented locally and installed by the Baltimore stagehands union.

Later that afternoon I meet my three freelance camerapersons, hired for the day. I go over how I want to shoot the band.

The rest of the afternoon, before doors, I spend practicing my show, cutting between the cameras and content until I'm completely relaxed with the system and *show-flow*. I'm so obsessed about cutting a smooth show I forget to phone London. By the time I think of it, I realize I'd have to call Beryl's flat again and decide to put it off.

Backstage is a flurry of activity, band groupies and stagehands bumping into the press hovering about *the talent*. Security guards hawk every egress and the venue's merchants are all scrambling, preparing for the crush of fans. There's a tour-launch press conference taking place next to where I've set up. I stand to one side with Phyllis while the cameras roll and *the ladies*, glow for the reporters.

At *doors*, while the subs are booming walk-in music, Vince stops by and looks over my shoulder.

"You good to roll video Slick?"

"Yeah."

He looks at me with a deadpan expression. "Don't screw the pooch Furey."

"Thanks." The hand-mic on his shoulder squawks and he leaves to *put out another fire*.

When the band hits the stage, I have James, my *stage right* camera operator, cover Georgiana; Liz, the *stage left,* cameraperson covers Bambi and VD. Tio, the *front-of-house* operator, on the telephoto lens, has been instructed to follow Bambi and cover the wide shots between songs. The fly-pack also has two small *lipstick* cameras. I set them up as *lock-off* shots on Tiny at the drums and Nigel at the keys.

The show is a good one, but I'm surprised by Georgiana's rather stoic performance compared to her vivaciousness the last time I saw them play in New York. It lacks the wild vitality I had seen that night at the Netherworld nightclub; perhaps the correct word is *joy*, her performance lacks the joy I remember.

Also different are the stage costumes the girls wear. VD no longer dons the blood-red leather suit and Bambi has shed her tight black leather pants and *see-thru* spider web blouse for a brighter, more *traditional* stage look; something closer to a sit-com concept of rock and roll.

However, Georgiana is still six-foot of solid black leather, her belt made of spent bullet shell casings; fingers adorned with silver skulls. She has a thick coat of black mascara running along the eye-channels. Her wild black hair frames her shoulders and she looks like an ax-wielding pharaoh-queen from Hell.

The evening's excitement is shattered when an unnerving event transpires during a pause, between songs. While James is adjusting his equipment, I see distinctly on the edge of his frame, a black shadow loitering in the crowd; the *Hollowman*, the hideous man without eyes! He mockingly stares at me, down the barrel of the lens and grimaces, terror permeating the moment.

When he moves, the cameraman is oblivious to my request over the headset to reframe his camera on the crowd. When he finally does, there's no one to account for what I saw. I'm left wondering if it were merely a shadow, more of an optical illusion than anything real but the morbid feeling in the pit of my stomach *says* otherwise. I ponder this weird enigma the rest of the evening.

I see nothing of the band after the concert and it isn't until after load-out and we're showered and rolling down the highway on route to Atlantic City that a few of the pieces of *the puzzle* begin to fall into place.

I'm in the front lounge of the bus with Waddles and Giles watching a show-cut of the night's performance on the television monitor when we're interrupted by Desi –in only underwear- being chased by Dominic. He *catches* her at the curtain that separates the driver's compartment from the lounge, and they play a short touchy-feely game until Waddles shouts at them for standing in front of the monitor, blocking his view.

They quietly recede back into the bunk area when Waddles throws the remote control against the couch causing the machine to stop. "Why the hell is that bitch back on this tour?" he shouts at Giles.

"Ask Nyle."

"I thought he was supposed to get rid of her after the shit she pulled in Europe, why is she still here?" Both men are silent while Waddles cracks open another *Corona*, grabbing up a second piece of cheese pizza.

"What happened in Europe?" I ask to break the silence but both men seem oddly reticent about answering my question.

"You watch what happens on this US leg," Waddles says. "Just because of that stupid bitch. This is how I earn my living man! What the fuck am I going to do if I lose this tour?"

"Easy."

"It's all fun and games until we all get collectively fucked in the ass Giles, just watch." He swears beneath his breath exiting into the bunk area with his beer and pizza. Giles exhales, shakes his head.

"What happened?" I ask and he grimaces.

"Desi wasn't supposed to be on the US leg. She pulled some real shit in Europe."

"Like what?"

"Sleeping with Dominic *and* the guitar player."

"*Guitar player*?" I ask, totally confused. "What guitar player?" He looks at me like I was stupid.

"Victoria, the guitar player."

"But? I thought Victoria and Georgiana were-" I catch myself, but Giles is staring a hole through my head. "I thought they were a couple?"

"They are...or were. That's messed up man. What a bunch of shit, right?" He waits for a response.

"I don't get you Giles."

"She got on the tour because Dominic has a thing for her. Don't get me wrong, Desi's a hard worker, and a pretty damn good lighting tech, just not a very good person."

"What do you mean?"

"You think screwing a guy on the tour while sleeping with a member of the band is acceptable behavior?"

"You're telling me Victoria and Desi...Georgiana is all right with this?"

"Hell no. It blew up in Europe when it came out, how could it not?"

"What happened?"

"Nyle and the European promoter told Georgiana to shut up and pretend all was hunky-dory or they'd sue her for breach of contract. They promised to replace Desi on the US leg. You can see where *that* went."

"Why is she still here then?"

"Why do you think?" he asks and waits for an answer, I just stare at him. "Victoria. She obviously wants her around, Nyle probably caved."

"What about Georgiana?"

"Pretty messed up. That's why she collapsed in France, shutting down the tour, she was hitting the stuff hard." In my mind, I see her on the rooftop again, in the rain.

"That's why she was on the roof..."

"What was that?" he asks, snapping me back into the present.

"The rest of the band is doing nothing about it?"

"Like what?" he laughs. "Bambi's a narcissist and Tiny a malcontent, she hates people. You probably think she just hates men, but she gives Flo and Yolanda a hard time. She doesn't give a fuck."

"But Georgiana is the band leader."

"Not anymore," he says cryptically. We both drift into our own thoughts. "How screwed up. The founding member of the band. She writes most of their material, their best stuff anyway, and she has to sit there and take this shit. I feel for her."

"It's like a *one-eighty* since I saw them last."

"Did you hear about the television interview in New York, what a fiasco that was?" I shake my head. He rolls his eyes and whistles.

"What happened?"

"They did one of the morning television shows, one of the big ones. Bambi takes the reins, of course. Well, she looks pretty good for the camera as you know, so, when they ask her to introduce the band she says: '*This is Tina Denton the founding member of the band and this is Victoria Denise Stockton our guitar player, VD studied at Julliard,*' etcetera, blah, blah…when she gets to Georgiana she says, and I state verbatim: '*and this is G, our bass player.*'" He stares at me.

"That's all?"

"Yeah, no shit. The person who created and drives the band, writes the stuff that gets on the radio, right there on national television relegated to being just *the bass player* without a name. She didn't even use her freaking name bro, not that anyone watching will ever know." He grows quiet, lost in thought. I voice the question that I believe is on his mind.

"Was that intentional? Bambi's not the brightest bulb in the shed."

"C'mon man, '*this is G our bass player,*' I don't know what *that* was." He finishes his wine, stretching. "I'm hitting the sack. Atlantic City isn't that far. I can't fall asleep if the bus isn't moving." He slips into the dark confines of the sleeping area, Waddles already snoring. After awhile, I decide to do the same.

Heavy-metal is blasting away in the back lounge, vibrating the wood paneling and cigarette smoke is issuing from the cracks, the sound of Dominic and Desi laughing and Rickey, Flo and Buzz talking non-stop.

I button the curtain closed to my seven-by-three-foot box and sleep in my jeans. The small television monitor has nothing but white noise–*Bob2* has deactivated the satellite, perhaps it's the road.

Switching off the white noise, the darkness absolute, I stare into the past, thinking about the things Giles has said, recalling the pain in Georgiana's face, on the roof of Morgan's building. I also can't shake the notion that the concert was visited tonight by the *Hollowman*, the man without eyes. Was it actually him, or my mind playing tricks? It was only a momentary glimpse, on the edge of the frame just for an instant, a dark face in the crowd staring fixedly down the lens; my mind harps on it incessantly, a *heavy* feeling following me into sleep.

Atlantic City is a rinse-and-repeat of Baltimore with one interesting exception. Just after load-in, Georgiana surprises me at the video racks. "You up for a walk?"

"Where?" I ask and she shrugs.

"I just wanna walk around."

Our *uncertain destination* proves to be a condo just off the boardwalk. She leaves me on the stoop for an hour watching people come and go from the shops and casino. The day is sunny, brisk, with a wind blowing off the ocean carrying the scent of the sea and the air feels pure and clean.

When she returns, I ask about the reason for the visit. She removes her leather jacket, showing off a freshly laid tattoo under plastic bandaging. Against my advice, she pulls back the plastic exposing the artwork, a tiny faerie and nymph, encircled with barbed wire.

We amble the boardwalk, the scent of the ocean mixing with the miasma of smells from the shops and kiosks. As we pass a *palmistry* shop, Georgiana pauses, studying the marquee. "*Madame Clarice*, she must be kidding. That's too cheesy to be real."

"I don't know, looks like she's been here a long time. They must be doing something right."

"Hey Willem, spot me *a Jackson.* I want my fortune told. Might be good for a laugh." Reluctantly agreeing, we enter the small innocuous shop.

A tiny bell summons our arrival. We're greeted by none other than the good Madame herself and entreated to a darkened antechamber with four chairs stationed about a circular table covered with a dark cloth.

"What, no crystal ball?" Georgiana asks and Madame Clarice smiles.

"Which of you is seeking advice today?"

"Can't you tell through your spirit medium or whatever?" Georgiana says and Madame Clarice points her toward one of the chairs.

"Please have a seat my dear, what can I do for you?"

"That's what I'm paying you for, you figure it out."

Madame Clarice is beginning to frown. She takes up Georgiana's hand and placidly gazes at the palm.

Then, a most remarkable thing happens. The woman adopts a noticeably severe expression, her eyes tracing the contours of the lines etched upon Georgiana's hand. The change in the old woman's expression is rather unnerving.

"What? What is it?" Georgiana inquires. Obviously, the change in the old gal's countenance has not gone undetected by my gangly companion.

The old woman recoils subtly, staring hard at her charge. "Today's not good, come back tomorrow."

"I won't be here tomorrow."

"So it goes," she says with a slight shrug.

"*So it goes*? That's your forecast for my future?"

"For today," the old woman says.

"You're a lousy hack lady. You give the racket a bad name," Georgiana says with a sudden vindictiveness.

The old woman's eyes narrow, "What is it you want?"

"I want you to tell me my future, isn't that what you people do?" It's a stare-down.

The octogenarian takes up her hand again, gazing at the palm intently before closing it. She leans back in the chair, her eyes fathoming Georgiana.

"I doubt you want to hear what I have to say."

"I'm paying you for it."

"Ah, so you are…and therein lies the contract doesn't it dear? The *contract*. Therefore, I'll say this…*you have no future.*"

"What's that supposed to mean?"

"What was said…you're *the Wicker Woman*," she says smiling.

"The what?"

"Yes my dear, you *are* the *Wicker Woman*."

Silence.

"What the hell are you babbling about lady?"

"*You* know. The woman made of sticks, with hair of straw, she sits amongst the cinders, minds the house whilst the master is away," she says and cackles softly. Georgiana suddenly explodes, pounding her fists upon the table.

"What sort of bullshit is that? *Wicker Woman*? Screw you lady. I'm not giving you fifty bucks for a bunch of bullshit." The old woman holds up her gnarled hand.

"On the house my sweet," she cackles anew. Her dark eyes glint. Georgiana storms out of the tiny shop and won't say a word the entire walk back to the venue.

The night's show is well attended and very loud. Georgiana's bass is more *present* than the previous night. She plays with an inner rage, her fingers drawing blood. The band is escorted off-stage to a standing ovation.

Also *present* was my dark mysterious intruder again, just on the edge of one of the hand held cameras in the front row. When I ask Shields, that night's operator, to reshoot the crowd, there's no one that even resembles what I saw, the only difference this time, I've recorded it.

When I look at the show recording with Giles later that night on the bus ride through New Jersey, he's there, for just a fraction of a second, before the camera strangely glitches. When the operator turns and reshoots the group there's no one that resembles –or explains- the dark image recorded mere seconds earlier; it's a conundrum and, for me, a very unsettling one.

Atlantic City soon gives way to Jones Beach. By now I'm becoming acquainted with the tour and its *flow* finding more time for leisure. During breakfast, I borrow Giles mobile phone and finally connect with Beryl Collins at the ISO office in London. She's beyond cynical.

"So, you've managed a trip abroad, and without a passport? Cheeky Willem, I'd love to learn that little trick."

"There's no *trick* Beryl, I'm in the States."

"Willem, I would certainly know if you left the EU."

"Beryl, will you pay attention. I woke up on the floor of Morgan's apartment in Manhattan, I'm on my way down to New Orleans now, to see her."

"Lucien's niece, the photographer? Why?"

"What does that matter? Beryl, I need you to reactivate the credit card and help me arrange my passport. Everything is missing. I have no money or identification, or-"

"Willem honestly, if you're on a binge somewhere just admit to it. If you need a car or a train ticket back to London…"

"There's nothing to *admit* Beryl, I told you. I was shot in my flat in London by the…*Hollowman*; then woke up in New York. Why would I make up something like that? I need help."

"Who shot who?"

"A man, I don't know who he was. He looked approximately *sixtyish*, had sunken eyes…actually, I don't think he has eyes. He carried a pistol with a silencer. He was going to shoot Lucien from the window of my flat."

"Who was going to shoot who?"

"The Hollowman."

"A man with no eyes?"

"Yes."

"You're serious?"

"Yes, of course."

"Willem, you're pissed. I mean really, this ridiculous scenario. You've been on a drunken binge for a couple weeks, just admit to it so we can-"

"Beryl, where's Lucien?"

"As I said, the Indian reservation, in the States."

"He's still in Arizona?"

"Willem, this has been a scream but I've a deluge of work; there's a queer little man sitting in the foyer and the phones are ringing off the hook. Philippe is in France and Millicent is on vacation. I'm fit to be tied. Get back in here as soon as you can. All will be forgiven, got to go."

"Beryl, don't hang up this phone." She does anyway.

Cursing under my breath, I hand the device back to Giles, giving me a strange look and the thought occurs to me he may have overheard some of this rather bizarre conversation.

The Atlantic Ocean backs up to the venue at Jones Beach during high tide. While I'm wandering around behind *the shed,* the covered stage, I spy Georgiana sitting on the dock amongst the pylons staring out to sea.

"Hey, how's it going?" I ask. The silent look in her eyes brings back Giles' words from the previous evening. After several minutes of my one-sided conversation she begins to open up. She tells me the afternoon reminds her of going to Coney Island when she was a kid growing up in Brooklyn, something about the air.

I sense she wants to talk. When I address elements of my conversation with Giles the previous night she explodes.

"Christ, can't I get a little peace and quiet around here?!" She throws the beer she's been drinking into the surf and storms off.

I shake it off, returning to the video racks and try to concentrate on the book I borrowed from Morgan's apartment, but the words keep changing into my own mind's thoughts. I'm forced to just sit and watch the tide roll out. I long to talk with Morgan but each time I borrow someone's phone to call, the recording on the other end indicates the line has been disconnected.

Chapter *3*: North-Central Nowhere

Finally, Atlanta. After tonight's show we'll be heading to New Orleans, and Morgan. I've seen nothing of Georgiana since our *chat* at Jones Beach, so I'm surprised when she takes the chair next to mine at the video rack.

"Hey, long time no see," I quip. She looks *very far away*. "Everything all right?"

"Yeah…sure," she says lighting a cigarette despite the no-smoking clause inside the arena. When the security guy mentions this fact to her, she acts like he doesn't exist. "Um…we're heading for *Nola*…after the gig tonight, into a day off. Rumor has it you're leaving tonight."

"I'm taking the tour down to New Orleans, but I won't be *cutting* the show."

"I know, you'll be hanging in the crowd with Morgan." I look into her opiated eyes.

"You spoke with her?"

"Yeah, you guys are coming to the show."

"The phones are disconnected, how'd you get through?"

She tosses her half-smoked cigarette into the morass of feeder cable behind the power distro. "Awhile back, we arranged a secret emergency message system thing." I don't ask her to elaborate. "Nyle is renting you a car. Vince wants me to ride down with you after the gig."

"Oh? He didn't mention it."

"I know." She disappears into her own thoughts, her strange vacant aloofness.

"What's wrong Georgiana?" She explodes, slamming her fist on the switcher, breaking several of the buttons.

"Why do you keep asking me that? Why does everybody keep asking me *that* question?" Her outburst freezes the stagehands routing the signal cables to the projectors. She leaves; I've no choice but to continue my load-in. Twenty minutes later Vince asks if I've a minute to talk. We sit together at the racks while my stagehands unpack the cameras and tripods.

He stares at the *color-bars* on the video monitors, chewing on a toothpick. When he looks at me, I see the seriousness in his face. "Look, I don't expect you to memorize any of this, but Georgiana's mom was my aunt Myrna. We're not just *like* family, we *are* family." He studies me a moment. "The tour is renting you a car. It'll be here in an hour. Immediately after the show, I want you to drive Georgiana to New Orleans with you, straight to Morgan's place. I was told you know the way?"

"I've been there."

"Drop the car off or bring it to the show. I'll have Flo set up tickets for you and Morgan at the venue down there."

"Okay," I say and wait for him to continue.

"That's it," he says in response to my expectant stare.

"Is everything okay?" He breaks the toothpick between his teeth.

"How should I know? I'm not a shrink, but I've been around this meat-grinder long enough to know when someone's walking a razor. This shit will do it to you." He tosses the toothpick aside. "Just get her down there with Morgan for a day. Get her to relax, open up. Personally, I think she takes this shit way too seriously, but what do I know? I don't have to get on stage in front of ten thousand people night after night, city after city."

"Yeah, okay Vince. One small problem though, I don't have a credit card, only the per-diem the tour gave me, most of which is already used up." His stare burns a hole in me.

"Are you freaking shitting me?" How do I explain to him my sudden *re-emergence* in New York? "I was using the company's credit card, *Karras and Corbeau*. I don't work for them any longer," I murmur, a half-truth.

"Furey, you're a worthless sack of shit," he says grinding his teeth.

"Sorry, bad timing."

After stewing a moment, he pulls out his wallet and hands me a Visa card with his name on it. "Here hot-shot. This is my personal card, make damn sure I get it back."

"No worries."

"Don't get any grandiose ideas with that card Furey. If you screw me, *I will* track you down and get my money back, in spades."

"I won't screw you Vince."

"I know, otherwise you wouldn't have my freaking card in your grubby little paws. Give me your pass." He takes the Sharpie from beside my switcher and writes four numbers on the back of my touring credential.

"That's the pin number, gas and food, or anything she needs...except drugs, no fucking drugs, you got me?"

"Okay. What about my load-out tonight?"

"Forget about it. I have it covered. Soon as the show is over, I want you and Georgiana on the road. And no stopping for booze either, drinking and driving is illegal in this country." I nod placing his card in my pocket. He goes to leave then returns. "I mean it Furey, straight to Morgan's. Keep her away from the dope. She'll try to talk you into going downtown, some nightclub or whatever, uh-uh, straight to Morgan's, capese?"

41

"You got it."

Just before *show*, I knock on their dressing room door to discuss these plans. Phyllis lets me in. CNN or some Atlanta news entity is interviewing the band. I spy Georgiana sitting off to one side in her leather stage costume.

"Hello," I say, she gives me a glance before returning her attention to the news crew. They hover around the rest of the band, Bambi doing all the talking. I study Georgiana. She's sipping a can of Coke; I can smell the alcohol.

"Is that rum in that?" I whisper.

"No, this is Coke's newest formula."

We watch as Bambi struts her stuff for the cameras.

"Have you already been interviewed?" I ask. She stares at me blankly a moment then abruptly leaves the room. I follow her out into the hallway. "Hey, where you going?"

"Where do you think? We're on in twenty minutes."

I can barely keep up with her long steady pace, her boot heels sounding on the concrete until she's delayed by a group of fans backstage asking for her autograph.

"Are you ready to roll tonight, after the concert?" She glares at me between smiles for the photographs.

"Yes."

"Did Vince tell you we're leaving right after the gig?"

"Of course."

She finishes signing their things, takes a moment to pose for another photograph before we resume our march backstage. I'm struggling to make conversation. At the door to the ladies-room she stops and glares at me, "Do you mind?" and disappears inside. I head for the racks.

The concert is a good one, however, Georgiana is less animated than the previous shows, as if alone in a crowd. When it concludes, I'm ushered to a Buick sedan and told to wait.

Within minutes I see Vince and Georgiana walking toward the car, her bass in the soft-bag over her shoulder. They get to the car and their conversation changes. I open the trunk and she places her guitar in and closes it.

"Georgiana, *Backline* can carry your ax," Vince says.

"Babe goes where I go." She gets into the passenger's seat and slams the door.

"You know your way outta here?" he asks. "Slip out through the service gate, you'll avoid the cluster-fuck out front."

"Okay."

"Remember, no booze, she needs a break from it."

"Okay, see you in New Orleans."

The service road leads us through an automated lift-gate onto a side street. We drive a few blocks in complete silence when she points at a liquor store.

"Hey, pull over." I drive past. "Hey, did you *not* hear what I said? Turn around."

"Vince said no liquor."

She glares at me, an incredulous expression forming on her face. "What did you say?"

"Vince said he'll break my arm if I stop for booze."

"I'll break your fucking face, turn around!" she shouts grabbing at the wheel.

"Whoa, calm down Georgiana. I'm just following orders."

"Willem, turn this goddamn car around, right now."

"No, no booze, not until we get to New Orleans." She looks as if she's about to explode. I prepare myself for the worst when she becomes strangely mute, staring out the windshield. "Sorry Georgiana but Vince made me promise." She's apparently unsure what to do or say. After a minute of this detached behavior, I ask what she's thinking. No response. We drive for several more miles in complete silence. Eventually her detached state of mind begins to creep me out.

"Hey, are you okay?" Nothing. "Georgiana, do you hear me?" This actually garners a response, a sullen deadpan stare then the same stoic disconnect for the next mile until she extracts a cigarette and *cracks* the window, the night roaring outside. "I'm sorry about the alcohol, I really am, but drinking and driving is illegal right?"

Eventually I surrender myself to the fact we're going to have a long quiet ride and switch on the radio.

"It's not your fault Willem," she says. "You're just a patsy, one of the *endless parade*."

"*Endless parade?*"

"Of soulless, spineless patsies without their own voice. Automatons for *the machine*."

"We all care about you. We worry about you."

"Yeah? So what?"

"So, you have friends."

"I've got friends huh?" she asks coldly.

"Yes, you do."

"Like you Willem, you're my friend?"

"Yes."

"Then go get me a fifth of Jack Daniels if you're my friend."

"That's exactly why I can't do it, because-"

44

"Because Vince says? How about because Nyle says…that I'm drinking too much. So Nyle is my friend too?" I wonder what she's getting at.

"Yes, I'm sure he is." Another scathing laugh.

"Want to know why they got me out of Atlanta tonight? Any idea at all *Brainiac*?"

"Because you need a rest…and to see Morgan." She laughs again and the laugh is unsettling.

"Try, because there was going to be a special guest on our bus tonight…and because Vince Giordano knows if that happens, I'll kill that fucking bitch! Strangle her with my bare hands. Or stick my shiv in her pancreas." I'm shocked by the sheer vindictiveness in her voice and words.

"You mean Victoria?"

"Desi, you fucking moron!" she shouts followed by a fuming silence. "There was a time Willem…not so long ago…if I said *yes*, then it was *yes*…or if I said *no*, then it was *no*…now, it's just…just fucked!" She slams her boot heel into the dashboard smashing the radio, which instantly goes dead. I see her pain welling, but don't know how to respond. I just drive. About a mile down the road she turns on me.

"Listen *friend!* You're going to take the next exit and find a liquor store and I'm buying a bottle. Trust me, *pal-o-mine*, I won't rat you out to Vince." I look at her, her bi-colored eyes, like a wolf's eyes in the dark. "Otherwise Willem, this is going to be the shortest car ride you and me ever share together."

"Georgiana…"

"You don't get a choice Willem. A drink on our little drive isn't going to ruin me. *Drinking's* not my problem at the moment. It's a lot bigger than a drink. Besides, like I said, you don't get a vote."

"What do you mean?

She glares at my wondering expression. "The minute you stop this car, to gas up or take a piss, I won't be here when you get back. Count on it."

What she's saying is true. She's exactly the kind of person who could walk away; walk away from the car, even the tour should it come to pass. She's right, I've no vote in the matter. There's really no choice.

"Alright Georgiana, have it your way."

I take the next exit that dumps us onto a long quiet boulevard filled with used car lots and junkyards. On a shady looking corner, lit by a broken and fragmented neon sign sits *Sullivan's Party Emporium*, coolly awaiting our arrival.

The *emporium* is a well-used room filled with outdated beer coolers from the sixties. She picks a fifth of Jack Daniels off the shelf.

The attendant looks at Georgiana in her leather pants and jacket like one might look at an alien stepping off a spaceship. When she makes the register, he just stares at her.

"What's your problem man?" she asks, annoyed by his attention.

"Damn lady, ya'll really tall," he says in a thick southern drawl. She looks at me and rolls her eyes.

"And a couple packs of Marlboro reds while you're at it *Jeaves*." He pulls two packs of cigarettes but just stares at her. "You got a problem buddy?" she asks, not masking her irritation.

"Ya'll look familiar." He glances back over his shoulder. "Hey Kenny, c'mere." A heavy-set man ambles over. "She look familiar?" They squint at her.

"Hey, *Tweedle-dee* and *Tweedle-dum*, we're in a hurry," Georgiana says opening one of the packs, tossing the wrapper on the countertop and lighting up at the register.

"That's one'a them wimmen on the television today," Kenny concludes. "Ya'll in a rock and roll band?"

"Nah, I'm an undercover narcotics officer, can't you tell?"

"Ya'll on teevee today. Ya'll played 'Lanta tonight dintcha? We seen ya on teevee. Ya'll the singer, right?"

"She's the gitar player," someone calls out from the back and a thin ragged looking guy with greasy long hair in a dirty baseball cap emerges and joins the duo at the counter.

"Damn, a real-life rock and roll star," *Kenny* proclaims showing a row of bad teeth. "What ya'll doing round here?"

"Where the hell is *here*?" Georgiana inquires and they all laugh together.

"Here? This here is *Nowhere*."

"*Nowhere*?"

"Yep, *Nowhere*." The three attendants laugh together. "*Nowhere*, Georgia."

"How about that Willem? We're in the middle of *Nowhere*."

"Not exactly the middle, more like north-central *Nowhere*." More laughing. "Where's that real purty girl, the singer, she with ya'll?"

"Nah, she's flying with the Producer on a private jet," Georgiana says looking at me. I know she means exactly what she's said.

"Yep, we seen ya on teevee."

"Hey ya'll played the Orpheum here while back," the skinny guy says. "A few years back, just up the road there aways."

"We played here? *Nowhere*?"

"Ya'll don't remember?"

"Do I sound like I remember *Gomer*?"

"Couple years back, 'cept there weren't no girl singer ner girl gitar player, it was a dude…least I think it was a dude, sorta hard to tell." More laughing. Georgiana looks at me.

"Nicci…" she says quietly, becoming very far away.

"Hey, ya'll wanna drive up to the club fer drinks? We's just closing up. The owner's there, he'll remember you betcha."

Georgiana grins. "What do you say, sound like fun?" I'm incredulous.

"No, not at all. We've a long drive ahead."

"Into a day off. What's the difference if we show up tomorrow morning or tomorrow evening?" then under her breath, "…or at all for that matter."

"Georgiana, what are you talking about?"

"I'm talking about having a drink with these guys." I pull her to one side and whisper low.

"Are you crazy? You can't go wandering off into the night with these people."

"Why?"

"Because they're total strangers."

"So what?"

"Georgiana, wake up."

"*Wake up?* What do you mean by that?"

"People don't go walking off into the night with complete strangers, sooner or later something will happen."

"Nothing is going *to happen* Willem, don't be a pussy."

"How do you know?"

She ignites. "So, what if it did Willem? So what?! What's the difference?"

"Hey, come on beautiful, if *Dickwad* don't want to roll, scratch him off the list. Let's rumble."

They begin turning off the lights and closing out the till. I watch as she actually prepares to leave with them, a morose feeling gripping my thoughts. "Georgiana…" I say but the heavy-set guy is pushing me toward the front door.

"Sorry feller but ya'll on yer own. We's closed." He uses his girth like a sumo wrestler and shoves me out the door, locking it and the lights go dark. I stand there numb.

"Fuck!" I shout into the glass wishing my voice could shatter the panes, but there's no one around to hear and the glass stares back at me, indifferent. "Fuck you!"

I return to the car, but the silence is deafening. A sudden intense remorse squeezes my chest. "Goddammit," I shout slamming my fist on the dash. "Not even past the goddamn city limits." I slam my fist on the dash again then swing the car around to the back. All the doors are locked, the windows dark. They've already left. Just a vacant beer store parking lot, *Nowhere* Georgia.

An automobile doused in silence; ripped up backsides of a forgotten place, and *the Silence* asks: '*What now*?'

Part of me wants to get on the highway for New Orleans. Not a chance, another part of me simply refuses to leave her behind.

I come to the sudden realization I've no way to contact her. I don't know her cell number. There are no phone booths even if I did know it. What was the name of the nightclub? For some reason the name is now erased from my mind. I curse myself for not paying attention.

Eventually I succumb to the realization that I'm going to have to wait it out in the parking lot all night. The thought tears at the twin sides of my personality, the one side furious, the other, the quieter side, anxious, waiting.

The minutes begin to drag on as I sit in the quiet solitude of the automobile and wonder. How could I let her do such a crazy thing? My mind harps on me incessantly. Eventually a sullen quiet surrender overtakes me. I just sit within the utter silence as if in some kind of trance. I begin to wonder if I'll ever see Morgan again, touch her, as if something–a weird series of circumstances-continues to keep us apart. I then begin to reflect upon my life, the strange course of events since I first saw *Karras and Corbeau's* ad for a business manager.

It's during this time, alone in an automobile in an eerily vacant lot, that a terrifying thing unfolds. It starts as a feeling, that strange uncomfortable feeling one gets when you're being watched. To my dismay I discover across the parking lot, beneath a lone streetlamp, just off from the edge of the beam, a shadow, vaguely human in form, is loitering in the shadows, as if waiting for someone.

At first, I wonder if it might actually be Georgiana, after all, she wears all black and this, person, is utterly black, void of any discerning features except the tall thin black silhouette of what looks to be a man. Just when I decide to check, he purposely steps nearer the light and I'm shocked to the center of my being. It's him, *the Hollowman!* He stands there like an ebony cutout, under the weak glow of the lamp.

There's no mistake this time, for he's not just a blurry image on the edge of a camera frame, but a dark shadow staring fixedly at me from across the barren expanse of the lot. I can literally *feel* his gaze focused on me. He's absolutely still, unmoving, as if frozen, except his attention; it grinds into my psyche. I feel my insides congeal.

As seconds turn into minutes, I'm forced to endure the incessant silent staring. I know this *attention*, this staring, is producing a vitiating effect; a chronic fear threading its course through my bones.

Then, the horrific happens. I watch, as if helpless, as he withdraws a large knife from inside his coat and begins to walk unrelentingly toward me. As he starts to cross the lot, he begins to pick up his pace until it's as if the man is nearly running toward me brandishing a horrid weapon!

A loud bang on the roof causes me to jump out of my seat. I'm face to face with Georgiana on the other side of the driver's window. She laughs like a crazy woman, circling the car before getting into the passenger's seat.

"You didn't split."

"How could I?"

"You start the car and drive, that's how." I canvass the parking lot; no one, not a person in sight anywhere in proximity of the car. "Why are you still here Willem?"

"I can't just leave you behind." I study the now vacant streetlamp; only the eerie feeling we're still being watched.

"What are you gawking at man?" she asks, irritation lacing her voice.

"Did you see someone, a man, walking toward the car just now?"

"There's nobody around here. *This place is a tomb.*"

After a thorough examination of the entire surround I inquire, "Where are your *friends*?"

"On their way to the Orpheum, I had to come back. I knew it. You dumbass. I knew you'd still be sitting here. I bet Willem, you'd be sitting here all night, waiting."

"We're a long way from home," I say still canvassing the parking lot now seemingly void of any other living soul.

"Next time I'll leave you a note," she says oddly. "C'mon, let's rock."

I turn the engine over and get us back onto the interstate, shaking off the experience as a bad dream.

She opens the fifth of whiskey and immediately starts pounding it. I'm amazed she can drink straight hard liquor in such apparent quantity. By the time we make the state-line over half the bottle is gone. Also gone is the dour demeanor she seems to have been in all week. She starts talking about music, guitars, touring and New York, primarily Brooklyn. I ask her about growing up in Brooklyn. She lights another cigarette.

"I don't talk about that."

"You talked about it with me before."

"When?" I remind her of our nocturnal walk through Manhattan after the performance at Klub Netherworld. "I forgot about that. That was a rare moment. Anyone who knows me knows I never talk about my youth, as a rule." After a pause she asks, "What did I say?"

"You talked about your *shattered youth*, your mom and dad, his drinking and hurting you." She stares at me darkly. "You don't remember? You said your aunt Barbara *saved your life* and you talked about your mom dying."

"I told you all that?" she asks, taking a slug from the bottle. "Yeah, well, so now you know everything there is to know *Zoltan*. Drive."

"Vince really cares about you, more than Bambi, I swear," I say to break the ensuing silence.

"Yeah, well, they don't like each other. Don't get it wrong, they *love* each other, just, don't *like* each other."

"Who else is there, in the family?"

"Who are you all of a sudden, *Joe Freakin' Friday*?

"I'm just curious."

"What's it to ya?"

"They don't have names?"

"Debbie and Mike. Deb's the oldest, Mike's the one with the band that got us all started, the one who bought me *Ginger*, my first bass."

"That was nice of him."

"No, it wasn't, he had to." She glares at me, I can see her doing so from the periphery of my vision. "You're a cagey bastard, know that?"

"I'm sure I don't know what you mean."

"Yeah right," she says, tossing her cigarette through the crack in the window, taking a slug from the bottle and settling back into the seat. "When we were teenagers, Mike used to pick on me, always making jokes about my height, because I was taller than him, and that I was born with two different colored eyes; jokes about my chest, that I didn't have any tits, no ass, no hips, no boyfriends, crap like that, you name it, on and on, it was endless. It would bug the shit outta me. So, one day, uncle Dick takes me aside and says: *'I've had it up to my eyeballs with you and Mike. Until you punch Mike in the chops, he'll just keep it up. Make a fist.'*"

"A what?"

"A fist, a fist," she says doing so and pressing it firmly to the bottom of my chin."

"Yeah, okay, I get it."

"He says: *'you're doing it all wrong, like a girl, make a fist like a boy.'* He shows me how to roll my fingers in tight to make a proper fist. *'So you don't break your fingers when you punch Mike in the mouth.'*"

"You're serious?"

"Uncle Dick says: '*you're left-handed so use your right. Next time Mike pipes off, punch him in the nose like this.*'" She demonstrates, rolling her fist counter-clockwise; landing it squarely on the side of my chin.

"Do you have to use me as a punching dummy? I'm driving." This remark makes her laugh.

"So, I practice a little. Couple days later we're all standing around the room while Bambi's going on about a dance coming up that Dil-" she instantly checks herself.

"*Dil?*"

"Um…some guy who used to go to our school…who had a crush on me for some reason…go figure."

"What happened?"

"Sure enough, Mike makes some crack about Dil having a thing for flat-chested chicks. I did what uncle Dick told me and popped him square in the nose; blood all over aunt Bab's new carpet. Aunt Barbara was really pissed-off; uncle Dick made everything worse because he wouldn't quit laughing." She takes a slug of whiskey and sits there, apparently caught up in memories.

"But…I don't get it. Why would he buy you a new guitar? Because you punched him in the nose?" I look at her and she's enjoying the moment.

"There was a kid at our school named Baxter, a real frickin' prick. He was big for his age and tough, always giving everybody a hard time. He'd pick on Mike because Mike had long hair; call him a girl, juvenile bullshit like that. So, Mike says one day: '*I'll buy you that gold Fender Jazzman you want so bad if you punch that fucker in the face, but it has to be in front of the whole school.*'"

"That's crazy."

"Why, what's crazy about it? I wanted a new bass and Mike wanted Bax to shut up, what's crazy about that?"

"Never mind."

"I always wanted my own bass, bad. The guy in Mike's band would never even let me touch his. I'm a southpaw so I had to learn on other people's guitars upside-down. That's why I play mine upside down. They were all beat-up pieces of shit with warped necks that never stayed in tune. So, sure enough, the next day we're in the gym watching Bambi's basketball game and Bax gets into Mike's shit about his long hair and won't let it go. He's telling Mikey to suit up and get on the court with the rest of the girls. So, I tell Baxter to shut the fuck up and leave us alone when he calls me a *rug-muncher*."

"A what?"

"You heard me. Don't make me repeat it." She drinks from the bottle, staring out the windshield. "It'd already started getting around, that I was, *a little different*." She glares at me. "That *is* the phrase isn't it? At that point in time it was all in the closet. I didn't even understand it. I made the mistake of trying to talk to Bambi about it little dreaming she would ever tell anyone. Of course, she went straight to the school loudmouth Suzie Kubiak, which was like announcing it over the school's PA system."

"Ouch."

"So, here's everyone at the school laughing at me. Baxter calling me that name and laughing, his stooges all laughing, everybody. I look over at Mike. Mikey ain't laughing, he's lip-syncing the words '*Fender Jazzman.*' Next thing I know, I'm squeezing my fist into a ball and letting Bax have it, except I was a little low and knocked out his front tooth, the guy next to him actually caught it in his hand." She becomes lost in her thoughts.

"So, what happened?"

"Something I wasn't exactly prepared for. He dislocated my jaw. I saw stars, like in the cartoons."

"He knocked you out?"

"I'd been hit before...my dad. And I'd scrap alongside my brothers and the guys on our street...but when Bax hit me, I lost it. I punched him in the eye, the mouth...wherever, I don't remember. What I *do* remember is sitting in principal Kitchner's office getting reamed. It was really weird. I was kind of dazed, from getting punched. Like being drunk. Seeing all sorts of strange things in the room, weird things moving around..."

"What do you mean?"

She seems to snap out of the reverie. "Aunt Barbara and uncle Dick are there. Babs is seriously pissed this time. I mean like, I'm thinking I really did it this time...they're going to send me off to juvey, or worse, back to the Snipes house."

She takes another cigarette from her pack and lights up, filling the car with smoke. "Hey, you want a cigarette? Don't wait around for a personal invitation," she says dropping the pack on the console.

"I'm all right."

"So, they bring Bax in and sit him down across from us. He's got a busted nose, a black eye and is missing a tooth. Uncle Dick starts laughing, you know, not right away but every time he looked at Baxter, it got worse. The more he tried not to, the worse it got. Babs is getting seriously pissed off, I mean it's getting bad and Kitchner is like: *'Mr. Giordano, I don't think you're grasping the gravity of the situation. This could lead to possible criminal prosecution.'* That's when uncle Dick grabs me by the arm and hauls me into the hallway. I'm like, oh shit, here it comes, the closer."

"Oh-oh."

"He yanks me over and says: '*Did you really do that to the Baxter brat?*' I'm like, '*I'm sorry uncle Dick, I won't ever do it again.*' He's like, '*you knocked his tooth out, the black eye too?*' I'm like, '*I'm sorry uncle Dick I didn't mean it.*' He's laughing, but trying not to, you know how that goes. Uncle Dick gives me this huge enormous hug and says, I'll never forget: '*Georgiana, as long as I have a roof over my head, so do you. You're as much my daughter as Bambi or Deborah. You're a part of this family, okay?*' Well, it was like shooting carp in a barrel, I start bawling like a baby."

"You cried?"

"Come on man, it was the first time in my fifteen years on the planet when I felt like I actually had a home…not afraid someone's going to drag me out of my bed and whip me with a belt, or throw me out of the house in the middle of a winter's night in only my pajamas."

She looks away, cracking the window, the roar of the night filling the car; reliving these painful memories.

"Uncle Dick doesn't miss a beat. He drags me back into Kitchner's office crying like a little kid. The whole mood changed. Now Babs is chewing on uncle Dick for '*being too hard on the kids*' and Kitchner's like: '*I believe everything's been resolved.*' Even Baxter's patting me on the shoulder: '*It's okay Georgiana, it was my fault.*' I remember him saying that, this gaping hole in his teeth." She takes another swig of whiskey, becoming lost in her memories. "That's just the tip of the iceberg. Brooklyn back in the day. The Giordano family…and the Snipes brothers, Ray, Joey and Lenny…sorry, *Raymond, Joseph and Leonard.*"

More silence.

"Tell me about your brothers." She becomes severe, deep in thought. "What is it?" I ask in response to her sudden change in mood.

"I don't want to talk about my brothers. I think you've heard enough for one night."

"Which one was Deborah? The oldest?" Nothing. "Was Deborah hard on you?"

"No. Why did you ask that?"

"I'm just curious."

"Debbie was sweet, and gorgeous…long hair, dreamy. Guys lining-up down the block to date her."

"What does she do for a living?"

"She still lives in Bensonhurst. She got Grandma's old house. She's got four…wait, no, five kids now. Hah, that's hilarious. Deb used to say: '*I can't wait to get out of this house and away from all you bratty kids.*' Now she's got five of her own."

"Tell me about Vince, what was he like growing up?"

She stares out the windshield at the on-rushing road. "Vince could scrap man, still can." She suddenly turns on me. "Not another word about my youth," she says returning her fist below my chin.

"Hey, I'm driving here."

"And not a word of this to Vince or Bambi, I'd never live it down. They'll dig up all the dirt they got on me."

"Okay, okay," I say rubbing my chin. She stares into the night, growing quiet. "What about Morgan?"

She gazes at me placidly. "What about her?"

"Why did you become friends?" Same weird stare.

"*Why*? You asked me *why* we became friends?"

I shrug. "Yeah…"

"No one's ever asked me that before. *Why.* That's a really good question. I've gotten *how* a lot, but never *why?*"

"Okay, *how* did you become friends?"

58

"You know, that's still sort of a mystery to me. We're like opposite ends of the spectrum. It doesn't really make sense we're friends."

"What do you mean?"

"C'mon man, what about me reminds you of Morgan? Name one thing."

"I don't know."

"Because there is none. We're like opposites. She's beautiful and sensitive. I'm coarse and intolerant. She's artistic and intelligent, has a Masters-degree in fine arts from Edinburgh. I dropped out of Canarsie High my junior year. I don't even have a high school diploma. She knows everything about anything, everybody who ever lived. I know nothing about nobody. She makes friends, I make enemies…the list goes on and on."

"How did you meet?" I ask and she laughs taking a moment with her cigarette.

"At *CBGB's*…before they shut it down."

"Tell me about it." I can see her watching me from the periphery of my vision.

"We were performing on stage when an argument broke out. Our *manager,* and I use the term loosely, is giving her a hard time because she's shooting photos of us without *his holy* permission. So, I tell him to leave her alone and let her shoot, if she gives us copies. So, she invites me over to her studio to look at the stuff. I'm thinking, this chick is some fashion whore who thinks she's tough-shit shooting metal bands in the lower east side right? No. Her *studio* is this tiny room in Soho with no furniture, just a futon on the floor, the rest film gear."

"She was broke?"

"She shows me her portfolio and there's no fashion BS in there at all…it's all black and white shots of orphans and junkies…street people and the homeless…bums along the Bowery."

"*Bums?*"

"I'm thinking, holy shit, this chick isn't your run-of-the-mill wannabe *ass-in-the-clouds* photographer, she's really fucking good man, and obviously *real* since you don't get photos like that from those people unless they trust you. Street people aren't like you and me Willem, they're a whole other breed, totally fringe. It's all based on trust."

"What happened?"

"I said come on down to our next gig and shoot. I figure that's the last I'm going to see of her right? Wrong. She's at the next gig and shoots these amazing photos of us, the best we've ever had. I get the girls to throw-in. We actually manage to scrape up a couple hundred bucks to pay her, which, if you knew us in those days, was a shit load'a dough, considering every spare dime went into booze and dope."

"Right…"

"Anyway, she says *no*, she only wants free admission to all our shows and to shoot whenever she wants. I'm like, fine…have at it girl. We've been friends ever since. Guess you just hit it off with some people sometimes…despite the differences." She's filling the car with cigarette smoke, making me cough.

"Do you mind cracking the window again?"

"She ended up shooting for this fashion rag on Park Avenue. They hired us once to perform at one of their *soirees* at some trendy uptown dyke-lounge. Big fashion BS, fashion gurus from all over the world, everybody's wearing Gucci and Prada…all that crap."

"What happened?" I ask during the ensuing silence, her smile catching my eye.

"Bambi gets tanked and VD gets so high we can't perform for their runway walk. Morgue's employer, this dazzling blonde chick with enough jewelry to stock Tiffany's, goes ape-shit and fires us on the spot, tells us to leave immediately or she'll have us arrested. What does Morgue do? She leaves with us and we run around *the Village* until three AM. She goes to work the next morning and no one says a fucking word."

"Really."

"I'm not condoning our behavior, just saying that's the kind of person she is. They don't make 'em like Morgue no more. Everyone's in it for themselves now days."

"Is the woman you referred to just now named Severine Marchaud?"

"You know her? You've met?"

"Once, briefly."

"I hate that bitch. She was always breaking Morgan's heart."

"What do you mean?"

"What do you think I mean?" she asks growing fiery.

"*Break her heart?*"

"Yeah. You've never had your heart broken?"

"I suppose."

"You *suppose*..." she says sardonically. "Obviously you haven't." She suddenly grows agitated. "Why are we talking about this? I don't want to talk about this anymore. Change the subject." I decide to address the topic that's been on my mind all week.

"What about the band Georgiana, how are things going?"

The question freezes her. She lights another cigarette with the one she's still smoking. After a minute, I repeat my question.

"You seem like an intelligent guy," she says, "aware of people, the things around you, at least I thought."

"Yes."

"Then you have your answer."

"What answer?"

She glares at me, the dark unsettling expression returning to her eyes. "Use your fucking brain."

"Pardon?"

"Are you blind? We're falling apart man. We'll never make it, not a chance in hell." She throws her cigarette out of the window and stews. "When we were a club band, doing clubs, we were tight. We moved together, ate or starved together…loved together. Now, we don't even talk…don't even look each other in the eyes anymore. All our lives, we wanted fame and money. Now that we're knocking on that door, we're killing each other, like an animal starving to death turns on its own kind." She takes a huge draught of whiskey.

"Hey, take it easy," I say and it's like lighting a fuse.

"Don't tell me what to do Willem. Don't ever fucking tell me what to do!"

"Okay, okay."

"I'm sick of people telling me what to do." She lights yet another cigarette and proceeds to fill the car with smoke. She pounds her fist on the dash. "Georgiana do this, Georgiana do that! *We're trying to refine our look Georgiana can't you dress a little nicer? That last song you wrote sounded a little harsh, can you soften it a little?* Fuck you!" she shouts giving me *the finger*.

I regret instigating the conversation. After about a minute of silence she glances over. "Sorry…I wasn't shouting at you." She draws hard on the cigarette then throws it out the window, stewing silently for several minutes. I just drive.

"Little while back, right after Tiny and I reformed the band, a guy named Hughes, a writer for one of the New York rags wrote a scathing review about us."

"Oh?"

"His headline said: '*More guts than brains*,' with a couple lines about us having enough guts to get up on stage to perform but no brains in doing so. *That* became our mantra, our rally cry. Before every show we'd put our hands together and say: '*With more guts than brains, rock on.*'"

"I know. I heard you say it that night at Netherworld."

"*That* was us; something that was *us*. We don't do that anymore. It's not *cool*. We were always a leather band, our fans are leather, now we're supposed to dress up in girl clothes and look pretty."

"That's absurd. Says who?" She suddenly seems like a caged animal, nervous, pulling yet another cigarette from her pack and lighting it.

"Bambi's sleeping with Nyle, they've formed a little *compact* with VD, and VD…VD's enthralled with someone else."

"What about Tiny?"

"*Tiny*…Tiny is throwing away our past, all that we were. We're losing our originality, becoming a cover band again. They've asked me to leave."

"What?"

"If I don't change."

"That's ridiculous. You *are* the band Georgiana. I doubt the girls would do that," I say, and she screams, a deep painful, penetrating scream, then silence.

When she's collected herself again, somewhat, she glares at me. "You know what your problem is Willem? You put women on a pedestal. You better come to the realization that women are manipulative and conniving. Men are just stupid and arrogant…and aggressive, but women are cunning, evil." I'm shocked by her assertion.

"How can you say such a thing?"

"Because it's true."

"But you're a woman."

"That's why I can say it."

"Lucien says women will be integral in solving the earth's future problems. Problems *men* will be incapable of solving due to their nature."

"Who's Lucien?" I pause a moment unsure how to explain him to her.

"A friend of mine."

"Well your friend's smart, he's right."

"But, how can they be both?"

"Because they are." I mull this over silently.

She then goes crazy, kicking the dashboard repeatedly with her boot, bits of plastic and fake chrome littering the leg-well and the blower fan begins rattling until it seizes. "I can't change man, this is who I am, get it?! I could no easier strip off this leather than rip my face off and glue on a smile."

"Take it easy Georgiana."

"I can't change the way I write songs. I write from the depth of my body, and my body has scars…so the words aren't always pretty."

"You have two songs on the radio. *Lock and Load* is on Billboard's top one hundred. Giles said *Run* is currently in the top-twenty…isn't it?"

"You're not up on current events Willem. *Run* hitting top-twenty is just *a fluke, a lucky mistake*…like the rest of my life." She then wrenches the ashtray from its socket, scattering the contents. "If this goes down, if I lose this band…it's pretty much fuckin' over Willem. I've my entire life into this. What am I supposed to do, pump gas? Serve dogs at the Seven-Eleven? Sling coffee at Dunkin' Donut?"

"You could start another band."

"Oh, great fucking idea Einstein! Never thought of that. Yeah, start over, build from the bottom, work my way back up…what, to relive this bullshit?"

"Georgiana…"

She holds up her hand. "You know what? I don't want to talk about this anymore. In fact, I'm done talking for the night."

"I'm just trying to help, just…talk it out."

"Talk to the road Willem, the answers to all your questions are out there anyway." She climbs into the back seat and doesn't say another word until we arrive outside of New Orleans.

Chapter 4: Orleans

Golden light rims the spires of the distant city; it looks nearly dreamlike, cradled within the primordial twilight of dawn. I see her head pop up in the rearview mirror, a silhouette against the eastern horizon. "Where are we?" she asks in a scratchy voice.

"Just outside New Orleans."

"We're in New Orleans already?" She climbs back into the passenger's seat, smashing one of the plastic heater vents on the dashboard with her boot. "Oops, Nyle can pay for that." She shakes her hair and looks about. "Are we heading downtown?"

"No, straight to Magenta."

"Magenta?"

"Villa Magenta, Morgan's home." She grows quiet a moment.

"Let's go downtown first, a quick buzz through the French Quarter, it's been awhile."

"We're to go to Magenta first. I need to see Morgan right away."

"But it's so early."

"They'll be up, they rise at dawn."

"Morgue? Hah. I doubt that."

"No, she does Georgiana." She mulls this over while lighting a cigarette. I'm amazed she can smoke so soon after waking.

"C'mon Willem, don't be a drag. Let's shoot into the French Quarter, grab an espresso then head to the house…c'mon, I'll buy."

Espresso. The word sounds magical. "Actually, I would love a cup of good coffee. I can barely stay awake. I can't stand the gas station brands."

"That's not coffee, that's swill."

"Alright."

The teeming downtown district is a quagmire, traffic like glue. Georgiana puts on a thick coat of mascara using the car's rearview mirror. By the time we hit the French Quarter, the sun is rising, the day new and alive, full of anticipation.

I park the Buick before a small petite café that advertises French press coffee. When I step into the street I smell the city on the breeze. I'm forced back in time to my last trip; my luncheon with Lucien and Colonel Montaigne, the moment Morgan asked me to leave.

When I return with two cappuccinos, Georgiana is conversing on her cell phone. She leaves to use the ladies room saying oddly: *'Keep an eye on Babe.'*

After twenty minutes, I'm beginning to wonder what she's doing. Out of boredom I pick up the pack of Marlboros she's left on the dash; stuffed between the two remaining cigarettes is a hand-written note.

'Willum, don't wait up, c u @ the gig. Tell Morgue luv her n will c her tomorow @ the show. Don't forget Babe. Thx 4 the ride.'

She's gone. I crumple the piece of paper in my fist, swing the car around and head for the freeway.

The iron gates of Villa Magenta–the old Montaigne manor-contemplates my arrival with a keen and knowing reserve.

When I turn off the car, a near absolute silence permeates the moment; only the soft twitter of birds. The placard of the stately golden rooster above the front porch reflects the brilliant morning sunlight, the light radiating off its golden patina nearly white and time seems to have stopped. Silence.

What will she look like? How will she react to seeing me again? My concerns are quickly answered when I spy her on the porch between the tall white Corinthian columns as if she knew I would be arriving that very moment. I want to run to her but Majo, the old Rhodesian ridgeback, trots at me with his teeth bared. It's not until he's treated me to a series of pokes and jabs of his nose–and a hearty sneeze-that he remembers me, and I'm allowed to pass.

Her embrace is serene, her deep green eyes euphoric. The sun tints her dark hair a rich chocolate. Despite my exhausted state, I feel rejuvenated; kiss her; breathe her deeply into my senses, her smile like looking into a sunrise. "How are you Morgan?"

"Hello Willem. We're well. Aunt Monique and Montara are in the garden. They're excited to see you again. Where's Georgiana?" My silent reaction speaks volumes. She takes my hand and leads me to the garden.

We round the hedge and she gasps, tries to cover my eyes with her palm. I pull back her hand to witness a young dark-haired girl floating in mid-air! "Ohhh…Montara, come down from there, right now," she calls out racing over to where Monique Montaigne kneels, pruning a row of vine works. She too is immediately on her feet, waving at the young girl who quickly descends to earth. I recognize her from my previous visit, Monique's young daughter Montara, ten years of age.

As I walk to where the women dote over the child, she shouts and points. "Willem…Willem!" She runs, stopping before me, her beautiful face reflecting the sunlight and touches my cheek with the very tip of her index finger. When the women join us she points at me. "Willem," and Morgan takes the child's shoulders.

"Yes Montara, Willem's here."

Monique, removing her work gloves, kisses me on both cheeks, her eyes, including the one solid dark eye without an iris, reflects the morning sunlight. A knowing smile curves the edges of her thin mouth. Her long black hair is tied back, and she wears tall rubber boots soiled in mud. "Bonjour Willem, how grand you've come."

"Hello aunt Monique, how are you?"

"Filthy and perspiring," she says dusting the soil from her pants. She wipes perspiration from her brow with the back of her wrist. "The weeds simply go on and on, if only the vegetables were as vigorous." I smile and gaze at the three generations of women, a deep affinity for them saturating my being. Aunt Monique looks past my shoulder. "Georgiana, where is she?" I share a concerned look with Morgan.

"I'm sorry aunt Monique, but she's in New Orleans."

"You left her in the city?" Morgan asks placing her fingers across her throat. I gaze between them at a loss for words.

"He did nothing of the sort," Monique interjects, snapping her gloves across her thigh. "*That little witch*," she says to Morgan, "she gave him the slip. She's off into the city for a run of mischief."

Morgan's countenance hardens. "I knew it…"

"Don't dwell on it. Morgan, Willem has come. I'll get breakfast ready." She leaves for the old mansion and Montara gives me a beautiful smile.

"Mama," she says pointing at Monique's retreating form. When I return my gaze to Morgan she looks very far away.

"I'm sorry, I should have kept better track of her." She then smiles, lovingly, her eyes aglow.

"I'm certain it couldn't be helped Will, after all we're talking about Georgiana Snipes."

We both look at Montara and she points at me again. "Willem," she says, and Morgan kneels down, taking the child's long ebony braids in her hands.

"Your aunt Georgiana is a very independent-minded woman," she says to the child who smiles then points at me.

"Willem."

Morgan *swallows* her in her arms. "Yes, *Willem, Willem*," she says tickling the girl, the child's laughter filling the morning. "Go in and get ready for breakfast Montara." The girl gives me one more long adoring look then skips off in the direction of the ancient manor.

She takes my hand, leads me out into the expanse of the great yard rolling back from the house like a grand green carpet. "*Willem, Willem, Willem*…that's all we've been hearing since she found out you were coming." Our eyes lock. "She adores you."

"But we only met the one time," I say, and this makes her smile.

"She's a very special person Will, just like you, very gifted. You'll find out."

"Was she actually floating just now? Or was that some kind of trick?" She doesn't answer, her eyes fathoming mine.

"Did you drive all night?" she asks as I take her arms. "You must be exhausted."

"Morgan, I need to talk to you, right away. Something incredible has happened, something terrible."

"Shhh," she whispers placing her fingertips to my mouth. "You mustn't talk about that right now."

"But something's happened, something awful."

She gazes deeply into my eyes. I actually feel her penetrate my thoughts. "I know all about that Willem."

"Know what?"

"About the stranger in your room in London."

"How could you possibly know?"

"I was there, don't you remember?" I've no such memory in the least. She takes my hands, her pupils dilating wildly. "So much has changed…since we were last together," she whispers and the strongest desire to take her, kiss her, overwhelms my thoughts.

"Morgan," Aunt Monique calls from the veranda. "Bring Willem to the house. He needs to eat. You too." She returns inside and Morgan's countenance softens, the eyes becoming tranquil again.

"You better come and eat or I'll never hear the end of it."

Inside the grand old kitchen, I'm excited to see Magdalena, the Creole maid, once again. She embraces me, her black eyes glittering. "You look like ten miles of bad road," she says pointing me to a chair. "I've salt pork and biscuits on the stove. Or I can make flap-jacks. Montara, what're you hungry for sugar?"

"Cornflakes."

"*Cornflakes*. Why do I even ask anymore? Git up there." She helps the child take her place at the table. Morgan pours two cups of coffee from a French press, handing one to me.

"Where's aunt Monique?" she questions the maid.

"Upstairs. Morgan, who in God's name is Georgiana?"

"My friend from New York. Why?"

"Monique's up there mumbling something about Georgiana this and that."

"She's never even met Georgiana, Mag."

"Hmm…she's up there in her closet going on and on about *Georgiana*." We exchange a wondering look. I can tell this piques Morgan's curiosity. "What are you hungry for Sir Galahad?" Magdalena asks turning her attention on me, her broad smile filled with perfectly white teeth. Montara giggles and points.

"No Magda…Willem," she says pointing and Magda gently slaps at her hand.

"Stop pointing Montara, it's impolite."

"I guess a couple eggs over-easy would be good," I say and it's as if I had openly shouted an expletive in front of the child, all eyes instantly upon her. She glances from Morgan to Magda to me, the smile disappearing from her lovely face.

"No Willem…no bird…no," she says, and Morgan leans over and whispers.

"I'll tell you later."

"We'll fix up some flapjacks," Magda says placing a pitcher of cream on the table before Montara. "And *you,* young lady, eat your breakfast and quit berating our guests. Willem is a guest in this house, you keep your opinions private."

Morgan smiles over the rim of her coffee cup and we watch as Montara carefully manages the pitcher of milk. When the cream is covering all the flakes evenly, she pauses and looks to Magda at the stove.

"Magda?"

"Yes sugar?"

"Berries," she says kicking the leg of the table.

"*Berries* what?" the maid says without turning.

"Berries…please," the child says and looks at me with dark wondering eyes. Magda produces a bowl of blueberries from the refrigerator and sets it before her. While I eat, I watch Montara take one blueberry at a time between her thumb and index finger and carefully place each neatly atop the cereal. When she has a dozen or so evenly spaced in the bowl, she begins munching. The salted pork is excellent. I offer some to Morgan.

"No Will," she says sweetly, "we don't eat meat. Magda made that specially for you."

"I'm sorry to make you go to the trouble," I say and the maid waves away my concern.

"Please, my grandmother used to cook me salt pork and greens. Just the smell brings her back in the room." Monique suddenly enters arresting all our attentions.

"Morgan, how many tickets did they send you?"

"What *tickets* aunt?"

"The concert, Georgiana's concert."

"They don't send them, there will be two tickets for Willem and I. At *will-call*."

"How expensive would it be to procure a third?"

"A third? For whom?"

"Why, myself of course," she says. Morgan seems stunned.

"Aunt Monique, this won't be classical or folk music, it's hard rock. I doubt it's your cup of tea."

"It doesn't matter. Georgiana will be on stage performing. I want to see her." Morgan stares at her, then me.

"Are there tickets available?"

"No, I'm afraid not. I heard them saying in Atlanta that the New Orleans show was sold out."

"My word, she must be very popular," Monique says.

"It's sort of a festival aunt Monique, there will be two other bands there."

"Oh dear, why wouldn't she come? Why must she forever persist in such behavior?" she asks as if talking to someone else in the room. Morgan's expression is beyond incredulous.

"Aunt Monique, with all due respect, you've never even met Georgiana Snipes. Why are you carrying on like this?"

"That might become apparent if I go, which I fear looks rather unlikely at this point."

"Aunt Monique, would you like to go to tomorrow's concert?" I ask and they both gaze at me expectantly.

"You can get her a ticket?"

"I still have my all-access laminate, my back-stage pass. We'll give her the second ticket."

"Oh Willem, you are a gentleman," Monique says beaming. "I graciously accept."

"Monique," Magda says placing her fist atop her boney hip. "Not to throw water on your fire but…you losing your mind again?"

"Whatever do you mean?"

"This ain't no hootenanny. This is that ear-splitting rock and roll kids listen to these days. You'll stick out like a sore thumb."

"I'm not as *back-woodsy* as you would have me Magdalena. I'll remind you, I used to dance at *the Go-Go* in the ninth ward, with Ceci and Emerald. Oh Morgan, such wonderful times, the sixties. Despite the racial divides of the time, Emerald and I became back-up dancers at *the Go-Go*. We were only sixteen at the start. Ceci lied on the paperwork. Magda, you'll recall, we danced in those matching chartreuse and white outfits that Blanche made for us." She realizes Magda is giggling. "What on earth is so funny?"

"The *Go-Go* is a far cry from what ya'll getting yourself into tomorrow," Magda says, and Monique turns her cheek, addressing me rather formally.

"Mister Furey, I am indebted to you sir for arranging my passage. Please forward me the charges."

"There are no charges, aunt Monique. The tickets are gifts from the tour."

"Please tell them I appreciate their generosity," she says, her dark eyes glitter as she exits the room. Magda and Morgan exchange an odd look.

"Don't say I didn't try...*the Go-Go*," Magda laughs under her breath, pointing her boney finger at Morgan. "Make damn sure you take a load of pictures tomorrow baby. I want this in the scrapbook." She returns to the stove, giggling under her breath. I look to Morgan cradling her coffee cup. She rolls her eyes and shrugs.

"Where is Emory?" I ask during the ensuing silence.

"Grandpa," Montara says, kicking the table leg with enthusiasm.

"He's spending a few days with his friend Binford Grayson. Aunt Monique thought he should get out of the house for a while."

"And good riddance," Magda interjects. "That old bone's becoming a permanent fixture around here, and an irritating one."

"No Magda...Grandpa...love," Montara says and Morgan strokes her head.

"We love Grandpa too," she says, the child renewing her assault on the table leg.

"Montara, no kicking," Magda says, and the inquisitive child tries to gaze around her torso at the stove.

"Magda...no bird," she says, the maid giving her a fierce look.

"What did I just say? Don't be nosing into other people's business, you worry about yourself. You're not the one running this house little miss."

During their exchange I question Morgan. "Bird?"

"She calls eggs, *bird*. She gets very upset when anyone eats eggs."

I cock my head. "Why?" We exchange a rather strange look. As if intentional, Morgan changes the subject.

"Mag, did we prepare a bed for Willem yet?"

"Shoot, I forgot about that baby. I'll get at it after breakfast."

"Don't bother," Morgan says pushing her chair back. "Come up to the guest room when you're finished Will, I think you need to rest after your drive."

After breakfast I join Morgan in the guest bedroom, one of several bedrooms gracing the old mansion's extensive second floor. It looks unchanged since the last time; the room filled to capacity with antique furniture well over a century old. I reacquaint myself with the oak desk and watch Morgan as she dresses the bed.

I'm pleased to find Maud, Morgan's steel-gray tabby from New York, asleep in the chair. We exchange pleasantries, *talking* together. He purrs loudly, rising from where he's been dozing, and stretches in the sun. His vibrant green eyes study me closely. I'm certain he remembers me from our previous encounter in New York.

I watch Morgan gently smooth out the sheets, her articulate fingers caressing the linen almost lovingly; I take up those hands, kiss them, and her. "Come, lay down," she beckons, drawing back the cotton.

She lies beside me, her body half atop mine, and we kiss, a deep passionate embrace, and she strokes my chest. I feel that side of her I knew in San Francisco coming through.

When my hands–seemingly of their own accord-attempt to undress her, she takes mine in hers and smiles away all the worries weighing upon my mind. She brushes my eyes with the palm of her hand and a heavy weariness overcomes me.

"Morgan, it's important we talk, about what happened in London. You, Monique…Lucien, are all in danger."

"Shhh," she whispers. "There'll be time soon." Her fingers caress my eyelids, the feeling similar to snow falling upon them when I was a child and I fall deeper into quietude.

"Morgan…a man was there…an evil, horrible man."

"I know," she says, her head upon my chest.

"I'm being serious."

"So am I."

"I'm not trying to start a fight but how could you possibly know?"

"I told you, because I was there." She rises up, stares at me, her eyes growing dark, intense. "Willem are you saying you don't remember?"

"Well, I remember a dream…a very vivid dream."

Her eyebrow rises sharply. "*A vivid dream*, that's what you remember?" She sits upright and glares at me. "What did I say in this, *vivid dream* of yours?"

"You said…*come to me*."

"And here you are."

"Well, that's a coincidence."

"I travelled over three thousand miles for you, and you relegate me to *a coincidence*, worse yet, *a vivid dream*." She takes the other pillow and pounds it over my head. "Uncle Lucien is right about you."

"What?"

"Willem, why won't you open your heart?"

"To what?"

"To the energies around you. For goodness sake, you saw a little girl floating in mid-air today and you've hardly said a word about it."

"Yeah, what was that, a mirage?" She looks nonplussed. "It looked like she was flying but…that's impossible."

"You're *impossible*," she says and goes to leave.

"Morgan wait, don't go." She fathoms me a moment, a sublime expression forming on her comely face.

"You don't believe I came to you in London, do you?" I don't know what to say, so I say nothing. She sits beside me on the edge of the bed. "I'll make you a deal," she says mysteriously.

"*A deal?*"

"If you close your eyes, and fall asleep, I'll take you someplace very special. Close your eyes Willem. Imagine us flying…flying together…beyond this place…beyond this world, flying…" She touches the center of my forehead *and like magic* I drift into a dream world.

I'm dreaming. I know I'm dreaming; floating within a heavy mist so dense it supports my weight. Morgan is there, grasping my hand. I *feel* her thoughts, as if she were speaking to me with her eyes. We hold each other's hands and simply float together. When the clouds part and the ground appears, hundreds of feet below us, I panic and falter. She tightens her hold and her constant steady embrace quells my fear of falling.

We pass over a small town with translucent amber-colored roofs, an ochre tinted steeple as sharp as a spear-point surrounded by several stands of dark forest, a meadow gleaming lavender-gold under a tired yellow sun.

She points. I look up into the pewter-toned sky above and spy the object of her attention, a small dark figure high within the clouds. The distant doll-like visage rapidly approaches, soaring at a remarkable speed. Montara. She hovers near me smiling then giggles, seemingly about my presence, or is it my pensiveness about flying? I watch the child as she looks into the setting sun, the wind rattling her ebony hair.

She floats in near me and her eyes shine. '*Montara, love,*' echoes inside my head. I remain mute, afraid to use my voice. She then embraces me tightly and I awaken, shocked to discover the night staring through the bedroom windows.

In the twilight of the ancient room, I hear the soft sound of voices. I quit the bedroom and cross the expansive common overlooking the entrée principal. The muted voices are coming from the parlor below. I follow the flight of mahogany stairs to the lower floor and walk in on what appears to be a family gathering.

"*Look who's back from the astral.*"

Sitting about the flickering lamplight is Morgan, Monique, Colonel Emory Montaigne and a tall dark-haired stranger with stark gray eyes and a salt-and-pepper beard. I'm introduced to Binford Grayson. He wears a round-rimmed Stetson and silver bracelet with a turquoise stone; the keen knowing look in his eyes makes me feel they have been discussing me.

"Sit with us Willem," Monique says gesturing toward an empty chair, her dark eyes gleam in the lamplight. I shake hands with Colonel Montaigne dressed in a thin white muslin suit, smoking a long black cheroot. I take the chair between him and Morgan.

"Why didn't you wake me? I slept the entire day."

"You needed it," she says.

The old Colonel slaps a shot glass down sharply on the small teakwood table that separates us and pours some bourbon from the bottle waiting at his elbow. "Bin?" he inquires pointing it in his friend's direction.

"What the hell," Grayson says extending his glass and Colonel Montaigne tops it off.

The men raise their glasses. Both *down* their shots neat. The straight Kentucky bourbon fiercely burns my throat. I manage only half, coughing. Monique smiles, a wry expression on her lean face and Morgan raises an eyebrow in my direction.

"If you fine gentlemen have concluded your salutations, perhaps we might return to matters at hand?" I'm uncertain Monique's meaning until Grayson addresses me.

"This man, who appeared in your room in London, what did he look like?" I ponder this sudden and direct question, not entirely certain how to describe what I saw.

"Well, in all honesty, he looked like a corpse." This causes a remarkable reaction within the room as all in attendance share in a solemn exchange.

"That's a damn good description," Grayson says looking at the Colonel. "All means and purposes, he could very well be a corpse," he mutters, pouring another half shot.

"What did he say Willem?" Monique inquires, our eyes locking; the keen knowing look. I struggle with forming the words. "Tell us exactly what he said," she presses.

"He threatened you aunt Monique, *an eye for an eye*, were the words he used." Her calm meticulous expression remains unchanged. All share in a silent focused communion. "He's behind what happened to Morgan in the bayou, leading her into the *Island of the damned*, he said so."

"Yes, yes we know it," Monique says into the emptiness of the room, her jeweled hands neatly folded upon her slender lap.

"Can he be shot down dead?" Colonel Montaigne asks me directly, his hair like white fire embracing his thin stately shoulders. He pounds his briar cane on the floor. "I'll fill the rapscallion full of lead."

"Mon Dieu Papa," Monique mutters below her breath and Grayson gives his friend a good looking-over.

"If he's a living being, that would be murder Emory. They could hang you for it."

"So what. How much longer do you think I got? It'd be a fair trade. I'm happy to do it."

"Hush father, no one will be traipsing about shooting anyone. Besides, something tells me it wouldn't work with this one. Willem is correct. *He's one of the walking dead.*"

"Well I'll not just sit here gathering dust while some sonofabitch yankee *duppy* goes around threatening my daughter. I'm happy to put a bullet into his mangy hide, whether it works or not I'd be honored to give it a try." The old soldier rails on relentlessly, his black eyes like two beads of coal beneath their enormous white eyebrows. "Hell son, Morgan said he drew a gun on you."

"Yes sir, that's correct," I say looking at Morgan with surprise.

"And this is all related to this, *Burning Man* business Moni, the demon you eradicated from Emerald? That came from Bratislava?"

"Yes Binford."

"The demon was *annihilated?*" he inquires, his eyes narrowing and a piercing, knowing look is silently exchanged between them.

"Unequivocally," she whispers, and the room goes deathly silent. "There was no choice but to annihilate the entity. It tried to attack Aphelia. It was clearly far too vile, too caustic to be rehabilitated. There was simply no choice in the matter."

"This man claims to have been the demon's master?" he asks me. I gaze at all the faces gathered around.

"Yes, so it would seem."

"He's a'gonna be damn hard to kill. You better bring Lucien into this, where is he?"

"The southwest," Morgan says. "We've sent word." Grayson nods solemnly, stroking his beard.

"This is an open proclamation of war Moni. I wouldn't take it lightly."

"No one is Binford, however, I don't want persons rushing about half-cocked. There's no reason."

"I'll shoot the damn bastard!" the colonel interjects, slapping the table. "*Eye for an eye.* Hum, I'll give the scoundrel an eye for an eye, both of his."

"Father…"

"Murder? Hell with that Bin. You can't murder what's already dead. I'll get the bullets sanctioned by the priest. We'll send the rapscallion back to his maker for straightening out…*eye for an eye.*" He curses under his breath and relights his cheroot.

"I don't believe he has eyes," I say after a pause and the room becomes still. "What did you mean Colonel, he's a *duppy?*" The Colonel ignores my question, fuming, but Monique studies me intensely, as if sizing me up, the look in her eyes sending a tingle through my body.

"We believe this…*being,* you refer to as *the Hollowman*…is in actuality what is called in the parlance of this region and this culture, a *duppy.*"

―――

"A duppy?" I echo.

"*A disembodied spirit, in possession of a dead person's body.*" I feel like I've stepped into ice water. "Thus, your use of the word *corpse* is quite accurate." She sees the incredulous look on my face. "Willem, this idea of death as an end to things is incorrect. There is no such thing as *death,* as you think you know it. We all survive after death...*one way or the other.*" Her dark eyes reflect the kerosene lamps.

"What do you mean by that, *one way or the other*?"

"Those who die with lightness in their hearts, their state of being, become lighter. Those who die immoral, with weight upon their conscience, deeply mired within the material world, become heavier. Binford, perhaps you can explain it better than I?"

"Well, one day you see a man walking. You talk to him. He curses or laughs. Next day he's laid out on a gurney, or a body bag. No more cursing or laughing, no more anything at all, what's changed?" He actually waits for my response.

"He's dead," I answer.

"He still has two arms, two legs, his face the same as you know'd it, he looks like he's sleeping, the body no different. But something *is* different. The *he* you know'd ain't there no longer."

"What do you mean?"

"He still has a body like you. How come he can't do the things you do no more? It's because the thing that danced or walked or spit or howled ain't there no more. It's *this,* that makes him jump or shout, the duppy she's referring to."

"And this...*duppy*...is an evil thing?"

"Every person has the propensity for evil," Monique interjects. "It is our higher selves, our better natures, what we term *the conscience*, that prevents our instigating evil upon others."

"The conscience…"

"We know this to be correct intuitively, what's called *listening to one's heart*. All persons must overcome the potential traps of life until they become men of higher spiritual quality, removing the negative karma from their souls. Occasionally the duppy of a person is freed upon the world. If he was a man of *ill-intent*, it's capable of the most atrocious acts upon the living. This is the basis for much of the work we do Willem."

"The work?"

"Moving the dead onward. It's less often than not, that the ghost of a person *passed-on,* remaining amongst the living, may suffer threat of becoming *coerced* into enacting mischief…or worse."

"Unbelievable."

"Once upon a time, we had *persons* who were responsible for cleansing the earthen plane of duppies and such things that remain after the termination of their material existences."

"Who?"

"Seers, adepts…persons sought for their ability to *move* these entities onward."

"Witchdoctors," the Colonel chimes in.

"Nowadays, these persons are fewer and far between and the planet becomes more populated with *the passed*, benign spirits as well as…lost, *disenfranchised souls*."

"Like a clear spring of water becomes muddied, undrinkable," Binford adds.

"What happened to them, these people, that did this work? Where have they gone?"

"Hundreds of years ago, they were burned alive at the stake," Monique says her gaze penetrating mine. "This was the beginning of the fall of *the profession,* if you don't object to my using that word."

"I think I understand."

"It became more efficacious to *go underground*, than to take one's turn on *the rack*," she says with intent and a spike of energy courses my backbone. I sense, *see* actually, within her eyes the thousands of people who were murdered in this way. "So now, our world fills more than before with, *creatures*, like our *Hollowman*...and people of weak character, those who exercise immoral, or *unconscious* behaviors, fall prey to these energies."

"Incredible."

"This is the work Aphelia and Talluleh's families are engaged in, and the mandate of our order set down by the Queen Mother herself nine centuries ago."

"Our order?"

"*The Golden Rooster*. Haven't you noticed the placard above our door? The golden rooster haloed by the rays of dawn?"

"Yes, and Emerald pointed out the one in Prague, the one on the old clock," I say and her dark eyes glimmer.

"What did she say?"

"She called it, *'our symbol.'*" Her eyes smile.

"Indeed Willem. She is quite correct. The Golden Rooster has been the sign of our order since the time of Mother Lenora."

"*Mother Lenora?*"

"The original matriarch of our line. Our family hails directly from France. *Aquitaine is my true name.* The Order, maintains an unbroken lineage dating back to that time, 1157 to be precise, nearly nine centuries ago, when the *Empress Regnant–suo jure*-put into action by the force of her pure and indomitable will, the very first of our sect."

"*The Order of the Golden Rooster*," I mutter, suddenly feeling very distant and timeless. "Somehow I know of it."

"The symbol represents the emergence of spiritual light into the world. This animal, ushers in the dawn, every morning, without fail."

"So, the rooster represents spiritual enlightenment," I conclude matter-of-factly. Her gaze intensifies, the one black eye reflecting the kerosene light.

"At face value, it served this purpose…to protect the members of the guild from…persecution."

"Persecution?"

"After all Willem, who wants to be dragged before the auto-da-fe…skewered alive upon a lance, drawn and quartered like a side of beef?"

"You're alluding to a deeper hidden meaning behind the symbol?" I ask to avoid conversation about this sordid chapter in human history.

"Quite indeed. Can you fathom what that might be?" I shake my head. "Would it help to mention Camille Saint-Saens?"

"The famous French composer?"

"The same. He was quietly a member of the guild."

"That's rather remarkable. How does he fit into this?"

"He was one of our order. He conveyed the symbols in his musical scores."

"How could he possibly convey such symbols musically?"

"His most famous composition, *Danse Macabre*. Recall how the piece ends, the crowing of the rooster and the scattering of the minions of the damned."

"Yes, but…what does it mean?"

"The Golden Rooster Willem, it scatters the ghosts of the dead. This is our charge. For over eight centuries, the members of the *Guild of the Golden Rooster* have done this charitable deed for humankind."

"That's truly remarkable."

"Hardly remarkable as you state it. More a tremendous burden frankly, after all…" and it's as if she were looking directly through me, her slender fingers lacing her throat, "*we're talking about a cause long ago forgotten*," and a sudden and inexplicable feeling of sorrow penetrates her expression and the moment. "I'm a poor substitute for what Aphelia and Talluleh's families are accomplishing."

"That's bull," Binford huffs, addressing me. "This woman, who modestly sits a'fore you, is of exceptional ability and there's a string'a folks between here and Mobile far-off better to prove it."

"Binford, no one wants to hear about old news."

"I remember one time, o'er in Lafayette. There was a mean old woman there, mean as spit, she died there at the convent, was carrying on a holy fuss…the sisters and the Mother Superior all at the end of their tethers about what to do next."

"It wasn't Lafayette Binford, it was Lake Charles."

"Lafayette. We went over, dead of night. I remember, there was no moon, the night, black as a raven's eye."

"Stick to the facts Bin."

"Monique was called over because Aphelia won't never go to the city. Anyways, we went down there, late, late at night. I remember it was as cold as a dead man's hand." Suddenly the telephone rings causing the women to start. They exchange a look before Morgan answers it.

"I loathe that contraption," Monique says low, her hands gripping the chair's scarlet arms. "Why must Magda forever persist in turning it back on?"

"Hello? Yes." She glances at us. "Where are you? Why did you ditch Willem?" Morgan exchanges eye contact with me. "That's just an excuse, and a bad one."

"Morgan, is that your friend Georgiana?"

"When? That's in an hour. Hold on a minute…yes aunt."

"Willem, would you be kind enough to escort my niece to the city?" she inquires. I look at Morgan.

"She's playing with some blues musicians on stage tonight, one of the clubs in the French Quarter."

"Splendid," Monique says, returning her gaze to mine.

"Of course, aunt Monique, if Morgan would like to go," I say. A smile curls the corners of the aunt's mouth.

"Morgan, tell her you and Willem will meet her tonight."

Morgan stares at her. "What about our meeting aunt…Mr. Grayson?"

She waves her fingers, the rings reflecting the lamplight. "All's been said that needs saying, for now. You children go have fun, it's a lovely invitation."

Morgan scrutinizes her aunt before returning to the receiver. "Did you hear that? Okay. It'll take about fifty minutes if we leave now…yes…yes, me too." She hangs up. "We have to leave immediately if we're going to make it," she says, and we look at Monique.

"Take the Mercedes. Enjoy yourselves."

An hour later we're parking the car near the Apollo, the streets festive, alive with humanity. The miasma of seafood and music wafts through the warm evening air.

I'm carrying Georgiana's bass over my shoulder. We get several inquisitive looks as we take our place in the queue at the club. Our conversation returns to San Francisco and our time there together. As I gaze into her eyes, I feel I'm travelling back in time, back to those carefree days, the house on Sutter Street, the cinema, the coffee shops and her.

The venue is a dimly lit blues club. Unlike my experience in New York, tonight Georgiana has impeccably included us on the guestlist. We're shown to a small table near the stage.

We're having drinks, Morgan red wine, I a Guinness, when Georgiana enters the bar through the backstage door. She embraces Morgan, a long loving embrace. I'm touched by the women's affection for one another. I see it in their eyes. She sits at our table, ordering a straight Jack Daniels on ice and lights a cigarette.

"You look great man. You always did. You always looked great Morgue," she says, offering her a cigarette.

"I don't smoke anymore Georgiana." It's as if she's momentarily stunned.

"I know," she says snuffing her cigarette in the ashtray advertising Martell cognac. "You're different."

"So are you." Silence. "What's the matter?"

"Everything Morgan. Everything's going to hell around me. The more I try, the worse it…" She goes blank.

"What's going on?" They exchange deep eye contact before Georgiana looks away.

"Maybe after the gig."

"No, now."

"After the gig, we'll talk then. We go on in a few minutes." She gives her wild head of hair a shake, downing her drink straight. "Thanks for bringing Babe." As she goes to leave, Morgan takes her wrist.

"Are you mad at me?"

"Where did you go?"

"I told you on the phone."

"In three-minute intervals, thanks."

"I talked to you more than Willem."

"Lucky him!"

"Georgiana, I'm not going to apologize."

"Who's askin' ya?" Silence.

"Georgiana…I don't know how to say what I'm feeling." Her eyes open like rain.

"Aw hell." Georgiana embraces her tightly and the moment is somber.

"Know what I figured out Morgue, after you'd gone?" she whispers, loud enough for me to hear. "I've not been the best friend you've ever had. I sure as hell thought so but…I was always wrapped up in my own thing, my own stupid, meaningless bullshit. I was never there for you, through your hard times. The stuff that really matters."

"Yes, you were."

"No, I wasn't." She takes Morgan's face, a sudden lucidity in her opaque eyes. "I didn't realize until you were gone. When I knew you had left New York for good. It was like…dying."

Silence.

"I was standing there, in a crowd, alone. Walking around a city filled with people, and all I kept thinking about, wherever I went, was you." Morgan begins to cry again. "Why are you crying?"

"I don't know."

"Morgue…I gotta go. Wait after the gig, we'll talk then okay?" She kisses her head and leaves.

"Are you all right?"

"We've been friends for a long time Will. She's hurting but won't say it, always keeps everything bottled up, afraid to let it out."

"I know."

"I've known that woman for over twenty years and I've never seen her cry, not once, not even when her mother died." She becomes quiet, reflective. I decide to change the subject.

"Do you know this band?" She shakes her head. "How does Georgiana know them?"

"I've no idea." I'm surprised by this admission. "Georgiana is a well-known session musician Willem. She's played with some very prominent artists, on stage and on studio recordings."

"Really? I had no idea. In New York?"

"All over. LA, New York, Nashville. She's an incredibly talented musician. Well respected, in certain circles," she says. "I've been in the studio with her, several times, and on tour." A genuine smile breaks through the tears.

"What is it?" I ask in response to that look.

"I was just remembering. I went with her on tour once. She was covering for a bass player in a well-known rock band while he was in drug rehab. She got me on the tour as their photographer." She laughs softly.

"What? Tell me."

"Where would I start? On tour with Georgiana Snipes, living the rock and roll dream. Some other time perhaps."

"So, she got her start with her brother Mike's band?"

She gazes at me placidly. "She said that?"

"More or less."

"That's not entirely accurate."

"Oh?"

"She wanted to be in Mike's band, badly. They were basically a Rolling Stones cover band. She helped them through a tough period, but they ended up dumping her for someone else. A rival band from New Jersey, a Beatles tribute band, heard about it and asked her to join, go on tour doing small clubs, parties, weddings, you know, money gigs. Within a month she was making more money with them than Mike's band made in a year."

"That's interesting. She didn't say a word about that."

"With the right clothes and wigs she could look and act almost exactly like Paul McCartney. Not only because she plays bass left-handed but also because of her height and boyish looks. Put her in a suit and tie with a Beatle wig and, well…I've seen photos and a couple old videos of her during that time and it's nearly uncanny, the resemblance." She sees the surprise on my face. "I thought you said she told you about this in the car ride from Atlanta?"

"Not about imitating Paul McCartney."

"But that's how she became such an outstanding bass guitarist, learning how to play like him, his bass patterns and licks. She told me once if it hadn't been for Paul McCartney she would *probably be working at Woolworths*."

The emcee's raucous voice cuts through her words like a runaway freight train. He welcomes the patrons and introduces the night's band as they emerge on stage. We watch as Georgiana enters with the drummer, guitarist and the keyboard player, taking his position at the Hammond B3 organ.

An old man in dark sunglasses, obviously blind, is lead onstage by a young woman and seated before an immaculately polished slide steel guitar. She helps adjust the microphone and exits as he fumbles with it, tapping on it loudly. His voice resonates like gravel.

"Good evening folks, good to *see* ya'll here tonight," he says, a smattering of laughter emanating from the audience. He tickles the slide, while the band adjusts their equipment.

When the musicians settle in, the old slide-guitarist takes the mic once again. "How ya'll doing tonight?" he asks. "We're *Black Bone*, from the north delta." The audience welcomes them with a thin round of applause.

"Good to be back here at the Apollo. Want to thank Miss Georgiana Snipes for stepping in to *hep* on bass. Her band *Concrete and Steel* is playing tomorrow night at the arena so ya'll come on out and see 'em." He speaks quietly to the side, eventually getting the go ahead from the guitarist. "This one's an old tribute song, just to getcha all warm inside, called *Howlin' For My Baby*."

The band launches the tune and I'm amazed how well Georgiana can play the blues. She *climbs the neck* keeping a steady pulse-like rhythm that drives the song. No leather tonight, she wears tight black Levis with a black t-shirt that reads, *Detroit,* in cursive. The singer's voice has a deep guttural tonality and *the blues* sends me somewhere timeless.

The rest of the evening is spent in near silence as we quietly listen to the pulse of the delta blues. When the performance is over and the club begins to thin out, Georgiana rejoins us at our table, inebriated and very *far away.*

"Whaddya think? All right?" she queries.

"It was good, really good. You sounded great."

"Thanks," she says lighting a cigarette.

"You really sounded good tonight Georgiana, you're good with this band," I add.

"Yeah, they're sexy. We mesh." She offers Morgan a cigarette again.

"No, thank you."

"Right, not smoking. That's a big change for you."

"Georgiana, come back with us to Magenta tonight. We've a room already made up for you. Don't worry, we'll get you to the concert tomorrow."

"I can't. I'm hooking up with some friends. We're gonna hit the town."

"Are you sure? Wouldn't you rather-" Morgan is interrupted mid-sentence by two rather questionable looking women, oblivious to our conversation.

"Hey. You coming or what?" the blonde asks, the brunette praying to her smartphone.

"Yeah, just a minute," Georgiana says and embraces Morgan tightly. They're head to head, whispering together. The blonde pokes Georgiana on the shoulder.

"Hey c'mon, the car's leaving."

"I said just a minute."

"Okay dude, suit yourself, it ain't waiting." Thankfully they leave. When she tries to pull away Morgan won't let go.

"Georgiana, don't go with them, come with us." They exchange a moment before Georgiana forces herself free.

"I'll see you tomorrow at the gig. We'll catch up then, promise." Her and Babe walk away. I can see the pain in Morgan's eyes. I take her hand and we quietly leave for home.

The following morning I'm awakened by a buzzing in my ear. When I open my eyes, I'm face to face with a beautiful young girl holding a beaten honey-colored teddy bear. Her lustrous ebony hair is tied back with a pink and white bow.

"Hello Montara," I say yawning.

"Me," she says pointing at herself. She touches my nose with the very tip of her finger and smiles. "Willem."

"Me," I say, and her laugh is as soft as a spring rain. She then sighs, gazing about the room.

"Willem…sleep?" she asks.

"Very well," I say, and her dark eyes scrutinize me.

"Willem…dream?" she inquires and I'm uncertain exactly how to respond, trying to choose the proper words when there's a gentle voice from behind us.

"I don't think Willem would appreciate you poking around his bedroom while he's sleeping." Our attentions are diverted to the door. Morgan joins her at the bedside, pulling the child lovingly to herself, kissing the top of her head.

"Montara...love," the child says softly and her eyes like polished jet-stone study me from within Morgan's arms.

"Yes, Morgan love too," she says, her tranquil gaze penetrating mine. "Montara, the girls are in the kitchen starting breakfast." She reaches up, pulling Morgan's neck to her mouth and whispers something in her ear.

"I don't know, you could ask him," she says, and the child addresses me somewhat formally.

"Willem...cornflakes?" she asks, expectation on her face.

"Sure Montara. I'd love some cornflakes." She gazes at Morgan, beaming.

"Willem...cornflakes."

Morgan brushes the bangs from the girl's deep brown eyes. "Okay, then go do it." The child immediately exits the room. "You better get dressed, she's going to make you breakfast," she says sitting beside me on the bed. "My, my, not everyone gets such superlative treatment. She loves you you know." I take her hand and pull her to me.

"So, I'm beginning to gather. But we hardly know each other." She smiles, her eyes glinting in the morning sunlight.

"Oh, she knows who *you* are." Her eyes dilate wildly. I'm caught, mesmerized by that look.

"Who? *Who am I Morgan*?" I ask and wait on her answer.

"The handsome knight who rescues maidens in distress. Who wouldn't fall in love?" I cup her cheek in my palm; gently kiss her. "Did you sleep well?"

"Very well, in fact, I had a very poignant dream," I say. She smiles, walking to where my journal sits open upon the desktop, picks it up, leafing through a few pages before placing it back atop the desk.

"Don't be late."

Breakfast is like being at a boarding school, there are three other girls at the table. In addition to the older girl, Sadie, I had met on previous occasions, there is a black girl, perhaps twelve years of age, named Lulu and a young red-haired girl with freckles named Rosemary; all talking non-stop and at the same time.

Montara pours a hefty bowl of cornflakes into an antique soup bowl and maneuvers the milk pitcher into position. Sadie dotes over her causing the ten-year-old to chastise her for doing so.

"Sadie...no! Montara...do!" The older girl looks to Magda.

"Just let her do it," the Creole woman says. "If she spills, she gets to clean it up." Montara manages without spilling then begins to apply blueberries, one at a time, meticulously across the entirety of the cereal. When Rosemary *tries to help* by dumping a handful of the berries into the bowl, Montara scolds her fiercely and all the berries are removed, and the process repeated until she's satisfied with her work. She looks at me somewhat formally and points.

"Cornflakes."

"Thank you." She waits until I taste them. "Mmm, yum," I say and the child beams.

Magda shakes her head and gently paddles her rear with the spatula. "Don't stand there staring at him."

Montara takes her seat at the table and the entire process repeats itself with her own bowl. Morgan watches from her chair sipping coffee and reading the morning paper, a pair of bifocals on her nose.

"What are you having sugar?" Magda asks her, placing a plate of grits and bacon next to my bowl of cereal.

"I'm not hungry Mag."

"Two cups of coffee is hardly breakfast baby-doll."

"I know but I'm not hungry."

Magda huffs as she passes, catching my eye. "Same thing every morning, two cups of coffee on an empty stomach, no wonder you're losing your eyesight."

"You're losing your eyesight?"

"Oh, she's exaggerating."

I study her closely, the glasses on her nose. "I didn't know you wore glasses. I've never seen you wear them before." She looks over the rims; her eyes are perfect, deep-green and lustrous.

"I've had them a year now. About six months ago I started switching from manual to auto-focus on some of my *shoots*. It's not a big thing. There's lots of professionals who shoot on *auto*, it's just-"

"Oh, my lord!" Magda interjects and all eyes divert to the archway into the dining room where Monique stands dressed in a pair of brown leather pants and a dark tunic blouse.

"Mama!" Montara shouts instantly on her feet hugging her. She also wears an authentic Navaho *conch belt* each silver conch adorned with an exquisite inlay. Montara, as if mesmerized, touches her fingertip to each of the bright shiny buckles on the belt.

"What in the name of heaven are you doing?" the maid asks pointedly.

"I beg your pardon?" Monique replies, somewhat indignantly. I glance at Morgan who looks dumbfounded. Monique strokes Montara's hair, returning her to the table, helping with her chair. I can't believe the transformation; Monique looks perhaps ten years younger and much more contemporary.

"Are you going crazy again?" Magda asks. "Where did you find that get-up?"

"These are my own belongings," Monique says, "I've always had them."

"Since when?"

"Magdalena, are you insinuating something?"

"I'm *insinuating* you're losing your mind." Monique disperses her words with a wave of her hand.

"Niece, what do you think? I need an unbiased opinion," she says over her shoulder at the maid.

"I hardly know what to say," Morgan stammers.

"Say the truth, do I look all right or not?"

"You look fine. Where did you get a pair of leather pants?"

"They're not leather. I bought them in France several years ago. Do they fit all right?"

"Very well."

"I'm not overstating myself, am I?" and Magda jumps on the question.

"Oh no Monique, not at all," she says with more than a tinge of sarcasm.

"Magdalena, if you've nothing constructive to add to the conversation then please refrain."

"Where did you get that belt?" Morgan asks. "It looks authentic Native American."

"It most assuredly is. Your mother bought it for me, from the southwest. I finally get to try it out. What do you think Willem, will I fit in?"

"Absolutely," I tell her. "You look very nice." This puts a genuine smile on her face. She takes Montara's cheek.

"What do you think dear?"

"Mama," she says pointing.

Monique absently strokes the child's hair as she studies us. "I wanted to wear something that would blend in."

"You're very becoming," Morgan assures her.

"Better be careful, they might take you away on the tour with them."

"Yet another sarcastic remark Ms. Tousseau?"

"No, I'm dead serious."

"I've been to concerts before I'll remind you."

"That's right, the Supremes," she says returning to the stove and giggling beneath her breath.

"What is so humorous about the Supremes pray tell? The so-called, *girl groups,* of the early sixties were the foundation of the new music to come, although no one ever credits them for it. What would *not have been* without these women breaking down the gender and social barriers of the time?" She realizes Magda is giggling into her apron. "Magdalena, are you laughing at me?"

"Why not get the chartreuse mini-skirt out of mothballs?"

"That's why I'm dressing like *this* Magda, I couldn't find the matching white go-go boots," the aunt rebuffs.

"Pay her no mind aunt," Morgan interrupts, "you look just perfect," the aunt smiles, exiting the room.

"Mama," Montara says pointing and giggling into her hands, Morgan shushing her.

"No, you go right ahead sugar, laugh, it *is* funny," Magda says and Morgan frowns.

"She looks perfectly fine, very modern."

"Who listens to me in this house anyway?" Magda says and cracks two eggs into the skillet and Montara stammers, pointing.

"Magda...no!" she shouts, a most concerned expression forming on her face. "Magda...bird!" she then starts into the most heartfelt sobbing. "Bird!"

"Oh good lord," Magda exhales looking up at the ceiling. Morgan drops her newspaper, embracing the child.

"Montara, aunt Magda is just making Willem an egg for breakfast," and the girl directs her wounded gaze upon me.

"No Willem!" she wails, tears pouring from her beautiful dark eyes. "Bird!" she cries, and breakfast comes to a crashing halt.

Chapter *5*: *A very strange occurrence*

Early that afternoon we're backstage at the concert. We park the Mercedes and make our way past the tour buses lined up along the VIP parking lot.

"What are those?" Monique inquires.

"Those are the tour buses, for the bands and crew."

"Each person gets their own bus?" she asks, and I laugh softly.

"No, each bus holds eleven or twelve crewmen."

"Twelve people live and travel on that contraption?"

"Sometimes."

"I'm sorry Willem but how is that even possible?"

"There are twelve bunks on each bus," I say but she's incredulous.

"Hey, look what the dog left in the yard, Willem Furey."

We turn to see Vince stepping off the Concrete and Steel #1 bus. He gives Morgan a big genuine hug. I see the affection he holds for her.

"Good to see you again Morgan. You're looking really good," he says and extends his hand toward Monique.

"Vince, this is my aunt Monique," and to the aunt, "Vince is Georgiana's brother. Sorry, half-brother."

"Hiya aunt Monique, thanks for coming." She clasps his hand in both of hers. I can tell she's *looking* into him. He senses it but doesn't pull away as I've seen other people react.

"Vincent…"

"Yes?"

"You're at a very precarious point in your life, a kind of…crossroads." She studies him intently and he doesn't move. "You've a very big decision to make, soon. Please correct me if I'm wrong, but you're very divided about it."

"Go on aunt Monique, you're not too far off," he says sharing a glance with Morgan. I see something in that look.

"Vincent, the decision is yours alone, no one can help you with this. However, I would like to point out something you already know." She holds his thick tattooed hand in her thin ivory fingers. I'm struck by the tenderness of the moment. "Every sentient being has a spark we call *spirit*, and every spirit must do its duration in the material world, there's no exceptions."

"I'm with you there aunt Monique," he says.

"Vincent, the temporal mind belongs to this earth, your spiritual mind, your inner voice, comes from the stars. It is the exchange between these two extremes, the finite and the infinite within ourselves, we call *our life*; our souls, formed of this dichotomy, the twin natures of humankind."

"What is the answer?"

"You know the answer Vincent, your heart knows. Your grandmother taught you this when you were a boy. Remember her words, never forget them. These relations we share are eternal, it's called *love*."

I actually see moisture forming in the tough Brooklynite's eyes. "Thank you aunt Monique. I appreciate that, very much," and they actually embrace. He looks at Morgan. "You get your tickets squared?"

"We just arrived. We were about to find *will-call*."

"Forget about it…come with me."

We follow him through a series of checkpoints into the backstage area of the arena, yellow-clad security guards hawking our every passage.

Backstage is filled with a variety of people and equipment, men in business attire, greasy vendors, black-clad roadies. Vince converses with several different persons along the way, *House, Security* and the head of the stagehands union before we finally enter the *Concrete and Steel* production office.

Surprisingly neat and smelling of patchouli, the office has a craft service table filled with fruit, snacks and coffee. Yolanda and Flo are behind desks tapping away on Macbooks, Yolanda conversing over a headset attached to her iphone. Jody, the young tattooed PA with a full red beard is charging batteries for the walkie-talkies.

"Hey Flo, set our guests up with VIP laminates, if you're not too busy."

"For who?" she asks, freezing.

"Willem and Morgan, and her aunt."

"You're Morgan?" she asks and Vince interrupts.

"I just said so."

She looks over her notes. "I've two tickets for Morgan MacIntyre at will-call."

"I want them in laminates," he says, looking squarely at the aunt. "I don't want anybody giving aunt Monique a hard time," and her eyes glimmer.

"There are no VIP laminates left."

"Flush your head out Flo. There's twelve VIP laminates."

"Bambi reserved them." The look on Vince's face is priceless.

"Are you freakin' trying to be humorous Florence?"

"For the greet-n-meet."

"The greet-n-meet gets stickers Flo, not laminates."

"There's some big-wigs tonight, from the Press." It's a stare down.

"Give me three of those laminates," he says gesturing with his hand.

"I still have my touring credential Vince," I say over his shoulder.

"Gimme two of those laminates Flo, right now." She looks over at Yolanda, already shaking her head.

"Leave me out of it," she says. Flo begrudgingly begins to sign them out in her ledger.

"Bambi's gonna frickin' bitch Vince, at me."

"Tell her to come find *yours truly* and I'll explain why the Press doesn't get touring credentials." She reluctantly hands over two *all-access* VIP passes on nylon lanyards.

"I hate getting in the middle of you guys."

"There is no *middle* Flo. Everything goes through me. If you could get that one simple fact implanted into the thing you're using for a brain your dealings with *the talent* would be seamless."

"Vince, give it a break," Yolanda interjects.

"Here you go aunt Monique," he says placing the pass around her neck. "This gives you *Carte Blanche* anywhere on the tour. Anyone tries to get in your way, walk through them like you own the place. If they still give you a hard time, tell 'em to call me on the radio, channel one, I'll explain it to them in no uncertain terminology."

"Thank you, Vincent."

He gazes placidly at Flo. "Hear that? *Thank you Vincent.* This is how a real lady talks Florence."

Flo exhales loudly. "Whatever."

We exit the production office and stroll the curving hallway that skirts the backside of the arena.

"So, Morgan. How was the little chit-chat with Georgiana yesterday? Imagine she had a shit-load to talk about."

"I never had the chance Vince."

We come to an abrupt halt and he glares at me. "You didn't deliver Georgiana like I asked?"

"She dumped me when we got to New Orleans." For a moment, I actually think he's thinking about choking me.

"Wrong Furey," he says pointedly. "*She* didn't dump you. *You* didn't drive her straight to Morgan's like I said, ergo, you blew the assignment." The following silence is deafening. Morgan takes his arm.

"What's going on Vince?"

"I think she's going suicidal."

"I hope you're exaggerating."

"Morgan, when do I ever exaggerate?" he says, concern clouding both their faces. "It's exactly like when Nicci died and Ramona dumped her. Here we go again, the whole goddamn *shit parade* all over again," he says looking at the aunt. "Excuse my language."

"You needn't apologize Vincent."

"Oh my god…" Morgan whispers through her fingers when something catches his eye down the hallway.

"Speak of the devil." We watch as Georgiana emerges from the loading dock in black jeans and a pink *Hello Kitty* t-shirt. She wears dark aviator shades and Babe is strapped over her shoulder like a bazooka. When she makes it to where we stand waiting, she embraces Morgan.

"Sorry I bailed last night. It got a little crazy."

"Look what the cat dragged in," Vince interrupts. "So nice of you to grace the tour again your majesty."

"I was with some friends."

"Sorta figured that out by the lengthy texts."

"Vince…"

He takes up his smartphone and reads the screen. "'*C U 2nite.*' Here's another one, '*C U 2mrrow.*' Here's a good one, '*B in noon.*' Oh, hey, one more, '*B in afternoon.*' Gosh Georgiana, I'm all warm and fuzzy."

"Vince, I'm not in the mood for this."

"Yeah, you don't look like it."

"Gee, thanks man."

"Are you in the mood to get on stage and earn your dough tonight?"

"Have I ever not?"

"Not on any of my shows."

"Well then?"

"*Well then* what Georgiana?"

She seems confused or exasperated. "Did you get me a single?"

"Referee's locker room, third door down. There's a shower in there, make sure you check it out." She acts pained and goes to push past him. He grabs her bicep. "Hey, I said that with love. Phyllis put shampoo and soap and *girl shit* in there for you, sheesh."

"Thanks," she says and begins to leave.

"Are you freaking kidding me?" he expounds, both arms seeking the heavens.

"What now?"

"Have I gone stupid or is your best friend standing here in front of me? Maybe she came to see you."

"Let's hook up after the show. I'm sorry Morgue, I need to get some sleep."

"Don't worry about it, Georgiana. It's all right."

"Vince, can you give me a wake up call an hour out?"

"What a piece of work. Anything else your highness? Foot massage, blow job?" She turns and walks away, her boot heels sounding on the concrete.

As we head out into the arena, Vince stops abruptly where five thick power cables cross the entrance to the stage. He whistles loudly at Desi, hanging fixtures with the stagehands.

"Hey Dizzy. Come over here." She stops working and joins us at the cables. "What is this?" he asks pointing.

"Our power run," she says flatly.

"I know *what* it is Dizzy. *What* is it doing here?" She adopts a blank expression.

"We always run our power stage right."

He immediately keys the hand-mic at his shoulder, wired to the walkie-talkie on his belt. "Hey Dominic, can you drop what you're doing and join us stage-right…just a moment of your precious time…please."

"What's the problem?" Desi asks irritated.

"That's why they call you Dizzy."

"No Vince, *they* don't call me Dizzy, *you* do." Dominic joins us.

"What's up?"

"Dominic, did we, or did we not, have a production meeting at load-in, first thing this morning?"

"Yes."

"And in that meeting did I, or did I not, say to route your power stage-left tonight because we'd be *directing the artists on and off stage-right tonight?*"

"Yeah but-"

"*Yeah but* you went ahead and ran five legs of freakin' four-aught cable across my egress anyway?"

"But we always route power stage-right, it's quicker."

"Dominic are you freaking stoned? Did you not hear what I just said?" Silence. "Move it."

"But it's run already."

"That's not my problem." More silence.

"Can we just tape it off?"

"You can move it."

"Seriously? Why?"

Vince squares himself. "Because I don't like it..." I sense the discussion is closed. Dominic and Desi stare at the cables like they were covered in plague.

"Seriously Vince, let it ride. We'll cover it over with a piece of marley," Desi interjects but Vince ignores her.

"Dominic, who's on stage tonight? Who'll be walking in and out of here in her six-inch stiletto heels?"

"Bambi."

"And what will happen Dominic? You get one guess, make it a good one."

"She'll trip over it." Vince grabs the back of his neck, squeezing enough to make him wince.

"See? You're not as dumb as everyone says." Dominic curses under his breath. "I'll steal a couple *hands* from *Sound* to help out, but only because I'm a nice guy Dom, right?"

"Thanks," he says, rubbing his neck.

We head for the other end of the arena where Giles is tweaking the front-of-house mixing board. "Giles, send two of your *hands* to *Lights*. Our genius LD ran his power straight across the talent's egress."

"I told him not to do it," Giles says, "the idiot."

"Hey, this is my good pal Morgan and her aunt Monique, you got room for them out here tonight?" He's instantly enthralled with Morgan and very accommodating. At one point, Monique speaks to him in French.

"I'm sorry, I never learned to speak it, but my father was from France."

Vince's radio squawks. It's Chuck complaining on and on about the sudden changes erupting in *his world* stage-left.

"Waddles don't recite me a novel over *channel one*. I'm looking straight at you from front-of-house numb-nuts," he says into the mic, setting off in the direction of the stage like a hurricane making landfall.

Giles takes good care to secure our seats next to his board while we visit with some of the personnel on the tour. I make a point to visit Dave at the video rack and we congratulate him on the birth of his second daughter.

Eventually we end up in the band's dressing room. Morgan greets all the girls, Bambi, Victoria and Tiny. I'm impressed by how much admiration they harbor for her. Bambi, dressed in a tight-fitting body-sock that clearly shows her womanly figure, *finishes* with the hair-stylist. She shakes her ebony tresses and smiles, mischief in her eyes.

"Damn Morgan, you're looking good babe, *meow*," she says, pouring herself a glass of Glenlivet. "You want a glass of scotch?" We graciously decline, introducing aunt Monique. Bambi extends her hand and as Monique takes it, a strange reaction forms in the singer's face. Is it trepidation or something else? Whatever the emotion, she instantly retracts and refuses to acknowledge the aunt further. She won't even look at her the remainder of our time together.

Morgan also introduces Tiny, who seems heavier and Victoria who seems thinner. Only Victoria shakes the aunt's hand. When Monique holds hers longer than customary, a strange expression emerges on the guitarist's face and she subtly recoils, becoming quiet and disassociated from the discussion.

Minutes later, Nyle joins the gathering dressed in jeans and his patented Tommy Bahama shirt. The conversation instantly shifts to photography.

"Did you bring your gear? You can shoot tonight if you like," he says and Morgan smiles.

"No. I'm afraid I didn't."

"We'd love you to shoot something with us again. In fact, I hate to bring up business, since this is a social occasion, but we need to talk about securing rights to the work you've done for the band. Apparently, everything's been done on a handshake. Can you set a price for the material we've been using? We'd appreciate you be as generous as possible." He actually waits for a response.

"Just a formality Morgan," Bambi adds, downing her drink by half.

"I'm aware how well respected you are in the fashion world. What a body-of-work," he says canvassing Morgan with his eyes.

"Thank you, but it all belongs to Georgiana, I did it for her." The reaction from the collective group is odd.

"Oh, well, cool but I'll need your signature on an official release. We probably got one in the kit. I'll phone Yolanda."

"You're asking me to sign a release? Right now?"

"It'll only take a second." He starts to phone the office when Bambi interrupts him, infinitesimally shaking her head. She turns to Morgan and instantly has a different face in place, like turning on a switch.

"Goddamn Morgan, it's good to see you again…and looking so goddamn sexy…" she purrs, refilling her scotch. "God bless a beautiful woman."

After several minutes of Bambi's recounting the group's rapid *rise to fame*, she actually dismisses us under the guise of a headache. Once outside the room Morgan and Monique exchange a deep penetrating look. I ponder the silence in the exchange.

It isn't long before the second act has come and gone and we're anticipating *Concrete and Steel*. When they hit the stage the crowd responds loudly, adrenalin coursing my body and for a moment I wish I were still cutting the video for the show that night. I look at Morgan sitting beside me, a strange feeling encapsulates the moment, something about us sitting together amidst the raucous surrounds, her face serene, peaceful and timeless.

The first song is a cover tune I don't recognize; the second is their hit, *Hell on Your Doorstep,* and the crowd becomes livelier. When they follow with Georgiana's tune *Lock-n-Load,* the crowd is on its feet getting very loud.

The tumult is short-lived however as the band follows with a series of famous cover songs and Bambi engages in a kind of verbal patty-cake with the audience. It isn't until they return to a set of original numbers, *Lucyfer*, *Back on The Street,* and *East Coast on The Skids,* that I hear the special quality that underlies the band. Georgiana's head is bowed low over Babe, her fingers beginning to bleed. This is how it goes until about two thirds through the concert when a very bizarre thing happens.

Exactly half way into her song *Dumb and Fun,* Georgiana stops playing becoming fixated upon where we sit at the soundboard.

It's odd, feeling she's performing some kind of theatrics when very deliberately she drops Babe on the thrust stage extending out into the crowd and jumps the barricade, pushing through the crowd to where we sit under the front-of-house canopy, the crowd going wild. It gets even stranger when she climbs the front-of-house riser and stands fixedly before Monique.

"Georgiana, what is it?" Morgan says over the shouts and cheering from the crowd. She stands before Monique staring as if she's seen a ghost. "Georgiana, what on earth?"

"She..." Georgiana stammers pointing at the aunt. "You're..." she mumbles on incoherently. Suddenly Nyle bursts into the circle forming around the rock star.

"Georgiana, have you gone insane? What're you doing?"

"She's..." pointing at the aunt, "I specifically saw..."

"Get the bloody hell back on stage! Don't turn this into another Shepard's Crossing," he snarls through clenched teeth. She seems to snap out of her delirium.

"I want these three people in my dressing room before the end of the set."

"Fucking fine Georgiana! Now if you would be so kind," he says gesturing toward the stage.

With what appears to be an effort, she pries her attention away from the aunt and manages her way back through the crowd assisted by Vince and Barnes.

The crowd roars its approval as she climbs onto the thrust taking up Babe and rejoining the band on stage. Their expressions say it all, their non-enthusiastic response all too evident. After a brief moment of indecision, they break into a loud version of *Gloria*.

Several measures into the song, the same thing happens again, however, this time she remains on stage, managing to keep the bass-line going but I can clearly see she's transfixed upon our place at the front-of-house boards. Like watching a person go into a catatonic trance, she becomes motionless, staring directly at us. I listen-in as Morgan converses with Monique over the din.

"What's going on aunt Monique?"

"Whatever do you mean?"

"Why is Georgiana staring at you?"

"It would seem so."

"Why did she walk out here and stand in front of you?"

"I'm not exactly certain. Morgan I think something very deliberate has just transpired."

"Like what?"

"I don't know." They exchange intense eye contact. "Why do you think I understand her actions?"

"Of all the thousands of people out here, why did she walk up to you?"

"There's no doubt something quite profound is in motion. Hopefully we'll get to the bottom of it when we see her after the show."

Before the last tune finishes, we're escorted backstage by Barnes–the black security guard-to Georgiana's dressing room. He gives us an odd look and leaves.

When she joins us it's like a stranger entering the room. She glares at us before locking herself into the bathroom for several minutes. When she emerges, she's toweling the perspiration off her neck and arms. She doesn't say a word, just stares at us with wolf-like bi-colored eyes, the blue iris looking dull in the yellow light, the brown iris nearly black.

She pulls a chair, placing it squarely before us, lights a cigarette and points a skull-clad finger at the aunt. "You're a witch, aren't you? You're a frickin' witch."

"What's going on Georgiana?" Morgan interjects.

"Her. She's a witch, isn't she?" The aunt and niece share a discerning look. "Aw come on, are you going to deny it?" When Morgan goes to respond Monique stops her.

"And isn't *that* the pot calling the kettle black. I could easily say as much for you," the aunt says. Georgiana seems strangely *caught*. "The question then follows Georgiana, as the old saying goes, '*Are you a good witch or a bad witch?*'"

Georgiana rises and paces the room like a caged animal. "You gotta be frickin' kidding me. Go ahead, *aunt Monique*, tell me I'm seeing things. Tell me I'm losing my marbles, go ahead."

"What did you see?"

"Oh come on, like you don't know?"

"I most certainly do not."

"Bullshit!" she shouts, and Monique laces her fingers across her throat, her one good eye dilating.

"Georgiana, really," Morgan interjects, and our gangly friend begins to pace the room again, *eyeing* the aunt narrowly with each pass. She seems to be struggling with an inner tension. "Stop it Georgiana! What's happened?"

"Ask her," Georgiana rails, pointing at the aunt.

"Aunt Monique?"

"Morgan, whatever Georgiana saw is emanating from her subconscious, perhaps her higher self. I was merely watching the performance, nothing more."

"Georgiana, you need to share it with us. What is it? I insist you tell us, right now."

She struggles anew, considering something deeply, before sitting down, collecting her emotions and gazing into the aunt's eyes. "You're telling me you've no idea what I saw?"

"No, but you need to tell us. It's imperative you do so."

"I must be losing my mind." She stalks the room again, like an animal caught in a cage and Morgan adopts a distressing look

"Georgiana," the aunt says, "it's my belief your higher self is reaching out. It has chosen me, a sensitive, simply out of expediency, perhaps concentration, I was watching your performance with interest, after-all, we've more in common than you think. You believe us to be total strangers, that your friendship with Morgan is merely by chance."

"You're saying it isn't?"

"Come, come now Georgiana. Surely you feel, at least on an intuitive level, your connection with her?" Georgiana slowly regains her chair.

"Yes…I know…it's more than coincidence."

"Now I understand why I was desirous of seeing your performance tonight, an inner calling, but your vision emanates entirely from within you."

"What is it you saw?" Morgan inquires. Georgiana stares at them, a look I've never seen etched into her face.

"When I looked at you…I saw…I clearly saw…" She falters. "I must be going insane."

"What is it? What did you see?"

The question goes unanswered when the door is kicked-in and Bambi is instantly lording over Georgiana.

"G, what the fuck man?" she snarls. "What the hell was that?" There's immediately a renewed tension in the room as Bambi hovers over her band mate.

"Nothing," Georgiana mumbles.

"You walked off stage man, in the middle of the set! You call that *nothing*?"

"I had a moment."

"*A moment*? G, what the fuck?! It's bad enough you getting all morose and shit, but I can't have you walking off in the middle of a number. Am I getting through the dope?"

"Bambi, we were just talking about that," Morgan interrupts, "about what happened," but Bambi instantly sets upon her in a most vicious manner.

"Shut the fuck up Morgan! This isn't about you this time. This is about us, our band, our business," she shouts. Morgan instantly becomes silent, her eyes narrowing.

"Leave her alone!" Georgiana snaps but Bambi holds her ground. I'm surprised by the way Georgiana recedes back into her chair, staring at the floor. "I got back up there."

"You just stood there like a zombie! Georgiana, I need you pumpin' up there man, givin' it up. You know the deal. VD just stands there, Tiny sits on her ass. I'm all alone up there. You just left me hanging tonight babe." She glares down at her, kicking her leg. "What about it *bassy*? What do you got to say?" She presses on relentlessly and it's as if Georgiana were melting away into someplace dark and alone.

I'm shocked by the change in their relationship. Before, Georgiana was the band's leader, now clearly something had changed, and Bambi's haranguing was taking on serious–I would even say monstrous-proportions. When Georgiana doesn't respond to her last tirade, Bambi kicks her heartily in the leg.

"You hearing me G? Am I getting through the drugs and alcohol?"

At this point something completely unexpected happens when Monique rises to her feet, calmly addressing Bambi.

"Dear, I'm certain you have business matters to discuss with your colleague, but may I suggest you calm yourself; take a moment to think things through perhaps?"

"Who the hell is this?!" Bambi shouts at Morgan who remains steadfastly silent. She kicks at Georgiana again. "Well? Who the fuck is this woman?"

"You already met. Morgan's aunt Monique," she mumbles, and Bambi squares herself before the aunt.

"No shit? Well, *Morgan's aunt Monique*…I got a little message for you baby," I prepare myself for the worst when a remarkable thing occurs. Monique raises her index finger between them, and Bambi instantly freezes clutching her throat and begins to sputter and cough. When Monique lowers her finger, only then does *the grip* on the singer's throat subside. Bambi stares at her, in shock; or is it fear? Whatever the emotion she quickly leaves the room, Georgiana following her to the door, watching her recede down the hallway.

I'm uncertain what to expect next. When Georgiana turns, her expression is hard to read. Is it anger, or curiosity?

"You shut her up. Didn't you? You shut her up." She looks to Morgan. "Your aunt shut-up Bambi Giordano. No one, I mean *no one* ever shuts up Bambi…ever…this is a colossal first."

"I apologize about creating a scene, but it couldn't be helped," Monique says glancing at Morgan. "My word, such a wicked tongue." Georgiana suddenly takes up the aunt's hand in hers.

"Teach me how to do that. I want to know how to do something like that." The aunt gently pats her wrist.

"Georgiana, I don't mean to cause trouble but there just isn't time to sit through all this negative rhetoric. It's important you hear what I've come to say."

"Hear what?" she asks pensively.

"How proud I am of you. It was such a pleasure to see you perform tonight."

"*Proud* of me?" she says, apparently confused by these words.

"Of course." She smiles at our gangly host. "Look at you Georgiana, so talented. I can't believe how well you play your instrument. I'm a musician myself. I play the viola and a little guitar, from time to time. I know musicianship when I hear it. You my dear are a true musician."

"You think I'm a talented musician?" Georgiana asks, her eyes growing misty.

"More than that. You're a talented *human being*, a truly lovely woman. Lovely. I'm so pleased to have finally met you, *in person*," she says her eyes reflecting a deeper meaning behind these words.

Then a most incredible thing happens as Georgiana begins to cry, not in a loud ostentatious manner but in a quiet painful way and my heart melts for her in that moment.

"Georgiana, what's the matter, what's wrong?" Morgan asks taking her side. She struggles to speak.

"No one's ever said that to me before…and meant it."

"Said what, that you're talented?"

"That I'm…*lovely*. No one's ever called me that before."

"But you *are* lovely Georgiana," Monique says. "Look at yourself dear, so tall and proud, such a unique woman," and Georgiana breaks. Morgan strokes her friend's wild black hair.

When she lifts her face. I see the pain in her eyes. I also see the love being shared between the three very different women. After a moment the aunt whispers to her niece.

"Forgive me Morgan, I'm sorry but we must be going. I need to return to Magenta. All this chaotic energy today has me feeling faint." There's a brief tender moment shared by the women.

"I wish I could come with you," Georgiana says, oddly sincere.

"Why don't you?" Morgan says and Georgiana wipes tears from her eyes dreadfully smearing her mascara.

"If it were only so easy."

"It is that easy. If this is becoming unbearable to you as a person then get away from it. Come stay with us for a while."

Georgiana gently pulls away from her. "I can't, I've everything wrapped up in this...this is who I am."

"It's not *who* you are Georgiana, I've said it a number of times. Quit equating *who* you are with something so transitory. If you continue, something bad could happen."

"Something bad *is* happening," she murmurs and grows distant, lighting a new cigarette.

"Georgiana, might I propose something?" Monique inquires. "When does your project end?"

"My project?"

"The tour," Morgan says.

"Um...from here we go to Houston, Vegas, then LA for a week. Then from there...um, the Bay Area, Oakland. Then Seattle and Vancouver, then we close it out in New York."

"Why don't you arrange to see us when it concludes? Or are there pressing matters in New York?"

"There's nothing *pressing* in New York," she says staring blankly into space.

"Splendid, then it's settled. We'll see you after you're finished working." Her reaction is less than effusive.

"Maybe, I don't know," she says growing detached. There's really nothing more to be said.

"Shall we be on our way children?" Monique concludes and Morgan touches her friend's sleeve.

"We'll see you then, right?" For some reason Georgiana becomes trance-like, she doesn't even rise to say goodbye. We slowly, reluctantly, leave.

Backstage is bustling, filled with stagehands pushing wheeled road-boxes. We can barely communicate over the din of men's shouting and the slamming of aluminum staging as the show rapidly collapses onto set-carts and into road-boxes being loaded into semi-trucks.

At the dock we find Vince directing the flow of road-boxes to the appropriate trailers. He spies us and tells the men to wait while he embraces Morgan.

"Did you enjoy the show aunt Monique?"

"Indeed Vincent, a rare and enjoyable experience. Thank you for your courtesy."

"Did you get a chance to talk to Georgiana?" he asks Morgan.

"Sort of...not really." They exchange a silent look. "Watch out for her Vince, I'm worried."

"*You* are?"

"She's not acting like herself at all. The worst thing is-"

She's interrupted when a shouting match breaks out about the direction of certain boxes onto the appropriate trailers and Vince goes ballistic. "What did I just tell you guys ten seconds ago?" he shouts at the men. "*Backline* on number three, *Sound* goes on number two, set pieces on one. How can you not get this?" He turns to us. "I gotta go, I'll call your cellphone in a hour," he says. Morgan takes him by the forearm.

"I no longer use my mobile phone Vince. I'm sorry." There's nothing to be said, he shrugs, gives her a hug and leaves, shouting at the men. "I step away for thirty fucking seconds to say goodbye to a friend and the load-out comes to an absolute halt? You people are pathetic!"

We head down the ramp leading outside. At the door we hear a voice over our shoulders. Georgiana catches up to us and embraces Morgan in a deep loving embrace.

"I miss you constantly," she says into Morgan's shoulder.

"I miss you too," Morgan replies, her eyes tearing. Georgiana then embraces Monique, looking deeply into her.

"Do you want to know what I saw, when I looked at you? What I saw sitting there instead of you?"

"I'm beyond curious my dear," she says, and we all wait with expectation.

"I saw me."

"You? You saw yourself, as you are now?"

"No, younger…much younger."

"How old Georgiana, could you discern it?"

"When I was a teenager, maybe sixteen…seventeen, I guess. I was wearing that stupid yellow vest mom knitted me for Christmas."

"What happened when you were seventeen?" Morgan inquires. The question freezes her; she just stares at us as if unable to speak.

"You need to understand something Georgiana," Monique says. "You have a higher self, all of us do…well, most. This quality of our *selves* is very quiet. It communicates as softly as a whisper, softer. One must pay very close attention to hear its voice…to *feel* its voice, might be the proper way of saying it. When things become critical, it can reach out to a sensitive, oft times a pet. Sometimes Nature herself will convey the message, the Goddess herself. Either way, my belief is this is happening. Your higher self, the higher aspect of your being, is reaching out for help, trying to communicate something of extreme import."

"But what?"

"This experience you've had is *yourself talking to yourself*. It's used me as a catalyst merely because it's easy for me to…*step outside of myself*."

"But why?"

"Your higher self is forcing you to focus on an aspect of your life."

"What if it happens again? How do I stop it?"

"There's nothing that can be done. You cannot control it, nor would you want to. Its message is highly valuable to your life. It seeks your well-being." Georgiana disappears into her thoughts, staring into space.

"What happened when you were seventeen?" Morgan asks again and the look in Georgiana's eyes changes radically.

"*What happened?* Quid pro quo..." she mutters and begins wringing her hands. The aunt takes up her hands, stroking them lovingly.

"It's not necessary you tell us here and now. Meditate upon it and please arrange your schedule to visit Magenta as soon as you possibly can. Now, I simply must be going home. We'll see you soon, yes?" but Georgiana's response is shocking.

"No Monique, you won't. Something will get in the way." She looks at Morgan and her eyes grow dark, unsettling. "Don't you feel it?" she states resolutely and Monique's brow knits.

"What are you feeling?"

Georgiana shakes her head. "I don't know. I don't know why I know, I just know, *something will get in the way,*" she says, the women exchanging serious expressions.

"Georgiana, you need to relax, you're too worked up. I doubt you realize what you're saying," Morgan responds but Georgiana's manner doesn't waver, leaving a strange feeling in my stomach. The women embrace once more assuring their intentions of reuniting.

When Georgiana gives me a rare embrace, she whispers in my ear. "Look out for Morgan and Monique, don't let anything happen to them." I look into her eyes and know she's serious, the words intended to convey some kind of warning.

"What do you mean by that Georgiana?"

"Goodbye Willem," she says as one might say before departing on a long trip, and *like a rock-star*, she's down the hallway, her boot heels sounding over the din of the load-out, stagehands slowing or stopping their work to watch her pass, not even a glance, back in our direction.

Not a word is spoken between the three of us until we are well on our way back to Magenta. Morgan is the first to finally break the quietude of the Mercedes.

"What do you make of all that aunt? All that about not seeing us again."

"I'm unsure, but it's somehow disconcerting. What do you think she meant?"

"I think she's exposing her fears. She's forever been of the mindset that nothing will ever work out right in her life; that her life is perpetually destined for failure. I think it was the influence of her father. He was very critical of her."

"It could be that…yet…"

"Yet what?"

"I can't put a finger on it. I'll meditate tomorrow."

"I'm sure it's just the current state she's in."

"Yes dear," the aunt murmurs and gazes at the night passing outside the car window. "Thank you for driving Willem, I appreciate it," she adds, and this is more or less the last of the conversation until we return to Villa Magenta.

Chapter 6: *Funeral in the rain*

"Aunt Monique, do you realize the award ceremony is this weekend?" Morgan asks from behind her cup of tea, putting the newspaper aside and studying her aunt as she instructs Rosemary how to make a proper C chord on the guitar. We're in the sitting room at Magenta the next morning; it's a brilliant day filled with sunshine.

"It hurts Miss Montaigne," Rosemary says, stopping the lesson and sucking on the tips of her fingers.

"Of course it hurts Rosemary. To accomplish anything in this world requires a little pain. Now try again," but the child becomes obstinate.

"I don't want to learn the guitar anymore Miss Montaigne, I don't like it."

"Rosemary Enright, I'm shocked at you. You've only just begun, and you've made up your mind you dislike the guitar? Why?"

"Because it hurts my fingers."

"But I've told you dear, your fingers will get used to the task and complain less as the days go by."

"I don't want to play the guitar," the child presses.

"No girl leaves Magenta without learning to play music on an instrument of some sort and you've already said *no* to our piano."

"I know, but I don't like the piano either."

"Rosemary, for heaven's sake…"

"I want to play the accordion," she says, the women reacting with surprise.

"The accordion? Whatever gave you such a notion?"

"The party last week."

"Oh?"

"Uncle Cristobal showed me how to play *You Are My Sunshine*."

"On *his* accordion?"

"Yep. It was easy. I played real good."

Monique exchanges a curious look with Morgan. "That's a very rare and valuable accordion. It has magic inside of it."

"I want one just like that one, a gold and white one."

"Hmm, we'll have to see about that...perhaps I might arrange something. Somehow."

"Aunt Monique, did you hear what I said? The award ceremony is-"

"I heard you Morgan," she says taking up the instrument.

"Award ceremony?" I inquire and Morgan looks at the aunt from above her bifocals.

"Aunt Monique is being honored by the Women's League with a Lifetime Achievement award...in recognition for her work on behalf of young women and her foundation, *Magenta's Daughters*."

"You mentioned that in a letter awhile back. That's wonderful," I say gazing at the aunt who seems not to share our enthusiasm.

"That's all for your music lesson today Rosemary, please go and finish your French lesson."

"Cripes. Why do I need to bother learnin' French? It don't make any sense."

"Rosemary, once you learn to speak it, it will make an enormous amount of sense."

"I hate French," the child says crossing her arms and kicking at the air.

"Besides, if you learn the language you may travel there one day, perhaps meet a young Frenchman and fall in love."

"Yuck," the child says, *squinching* her nose, the freckles forming new patterns.

"Young man or other, it *is* part of your lessons."

"Geez, can't I go out and play? I need a break Miss Montaigne. Cripes, I'm still just a kid ya know," she says and Morgan smiles while Monique frowns.

"*Geez* and *cripes*, are not words Rosemary and certainly unsuitable vernacular for young ladies," she says and Rosemary squints. "Alright Miss Enright, if we're overtaxing your constitution, perhaps you could use a reprieve."

"What's a *reprieve*?"

"A moment of rest or relaxation from an arduous endeavor," Monique says. Rosemary rolls her eyes and exits the room. "She's so precocious it's almost endearing."

"So, the award ceremony is coming up and you've done nothing about an acceptance speech."

"I've told you Morgan, and them, I've not changed my position on the matter, not in the least," Monique says returning her beautiful handcrafted guitar to its hard-shell case, placing it within the old chifforobe in the corner used for the storing of musical instruments.

"Her position?" I whisper to Morgan under my breath and she uses the opportunity to express herself openly.

"She refuses to speak at the ceremony. Really aunt Monique, your *moment in the sun*."

"My, *moment in the sun*, as you state it, will be the day I *pass-on* to the next realm and hang my hat on the hook of this material plane for good."

"But I do insist you change your mind and say a few words of thanks for such a marvelous award. Just a simple thank-you would do volumes of good for all considered."

"Morgan, why must you persist so? Really, I'm quite resolute on the matter."

"Aunt Monique…"

"Morgan, what reason is there in even attending at all? Really, I mean it. I've no desire for such accolades. I do this work out of necessity. I've really no choice to the contrary. I took a vow to the *Lady on High,* that I'd stick to it and I've done that, I've done it out of love for my community and for society as a whole. Personal rewards are contrary to the spirit of the thing. There's really no need for all this fussing about over it."

"*Fussing about*?" Morgan says incredulous. "You've been awarded *Woman of the Year*…by the Women's League. Do you realize what an honor this is?"

"*Woman of the year,*" she huffs, "as if there were just one of us out here doing this essential work," she says placing herself squarely before her niece. "Honestly Morgan, I regret you failed to follow on my wishes to have the whole thing redirected to someone more deserving, someone who will appreciate it."

"But how can you not appreciate this aunt? This is a rare and prestigious award. You deserve it."

"They can send it via the post."

"Oh, honestly, this threatening not to attend is not going to get you out of going, and saying a handful of words, at least a *thank-you*. Willem, have you a suit?"

"Yes, the one I brought with me from the tour," I say and her expression is less than effusive.

"No worry, we'll rent you a tux," she says before readdressing her aunt. "I'm going to wear my magenta blazer over black, just to make a statement." She smiles and exits the room. I see the rather troubled expression on Monique's face as she turns and walks to the old fireplace and silently gazes at the collection of family photographs all neatly arranged across the entirety of the mantel.

When she takes one up and studies it, I feel compelled to look over her shoulder; its an older photograph in black and white of a beautiful young girl in a silk dress, her long black hair and dark eyes comprising a gentle face known to me, the phantom girl I had met in this very room, not long ago.

"Gillian?" I say softly and the aunt's gaze seems moist as if near the edge of tears.

"Yes," is all she says, studying the photograph, gently caressing the glass.

"Tell me about her. All I know of her is the night she appeared to us, as a ghost," I whisper. She replaces the frame to its place amongst the family.

"Gillian was a mere wisp of a person Willem, delicate, like a crystalline doll. So fragile to the touch one felt compelled from doing so. Like a tender blossom, one becomes afraid to touch it lest it crumble in one's grasp. We all knew she wasn't destined long for this world. How does one know such things? Like the *Goddess blossom,* she came into this world, pristine, and like all blossoms, too soon to fall…as if this world were incapable of sustaining something so beautiful. We all knew, in some mysterious way, her presence would be a fleeting thing. By her sixteenth birthday, she was gone from us, this world."

That afternoon, a very important meeting comes to order inside the children's classroom on the second floor. In attendance are the girls and myself. Monique taps on a water glass with a yellow number two pencil.

"This meeting of the *Magenta Garden Club* will now come to order," she states formally. "President Rosemary Enright presiding." I glance at our *president,* looking very *presidential*, as she sits attentively engaged, her hands folded neatly upon the desktop.

"Now, ever since Jerome took over sole care of the tomatoes–the *Prima-donna Regis* of the garden-the herbs and the rest of the vegetables are all clamoring for attention. Therefore, Mr. Furey has been conscripted as supplemental labor. Are you sure you're up to the task good Sir Willem?" she asks and Montara giggles.

"Yes, I'm happy to help out."

"Then it goes to a majority vote within the body of the club. All in favor of Willem joining the Garden Club raise your hand." Each girl instantly holds aloft her hand. "All those against?" We gaze at each other, not one hand raised, and Monique taps the table once with a plastic toy mallet. "The ayes carry. The vote is final, congratulations," she says and begins to clap, the girls all eagerly joining in. Monique rises from her tiny desk chair, standing formally before me.

"Good Sir Willem, you are now bequeathed the honorary title of *Tillerman*, first-form, of the House of Montaigne, by God, Queen and country" she says, touching both of my shoulders with the straight edge of her palm and the girls giggle through their fingers as I'm *officially knighted*.

"Here is the list of the vegetables chosen for your care. I leave you to your own volition." I scan the list written in Monique's elegant cursive.

a) *Eggplant*
b) *Okra*
c) *Cayenne*
d) *Red chilis*
e) *Chives*
f) *Garlic*
g) *Snap peas*
h) *Acorn squash*
i) *Zucchini*

j) Crooked-necks
k) Butterbeans

After Monique has left with the rest of the girls, Rosemary looks over my shoulder, scratching at a scab on her elbow.

"Mr. Willem, where's *Volition* at?"

"*Volition?*" I ask, surprised by the question.

"Miss Montaigne said she was gonna leave you there. Is it very far away from here?"

"Rosemary, *volition* isn't a place, it's, well, the motivation to do something, accomplish something."

"You mean like work?"

"Well, volition would be an aspect of work I suppose." She *squinches* her nose, the freckles forming undulating patterns. "I'm not doing a very good job of explaining. You yourself have volition, use it every day."

"Me? When?"

"Well, when you help in the garden for instance, or do your homework, or wash the dishes, things of this nature, that's *volition*." She adopts a rather blank expression, gazing at me deadpan.

"I don't think I'd like volition too much," she says and quietly leaves the room.

The gardens of Villa Magenta are vast, nearly an acre in size, half of it dedicated to tomatoes alone. Tilling my rows is tiring but rejuvenating, my body responding to the work. Halfway down the row of butterbeans I'm startled by Monique suddenly at my elbow.

"Oh, Aunt Monique, I didn't hear you walk up."

"Come to the house for lemonade Willem, before you dehydrate," she says.

I wipe the sweat from my brow and dust the perspiration from my chest with my t-shirt. "That sounds good."

"Are you enjoying the work, or is it taxing you?"

"Yes, I'm rather enjoying it actually." She smiles, her eyes penetrating.

"Willem, I would appreciate you doing something for me. From now on, when you till the plants, I want you to think of them as people."

"People?"

"Willem, plants are very much like human beings, especially *the garden club*, as we refer to them."

"I don't think I understand."

"Haven't you noticed? As you till the rows how some of the plants are vigorous and productive while others, well, dither along, not exactly productive yet not fallow either, and then again, some actually do lie fallow, some wither and die."

"Yes. I've noticed."

"Why do you suppose it so? Plants birthed together in the same environment, planted from the same stock in the same soil, the same watering and care?"

"I hadn't really thought about it. Do you know the answer?"

"I've already told you. Plants are exactly like people."

"I'm not sure I understand."

"It must be something within the plant itself, a desire to will and grow. Some possess this, magical ability. One gives forth abundance to the world while others seem not to care to produce that for which it was designed. Thus, the burden of the gardener, the Tillerman, for it's the touch of his hoe that reminds them, *I'm here watching and waiting, get busy down there, I've raised you from a seed, watered and nurtured you, let's get going.*"

She scans the rows, her hands atop her narrow hips. "Such prima-donnas...take any one of these seeds Willem and stick it in a corner somewhere with just enough sunlight and a splash of rain and just watch it grow...but God forbid you put her in a row in the garden. They think they've gone to heaven. Yet, let one little weed, one thin wisp of grass get into the mix and watch what happens...such complaining and consternation!" she says directly to the plants before turning her gaze back upon me. "The expectations of the plant itself Willem, *some expect nothing and give everything, others expect everything and give nothing*."

We share a knowing smile. "I understand."

"And what is the Tillerman to do?" I shake my head in response to her expectant stare. "He gives extra to the complainers of course, hoping they respond, while the vigorous souls, the productive, are often left to *tough it out*, content with what the garden gives. Exactly like people, don't you think?"

"Yes, it is. Exactly like people." I wipe my brow with my shirt. "I'll finish this row and be right in."

"As you wish it."

I turn and set upon the row when I remember a question about the pruning. However, when I turn, she's not there, in fact, she not even in proximity of the garden.

That evening a most terrifying event takes place. Just near twilight, as the children are preparing for bed, Montara walks into the kitchen where I'm having tea with Morgan and Monique, a most concerned expression on her lovely face.

"Mama...man," she says arresting our attentions.

"*Man*?" Monique echoes, confusion coursing her face and Montara nods pointing in the direction of the back yard.

"Bad…man," she says and Monique is immediately on her feet.

"Morgan, take Montara upstairs, check on the girls. Hurry, go now," she insists, and Morgan does so without question.

Uncertain as to what is happening, I follow Monique to the doors that open out onto the veranda and there, just discernable in the feeble light is a dark form, a man, standing beneath the chinaberry trees at the very rear of the yard. Monique fixates upon the spot. I position myself for a better look.

"Who is that?" I inquire but the aunt remains silent and still. I squint, trying to focus on the queer sight when a strange unsettling feeling begins to creep into my chest. "Do you know that person?"

She remains eerily silent. The man stares unrelentingly at our place near the door. He's dressed entirely in dark clothing and absolutely motionless. A feeling of unspeakable evil suddenly permeates the moment when I realize who the mysterious person is.

"My god, that's him…*the Hollowman,* he's here."

"Quiet Willem, don't make a sound." The moment is dreadful, the silence deafening.

"Aunt Monique, don't you realize who that is?"

"Shhh, *stone, stock, still,*" she whispers, and I'm forced to endure this seemingly endless waiting.

"That's him, *the Hollowman,*" I say breaking the quietude. She takes my wrist. I can feel the nervous tension in her grip.

"I know who it is, please be quiet."

"But aunt Monique, what is he doing there? How is it possible?"

"Willem, I beg of you, please quiet yourself," she insists, and a horrifying kind of stalemate ensues.

I try to calm myself, feel the blood coursing my veins. He's completely still, unmoving; I can literally *feel* his attention on us. Something deep within me knows that this *attention* is the cause of the dread permeating my mind and that I need to control it. However, fear and impatience takes hold. I can no longer endure the *chess game* and race into the house, enter Colonel Montaigne's private study, extracting the old Colt revolver he keeps in the drawer of the desk and quickly rejoin her on the veranda.

"For goodness sake Willem, put that ungodly thing away," she says arresting my arm.

"But aunt Monique, that's him, the man who attacked me in London."

"I'm perfectly aware of who, *or what*, it is...now please take hold of yourself, I need to concentrate."

"But what if he comes in?"

"Willem, that vile thing can't come within a hundred meters of this house."

"Why?"

"This isn't the time to explain. Please be quiet."

How long we stand there engaged in this silent vigil I have no idea; however, I eventually reach my breaking point. "I've had enough of this," I say, deciding I'm going to pay him a visit. When I go to leave, I'm brushed aside by what feels like a sudden gust of wind. I watch–incredulous-as a dark shadow races across the expanse of lawn on a direct course toward the man in the recesses. He either runs or disappears altogether. Monique is nonplussed.

"Topey, get back here, this instant!" she shouts across the lawn. I'm shocked beyond words when an enormous black animal-like creature, resembling a wolf but void of any distinctive features except its two glowing eyes, quickly returns, groveling at her feet.

"How dare you," she chastises the thing; the sound it makes reminding me vaguely of the purring of a great lion or one of the large predator cats. "You leap for your master only," she scolds, and her inflection is somewhat unnerving. She glances in my direction momentarily before readdressing the creature. "Now go, off with you."

The creature takes a moment to rub itself along her leg, but the aunt is obstinate. "I said off with you, this instant." Like the shadow of a bird in flight, the thing disappears around the corner of the house.

"What in the name of god was that?" I expound. She sees the utter shock on my face.

"Willem, I know this is hard for you to understand but there are *energies,* for lack of a more suitable word, at work within this house, that protects Magenta inside and out."

"What do you mean?"

"Nothing of malicious, evil intent can get anywhere near this home without a direct invitation, *the house simply won't allow it.*" I'm at a complete loss to understand what she's alluding to.

"What was that thing, that attacked the Hollowman? It looked like a wolf, except..." I go mute unable to describe the incredible creature.

"A conversation for another time. Excuse me, I need to check on the children." I'm left standing under the shroud of twilight like a man who has just seen an apparition.

The next night a strange group of people arrive at the house. The moment I spy the old Creole woman getting out of the car I know this is the medicine woman Aphelia I've heard so much about. She's withered beyond years but her eyes, like two shards of obsidian radiate an inner glow.

She's accompanied by two beautiful women of color, Magdalena's half-sister Aone and her mother Ceci, the women embrace and there seems a lot of attention over Montara who shows the ladies her current art project. They study me silently from afar. It's only when they converge on the north study that Aphelia stops before me in the parlor, gazing at me with deep penetrating eyes.

"Sista...da re de?" she inquires pointing a finger that looks like gnarled root wood.

Monique pauses, her expression growing inquisitive. "Dat Willem, ma Mer..." she says, the old gal giving me a thorough looking over.

"Hmm. Him Hounci?"

"*Hounci*?" Monique echoes, surprise forming on her face and her dark eyes glitter. "E-nay...nes pas Mama. L'apprenti."

"Hmm," the old gal breathes, resuming her deep study of my person and the area about my head. *"Him, baka heyla...he, la titi ney,"* she says over her shoulder to Ceci and Aone and the elder nods.

"Oui...come Mama," she says taking the old woman's arm, gesturing toward Monique. "Arete sista Monique, neh?"

The old gal gives me one more long discerning look before they slowly disappear into the north study.

"Guess I better go hide Majo before this one here decides to sacrifice him to Damballa," Magda says gesturing at me.

"Mags, really…" Morgan says, shaking her head, and they both join the women in the north study. I turn to Binford and Colonel Montaigne quietly sipping bourbon together.

"What was all that?" They remain silent. "What was she talking about?"

"You," the Colonel says.

"What did she say?"

"She asked Monique if you was a witch doctor," Binford says.

"*A witch doctor*? Are you joking?" Nothing in their muted responses indicates any humor is being interjected. "Is she a little…off?"

"Off?"

"Mentally unstable."

"She's a priestess. One part black, one part white, couple parts Choctaw and enough French for spice," the old Colonel says lighting one of his thin black cheroots.

"What did Magda mean by that crack about Majo?"

"Magda's full of vinegar."

"Does Aphelia sacrifice animals?" I ask and the men exchange a look before Binford answers.

"Of course not. *Any entity that seeks the spilling of blood isn't to be trusted.*"

The morning of the biggest change in our lives started quite routinely. We dressed, had breakfast together more or less as usual; the only noticeable difference was aunt Monique. I was quick to note she seemed uncharacteristically pensive. After lunch, while in the sitting room having wine cakes with coffee –waiting for the arrival of Mrs. Richardson- Morgan actually questions her about her mood.

"I regret they ever awarded me this."

"Aunt Monique, how can you say such a thing?"

"I told you before dear, I dislike such notoriety. I do this work because Universe demands it, there's nothing selfish in my motives."

"No one is saying there is. It's the League's respect for all you've done for women and girls. Aunt Monique, you're a treasure to this community. You've saved lives from despair."

"That's my reward, lives rebuilt, people having a better chance of leading healthy productive lives."

"And thus the lifetime achievement award. What's wrong aunt Monique?"

"I don't know."

"What are you feeling?"

"That's what concerns me. Strangely, I can't seem to delve my feelings. Why?"

"You're nervous about being in front of all those people?"

"I suppose that could be it…but then again…"

"But what?"

Monique shakes her head. "I don't understand it."

"I understand it," Magda interjects, "you've had too much coffee."

Montara enters the room wearing a lovely pink and white dress and carrying a dog-eared storybook. "Mama…story-time."

"No, your maw's got an event this afternoon sugar," Magda says and the child looks at her mother with concern in her dark eyes.

"No, Mama…no go."

"Hush Montara, let's not start this again," Magda says but the mysterious young girl can't disguise her concern.

"Mama…"

"Go play *game-time* with Rosemary," Magda says gesturing. The freckle-faced, red-haired girl instantly drops her study book and extends her hand.

"Come on Montara, Rosemary *game-time* with you," the girl says, and they reluctantly begin to leave together when Monique suddenly goes to her, clasping her daughter in a deep heartfelt embrace. She brushes the bangs from her lovely eyes.

"Montara, Mama loves you. Mama loves you more than anything else in this whole wide world."

"Montara…Mama…love," and they smile together.

"Mama will always be here with you, right here," she says placing her fingertips atop the child's heart. She then embraces her for several minutes seemingly unable, or unwilling, to relinquish her hold.

We arrive early and park the Mercedes in the ramp adjacent the hotel. As we cross the street, I see a disheveled man in a worn brown hoodie at the doors.

"You're Monique Montaigne?" he asks, less a question than a statement.

"Yes," she says stopping, addressing him fully.

"You took my daughter away from me, I hope you burn in hell you goddamn witch!" he exhorts and we're all shocked beyond words.

"I remember you Mr. Callis, quite well in fact, you beat your child, put her in the hospital if I recall correctly."

"You took my daughter from me."

"No Mr. Callis, we didn't take your child from you, you sent your daughter away. Your course and brutal treatment of your own child sent her away from your arms."

This statement seems to freeze the man. He stands as if uncertain what to say or do. I step between him and the aunt pulling open the door.

"Excuse us," I say and see the women inside. As they enter, I study the man. His appearance is extremely unsettling to some quiet aspect of my inner self. He avoids my gaze as he turns away and retreats down the concrete stairs and around the corner of the building.

The room is large and adorned in gold and white with hints of purple. There are approximately forty to fifty large round tables, with eight chairs apiece, draped in white satin covers and adorned with purple iris centerpieces, Monique's favorite flower.

We're beset by a group of women, *Magenta's Daughters* board of directors, including Regina Malcolm-Torres, the foundation's director. She is a stunningly beautiful woman of color with an enormous smile. They each embrace Monique lovingly while Morgan snaps photos with her Leica.

We also greet several of the members of the Women's League and are introduced to their chairman Beverly Taylor. She and a few of her officers gather around the awardee for a photo session and a lively animated conversation ensues. As the women converse together I see Monique's pensive mood rapidly dissipate and the moment takes on a joyous and optimistic tone, the room filling with laughter and a sense of hope.

There are several other young women of various racial distinctions all lining up to greet Monique. Morgan informs me these are all girls from broken and abusive homes that have gone through the program.

I look at these girls, women really, as they loiter near the inner circle. I see clearly their affection for Monique, I see it in their eyes and hear it in their words, the genuineness in their embracing of her.

Our table is immediately before the stage and adjacent the podium. We're directed to our seats and the visitations from a variety of men and women seem almost endless.

It's during this time as large amounts of people begin to pour into the room that I chance to see, standing near the entrance, the same man who verbally assailed us outside. He gazes about unaware of my attention upon him. I side up to Morgan who has been taking pictures of the women and whisper in her ear.

"Morgan, isn't that the same guy who shouted at us outside?" She stares at the man. I instantly see the trepidation on her features.

"Yes, I believe it is."

"Should I ask him what he's doing here?" She seems uncertain what to do. "I'll go say hello." She takes my arm.

"Just let it be Will. Aunt Monique has had to deal with this kind of person before."

"I don't know…something about him disturbs me." I see her concern about my stating this, her eyes returning to the disheveled man, somehow so very queer, so very much out of place.

"Never mind him Willem, let's have some punch."

At the punchbowl, Regina and her assistant, a tall thin young man in his twenties, engage Morgan in a lengthy discussion about an upcoming fundraiser they want covered by local media. They begin to outline a plan of action when a voice booms over the PA indicating the event is about to begin and requesting everyone to take their seats.

We watch from our chairs as one of the officers from the League introduces the evening's proceedings. She welcomes the special guests in attendance including a prominent congresswoman.

Regina is asked on stage and she addresses the gathering impeccably, a woman of ability and candor. She speaks about her ten years with the foundation starting as an orphan from a broken home before becoming an administrative assistant, eventually attaining the presidency. The audience becomes enthralled by her wit and rhetorical acumen. She talks extensively about the mentoring and tutoring programs and the girls they've placed in various homes, based upon Monique's original plan laid down twenty-five years ago.

She then introduces several of the young women who could make the event. I'm impressed by the scope and breadth of their collective achievements. What could have been under-privileged youth cast into questionable circumstances, are now all fine young citizens engaged in a wide variety of professions including business, art and music.

Three of the girls are asked to speak and each one expresses an enormous degree of affection for Monique and their time under her tutelage.

Two of the girls who had been trafficked as teens, come to tears at the microphone regarding the tragedy their lives could very easily have developed into had it not been for the efforts of *Magenta's Daughters*, Monique in particular. One of the girls actually descends from the podium to embrace Monique on the floor and a standing ovation ensues, the occasion deeply moving.

Next, the chairman of the League takes the stage and talks first about the League's current work then about *Magenta's Daughters*, culminating with the presentation of the award.

Morgan ascends the stage to accept on her behalf. She looks stunning in her magenta-colored blazer over black slacks and blouse. I'm surprised by her relaxed nature and eloquence as she addresses the group from the lectern.

Although brief, her words are passionate and heartfelt. She finishes by delivering Monique's acceptance speech but refuses to accept the award beckoning from the lectern for Monique to receive the award herself.

It takes a constant determined standing ovation to get the woman to take my arm so I can escort her to the podium. When she makes the lectern she lays her head into Morgan's shoulder and tries to hide her face. All in attendance remain on their feet and their applause continues, moved by either her shyness or humility.

"Say something aunt Monique," I hear Morgan say off-mic and Ms. Taylor helps *drag* the aunt to the microphone.

Despite her obvious discomfort, her dark eyes glimmer and a smile emerges at the edges of her mouth as she scans the people gathered before us.

"Thank you all so very much. I've no words to express how deeply I appreciate this so very fine a distinction. Forgive me, but I'm unequal to it, there are so many others who deserve this more than I. How I wish they could all join us here today but it would take the rest of the week I fear," she says and the audience laughs softly.

She then gazes at the girls sitting in proximity of the stage and a smile beams upon her face. "Really, it's not me, or anyone else up here on this stage, the thanks goes to you, you beautiful precious young women, all very fine ladies one and all. Just look at you, what you've done with your lives, of your own initiative. Each one of you, prove to the rest of us…it *can* be done, yes, yes it can. Bless you all, thank you."

Everyone rises as Regina gestures for the girls to stand and truly, each one looks beautiful and a sense of optimism fills the room. Then, like that, it's over as we all leave the stage and the assistant closes the event thanking everyone for attending.

I'm waiting in the lobby while the ladies finish socializing before we proceed outside.

The night is cool, comfortable. Just outside on the steps, the impossible happens. A moment locked within a moment, like a piece of film remains behind, a feeble reminder but indelible…*the man in the brown hoodie.*

I watch it unfold, moment to moment, like a movie, the glass doors, the stone steps, the man, his hand extracting a thin dark object and pointing it at Monique and incredibly…firing.

Time stops, comes to an agonizing crawl. I see this all happen before me, like watching a newscast on a television screen. There is a horrendous series of sounds, the gunshot and screaming, then a profound silence washing out all other sound except the rapid beating of my heart, and all of it happens within the fraction of a moment.

When my mind realizes what has happened, I have the gun in my hand. I bury my fist into the side of his head, knocking him down. It's a miracle no one else was shot but those thoughts never occur to me in that singular moment, only the gun, the man, his pistol now in my possession…and I'm going to use it.

My knees are atop his arms, pinning him to the concrete. I pull back the hammer and place the barrel directly against his head and begin to squeeze the trigger. *This will be quick and easy, without any lengthy legalities.* Then I hear her voice.

"Willem!" The microsecond before I do it, I see her eyes. "Good God, what are you doing?!" I return to my senses but I hear the words *'do it'* repeating in my mind.

'Look at the man, his face, stupid and ugly, do it...kill him.'

"Willem, please, put down that gun, or everything is lost, all our hopes and dreams will become nothing."

I look at Morgan, then at Alma Richardson bent above Monique, see the rivulet of crimson slicing the step, the concrete drinking up the *life-blood* as if it were nothing more than...rain.

"Willem, please..." I look at her, then down at the bastard under me, replace the hammer on the pistol and bury it into his jaw, shattering it.

We're in a kind of collective trance, a walking stupor. I recall talking to the police but remember nothing that was said. I know we're sitting outside an emergency room. The walls are painted an ugly pastel green, not natural at all. Why this color? Who would chose such a dour hue for a hospital, a place of healing?

I'm sitting with Mrs. Richardson while Morgan uses the phone near the nurse's station. I look at the temporary cast on my hand feeling the pulse of blood moving through it.

When the surgeon enters, Morgan immediately joins us. His expression is not to my liking.

"Although the caliber of the weapon was small, the bullet has lodged in the chest cavity. We've controlled the bleeding, somewhat, but...a very serious wound, you may want to prepare yourselves."

"*Prepare ourselves?*" Morgan echoes.

"We need to operate on the heart, however, your aunt is...well...she's indicating she doesn't want an operation."

"What?" Morgan says as if very far away.

"You need to talk with her, in fact she's asking for you. She's cognizant but heavily sedated." Morgan holds her hand across her mouth, unable to speak.

"What do you mean she's saying *no*? Is she in possession of her senses?" Mrs. Richardson asks the surgeon.

"I believe she's in shock, which could account for her state of mind. At this point we'll need permission to proceed. I recommend we do so immediately. I'm very sorry."

We follow the nurse into the room and a sickly feeling stabs into my gut when I see her in the bed, wired with electrodes, tubes and drips; only a handful of hours ago, smiling and laughing.

She lies still as death, IVs and oxygen being pumped into her thin frail body. When Morgan whispers in her ear, her eyes open slowly like a dreamer emerging from sleep. She weakly raises her hand and Morgan takes it, her tears falling upon the fingers, lacing their way along the length of her wrist.

"Aunt Monique," she says breaking. "This is all my fault. I should never have pushed you into it."

"Morgan…you mustn't."

"This can't be happening, it's like a nightmare. We'll all wake up together…at Magenta."

"Shhh," the aunt whispers, her eyes shining. "I'm so very proud of you, what you've accomplished in your short years…such a rich life for someone so young."

"Monique, best you stay quiet," Mrs. Richardson interjects but the aunt remains steadfast upon her niece.

"It's important you listen, we've such little time."

"What do you mean, *little time*?"

"Morgan…I'm dying."

"No, no you're not. The doctors are going to operate, remove the bullet. I'm giving them permission to do so."

"No."

"What do you mean *no*? It has to be done if…if…"

"Dear, listen to me. I need you to do *somethings*, before I'm gone." Morgan breaks. I hold her shoulders. She feels so thin and fragile in my grasp, like a willow frond.

"You're not going to die…there are so many things to do yet, we've only just begun."

"Please listen…this is very painful for me."

"Monique," Mrs. Richardson says, "you need to quiet yourself and gather your strength. The doctors are-"

"Alma, please…" the aunt says lovingly and the room goes silent except for their weeping. "Now, first…you know as I, father will seek retribution. I don't want it. I don't want the karmic responsibility of sending this young man to his death."

"But aunt…"

"This boy who did this thing was misguided. Let justice seek its due course and it's in the hands of a higher authority but this *eye for an eye* business will stop right here and now, do you understand me?" she says with a surprising intensity, Mrs. Richardson reaching out to calm her.

"Monique, I this necessary?"

"Secondly, I'm concerned for Montara's upbringing. You know as I, she's a uniquely special child, with special needs. I'm not talking about physiology, I'm talking about spiritual matters. The sisters are already discussing it, preparing for their trip to Magenta."

"Sisters?"

"Vivien and Vanetta, your aunts…the MacIntyre sisters."

"I doubt very much they know."

"Quite the contrary, they've already made their travel arrangements and are preparing to leave Scotland tonight."

"How could you possibly think that?"

Monique points into the emptiness of the room. "Grandmother has informed me…your great grandmother, Lisette Montaigne. She's standing beside you." The three of us share wondering expressions.

"I'm sorry…I don't…"

"You're distraught. Your mind clouds your finer senses, not to worry, you'll be hearing from them tomorrow morning…after I've gone."

"Aunt Monique stop saying that, you're not going anywhere. They're going to operate and remove the bullet that's in your…*your heart*," she breaks anew covering her mouth.

"No Morgan…I won't allow it. I won't be ripped open like a sack of beets. This is my time. There's a greater power at work. You would sense it if you weren't so upset." Morgan gazes at her through the tears.

"*Upset?*"

"Everything is in order. I've made some final arrangements you'll find suitable. Everything is on my desk, in my bedroom."

"You're saying you knew this would happen?"

"No, not *knew it*, that's what was so puzzling about the whole affair, there's a kind of…*shroud*, over the thing. "

"What do you mean?"

"There's a veil cast over the whole episode…all too clear soon enough my lovely, *all too clear soon enough*," she says, closing her eyes and we quietly wait.

"My intuition wasn't fooled. I was able to tidy up a few loose ends."

"Loose ends?"

"I want you to adopt Montara, raise her as your own. I've put it in writing. She mustn't be taken from the bosom of the family for any reason. When grandfather passes, Magenta will become yours, all of her splendors...and responsibilities."

"For god's sake why did you come today? Why didn't you talk to me about this? It could have all been prevented."

"Morgan, you mustn't carry on so. It's bad for your health."

"*My health*?" she repeats squeezing my hand. I feel the pain reverberating through her body.

"How very strange," Monique whispers. "I've always been ready to leave, even desired it at times...but now, here with you...life seems so, so much more precious...it's *Time*, that's what it is...*Time*."

"*Time?*"

"*Time.*" Monique gazes at us, her eyes deep and empathic. "*Time* Morgan, is so, so very precious. Where I'm going, where we all will meet again, there will be no *Time*. There is no such concept within eternity...but here, this fragile blue world, with its days and nights, minutes and hours...it is *Time* that becomes the details that become the fabric of our very lives." She drifts and we silently wait.

"Time..." she whispers. "Time for books...playing music, or just being together, talking together...brushing Montara's hair...oh, and walking in the rain," she says wistfully, "how I'll miss the rain. What profounder expression of love than *the very substance of life, just...falling on our heads.*"

Morgan averts her face into my shoulder. I watch the tears gently cascade across Monique's cheek and it takes all my resolve not to follow those tears to my own.

"Monique, rest yourself now. Garner your strength for the operation. We'll have plenty time for talking."

"There will be no operation Alma," she says lovingly. "I won't be seeing the sun rise I fear," and Mrs. Richardson begins to shudder. "How I treasure our friendship Alma. Despite our...*religious differences*...we were able to place those things aside and get to work. And such noble work indeed. Please continue on, without me."

"But how?" Alma says, her voice breaking. "How can I carry on without you?" and Mrs. Richardson covers her eyes with her hand.

"Now, one last thing...something has to be done about Georgiana." Morgan slowly removes her face from my breast and stares at her.

"Georgiana? Georgiana who?"

"Your friend, your sister in actuality, from New York."

"Georgiana Snipes? What about her?"

"She's one of us Morgan...the baby, the baby soul."

"Us?"

"Our group...our pack...the one that came up together *two hundred thousand years ago*."

"I'm afraid I don't understand."

"Morgan, there was so little time for us...and now all this. It's unfortunate."

"Aunt Monique what are you talking about?"

"Dear, it's time for you to fathom the depths of your being. It's buried deep within you, your DNA holds the record of our ascent into humanity, the last ice-age, two hundred thousand years ago." The women clasp hands and gaze into each other's eyes.

"What do you mean?

"Your spirit knows the way, your beautiful immaculate spirit," she says caressing her hand. I see a deep profound emotion surface in her eyes. "*Fast* for twenty-four hours, water from the spring only, seclude yourself within the northern study. Go into the deep state. Ask for your life to be revealed to you…you're ready…*your heart has become pure, purged of disdain for your fellow man and the living things of this world*. This is the key that opens that heavenly door…the pure heart, without which none of us will ever attain our destinies."

"But aunt, what does this have to do with Georgiana Snipes?"

"Morgan, forgive me…I haven't had the time to preface you properly but now…there is no time."

"For what?"

"Something has to be done about Georgiana. Why won't she ever learn? It's forever the same with her, the same lesson over and over again…she thinks a wolf's nature is to chase hares."

"*Chase hares*? Are you referring to rabbits?" Morgan asks, breaking.

"A wolf's nature, her obligation to her breed, is to follow the pack…move as the pack does, not be selfish and impetuous, go where one's own desires dictate, yet always the same with her…chasing hares, getting stuck in *the bog*."

"Aunt Monique, I'm trying to understand…I'm confused." The aunt seems to drift, gazing through the ceiling as if it no longer existed and in a very far-away voice she tells us this incredible story.

"Our pack was stalking the herd for days, our splendid lead male pitted against the herd's male…a wise old buck, many years at the helm of that great and noble tribe." She coughs up blood. We help her become more comfortable.

"We were committed to maneuvering them, to break or shatter their group, but the clever old buck was always able to outsmart us; take the high ground or the proper salient...keep his group one step ahead of ours...always keeping his herd moving, yet together...that's the nature and strength of the herd...to stay moving, together, at all costs, therefore, indomitable." She takes a rest to collect her breath and staves off our attempts to quiet her.

"A fast moving herd of caribou is a formidable force to reckon with, extremely dangerous. We had lost members on the hunt...gored to death, or trampled underfoot by shifts in their path. These animals are thunder incarnate upon the earth. Once committed to the *blood-chase*, there is no room for error in one's dealings with them."

"Monique, I think it wise to call in the doctor now."

"We bided our time wisely, looking for opportunity to entrap them. Our pack had managed a most brilliant maneuver, stampeding them into a low narrow valley, thus exploiting a unique weakness inherent within any large herd on the move, its inability to stop and retrace itself. To do so is death for them. Having accomplished this, it was merely a matter of out-distancing them to the gap, where it was probable, we could take out one or two of the infirm at the pinch, before they could make the open plains to the south." She coughs, the action obviously paining her.

"Once again, Georgiana, the young clumsy yearling, became sidetracked chasing a hare, which in reality Morgan, wasn't a hare at all, but a malicious nature sprite out on a lark." We wait while she coughs, helping her collect blood spittle in a catch.

"Shall I call the nurse aunt?"

"Despite the pack's repeated admonishments, off she went, yet again, got herself stuck in a bog, a watershed from the mountain. Oh, how she wailed, pitifully, calling out for us not to leave her behind. The pack had a very serious decision…abandon the baby, succeed in the hunt and therefore live on as animal nature dictates or halt the hunt and extract the young errant wolf. The snow had already begun falling when we ceased the chase and went back for her." She stares through the ceiling and seems to laugh softly beneath her breath.

"What is it aunt?"

"Imagine, wolves abandoning the blood-chase because of a silly yearling. You and young Willem crawled out on your bellies. Willem got hold of her by the nape and hauled her back, yelping to beat the devil."

She looks at me, a profound empathy in her gaze. I take her hand and we share a moment of silence together.

"Young Willem…such a fine, strong young wolf. Always reluctant to leave the pack, begin one of your own." She drifts for a moment before *her eyes* return. "Once we got Georgiana on solid ground the alpha-male had her belly-up and whimpering, a sorry lesson indeed but fruitless, for his actions had doomed us to starvation." She shifts, obviously in pain and her manner takes on a kind of urgency.

"Try as we might to make the pinch, it was too late. From the pass, we watched *the tail* of the herd recede into the plains. We had missed our chance for the easy kill and to gorge our bodies against the oncoming snow." Silence.

"The decision remained to pursue the chase onto the flatland, thus exposing our pack to the storm now severely upon us; or turn back to the shelter of the forest."

She pauses to collect her breath and I fear for her in that moment.

"There was no choice of course…our group's nature was contrary to the open plains. We were forest dwellers, *our spirits and guides were wood, not grass.*"

"Monique, perhaps you should rest."

"Within just a few hours a meter of snow lined the wood and by the morning of the next day, two. By the end of the week we were buried beneath ten feet of snow and hunting relegated to digging for rodents." Her good eye dilates, a strange light reflecting off it. "Slow starvation is a long drawn out affair, agonizing, especially if one is trapped within a virtual wall of snowpack, lean empty bellies, yet the pack was at peace with itself, the entire pack accepting its fate, each and every animal."

"Monique, it's best you quiet yourself now."

"As we lay together beneath the pines, dying…an extraordinary thing happened. Do you know what happened Morgan?" she asks and actually waits for her answer.

"No, I don't…why don't you tell us."

"The great one, the great wolf, *Lobos Invictus*, appeared to us, our tiny beleaguered host, a warm radiance glowing under the boughs buried beneath the snow. The great one told us that because of our *integrity*…we were *moving on* together, including the younger souls if we agreed to bring them up, they would be our collective responsibility." She pauses, a deep ephemeral silence.

"Go on aunt, I'm listening."

"The decision was made there and then to bring the baby souls up with us." She looks directly into Morgan's eyes and a kind of silent exchange occurs between the two women, a communion devoid of words or utterances.

"Then like that, the great wolf called the *Snow Woman*, the magnificent lady of white…you know her…you've seen her on those winter nights up north…the *deep twilight nights of indigo dreaming*."

"Yes…I think I know her."

"She waved her hand, her graceful hand, and the entire host grew frigid and died, all of us, together in that place, that moment. We passed on, together, into the next realm, the realm of human existence and spirit evolution. We had done it…in a very *un-wolf* like way, we had become very splendid wolves, the very best the species was capable of offering the world…two hundred thousand years ago."

No one speaks a word. Faintly, somewhere in the distance, a church bell sounds out the late hour.

"And look, here, in this lifetime, our family and friends, all very splendid human beings. People who care for one another, and their neighbors; *care about the innocence of the world*."

Her eyes suddenly tear, and we draw closer to her. "How deeply I love you, all of you. How I wish the very best for all your lives, past and to come." She tightens her hold on Morgan's hand. "Daughter…this is the end for me, I'll not be coming back, not again…this troubled but beautiful world."

"Aunt…"

"Morgan, dear, how I'll miss our time together within this life, so short, yet so very rich." Morgan takes her hand to her cheek and cries, the moment truly somber.

"This tired old ball of dirt," Monique whispers. "So much complaining and consternation…but yet look, all around you, love everywhere. The sublimated gold of the sun…azure skies…*her lapis midnights and amber dawns*…a planet rich in water, the very substance of life when so many others in the universe are so bare of it, so deplete."

"Why is it that people are so narrow and fearful when love is all about them, sustaining their very existences?" Her eyes seem to glow as she studies her niece.

"I don't know," Morgan says softly, tears forming channels across her cheeks.

"Alas, the great fallacies of humankind, so brutal to himself and the living things of this world...those tiny souls, God bless them all." We wait silently while she struggles to breathe. "This old dirt...you tired old thing...bless you for putting up with us...you most glorious living thing...her mauve-colored sunsets...her perfumes...Morgan, her perfumes...summer nights...wine and magnolia...never again..." then she quietly dies and our world shatters.

Outside in the waiting room, as Morgan valiantly struggles with the death of this remarkable woman, I take the seat next to Alma. "How are you holding up?"

She shakes her head. "It's so sad, so very, very sad."

"Her loss will be felt on many levels, by many people," I say, an odd expression forming on her face.

"Yes, but I mean her dementia, so utterly sad."

"Her dementia?"

"Of course."

"I'm afraid I don't know what you mean."

"All this nonsense about wolves and seeing her dead grandmother in the room. Who would have thought Monique Montaigne, of all people, would lose her sensibilities like that." She sees the expression on my face. "Mr. Furey, you don't think for one moment we as people were ever animals, do you?"

"Yes, in fact I do believe it."

"Mr. Furey, animals don't have souls, everyone knows that. They were put on the earth for our uses, it's in the scriptures." She apparently doesn't like my muted response for she shakes her head and joins Morgan at the telephone.

When I return to the house from grocery shopping the following afternoon I'm surprised by an incredible sight. Two flaxen-haired twins, both nearly six foot tall. Their long red hair flows about their shoulders and arms and their fingers and necks are elegantly jeweled. I'm introduced to Morgan's Scottish aunts Vivien and Vanetta MacIntyre, her father's sisters.

Vanetta, slightly fuller than her twin, shakes my hand, her smile genuine. Vivien remains seated, a glass of red wine in her hand, smoking a cigarette.

"He's a handsome lad," Vivien says, a gleam in her hazel-colored eyes. Her sister flashes her an odd look.

"Viv…let's behave ourselves shall we," she says and the twin's eyes glint.

"I just said he's handsome love, and so he is. Have a look."

"Let's keep our mind on things."

"You should give a man a try sometime Vannie, you might like it."

"Oh, what evil having her for a twin," Vanetta says to Morgan, "I must have done something terrible in my previous life…like murderin' a sibling."

"I got all the verve," Vivien says to me, "Vannie got all the weight." She then turns her thin body directly toward me. "Van 'ere's still a virgin." Her sister goes wide-mouthed. "Morgan, perhaps your man might lend us a hand with that?"

"Aunt Vivien, really," Morgan says. I sense this has been going on since their arrival.

"Well, it's not like he's asked for *your* hand yet," she says, and Morgan turns red.

"Ach, yer wicked sister. Vivien MacIntyre, your ways will be your fall, and sooner than you imagine it love."

"So you say."

"Yes, I say."

"Who made you lord and master? It's hardly my place but your constant tittering about like a devilish little wren is what drives your men to smoke and drink and the lot."

"How's that?!"

"Ye heard what I said."

"You horrid thing. I've half a mind to-"

"Please stop it, both of you!" Morgan interjects and I realize how fragile she is since Monique's death. Vivien extends her pack of cigarettes in Morgan's direction.

"You need one of these dear," she says and Morgan waves her off.

"No thank you aunt Vivien. As I've said, I'm not smoking."

"Well, that's a change. That's what I like about you niece, always unpredictable. You were always my favorite."

"I'm sorry to snap at you."

"Don't apologize to her," Vanetta says. "You're certainly in the right. Monique's death is, unimaginable. Even now I can't believe it. Good lord, whatever shall we do without her?"

"What's *unimaginable* is the bastard that done this, walking about like royalty, above it all," her twin interjects. "The sooner that one's *done-in* the better."

"Monique asked us not to seek the death penalty," I say. She stares at me as if I said something ridiculous.

"Niece, is yer man daft?" Vivien asks.

Morgan looks at me with wounded eyes. "He doesn't understand the *he*, you're referring to aunt Vivien."

"Well then, let me inform him." She stands, closing the distance between us. "The devil who killed Monique Montaigne isn't the poor dumb bastard sitting in a jail cell in New Orleans." This statement effectively ends the discussion as all become lost in their private thoughts.

The house is in turmoil, dozens of people arriving, everyone in tears and I've been informed Colonel Montaigne has collapsed and has been taken to the hospital, the other sisters Pearl and Angeline accompanying him. The orphan girls, Sadie and Rosemary, seem as if in a catatonic state.

At twilight, I spend an hour with Morgan in her room in a deep silent embrace. Once she's gone to sleep, I wander downstairs and gaze at the pictures of the family on the mantel above the fireplace; the blind sister Pearl and silent Angeline I had met on my previous visit, the mysterious, ghostly Gillian and their beautiful raven-haired mother Magenta. There are several photographs so old as to be barely discernable, the great-grandmother Lisette Montaigne, handsome and poised, her father and his two brothers in civil war regalia. The oldest pictures in the collection, Lille and Alfred Montaigne, are actually intaglio prints, finely crafted and framed in silver and gold.

When I study the photographs of the two twins, Emerald and Monique, young, beautiful and spirited, I can't hold back the immense sorrow that engulfs me and have to retire to the back garden.

In my sorrow, I find myself wandering the woods where I chance upon the Creole cousins Jerome and Cristobal sitting with the two Cajuns, Robert Anthony and his lazy-eyed brother Carter before a bonfire moaning over their instruments.

"Allez Bonaparte," Jerome calls out using the nickname of the famous French general they had christened me during my last visit; the night I brought Morgan back from the *island of the damned*, that hideous and scornful place Morgan had been tricked into going.

They extend me an old canning jar with a chipped rim, filling it to capacity with a dark red wine. I listen to the dirge-like music issuing from the very depths of their psyches; the sorrow we share, profound.

I sit before their fire, completely lost in this exchange deep into the night, the tones of their instruments and the pathos in their voices, sometimes singing in English, sometimes French, carries me away, into another time, another place.

The next morning after breakfast, while sitting on the veranda overlooking the back garden, Vivien joins me, a large mug of black coffee in her fist. A slight wind lifts the finer tendrils of her ruddy-toned hair and an odd sense of familiarity encompasses the moment.

"Beautiful day init?" she says and I agree with her. She studies me a moment. "You lovers?"

"Pardon?" I say feeling my face flush and she laughs.

"Of course you are." She lights a cigarette. "You know, I love that lass dearly, always have. She's got her dad's spark. I like her sister too, the half-breed," she says oddly. "A bit cheeky, but spark as well."

"Audrey?" I ask. She studies the surprise on my face.

"What's the matter love? You look as though you've seen a ghost." I have no idea as to her meaning.

"*Half-breed?*"

"Her father is a *supreme materialist*. He has no conscience. Emmie had no business getting hooked up with that one…what with Seamus dying…he manipulated that situation. Some people have no decency."

"What do you mean?"

"He nearly ruined that girl. Emmie too. The greatest threat to anyone with *insight* is a conscienceless person. They see nothing except their own reflection in the *mirror of life*." Her eyes catch the sunlight, the irises radiating the colors of autumn. "Sometimes life requires a modicum of faith, right lover? Have you met him?"

"I've only heard things."

"It took an effort by the family to get that girl out of the hell he was creating for her. Thank Morgan and the Holy Muse she's come round. Now, it's only a matter of time before we get the daughter back with us."

"*Rain*," I mutter, "…her daughter, in Los Angeles."

"She's gifted. Poor Audie. You know, a lifetime is precious. There's really no time to waste dithering about."

"Dithering?"

"Drug addiction, obsessions…chasing illusions, especially when you've been blessed enough to be born into a family like this one," she says.

"I see."

She closes the distance between us. "You're a handsome lad, you know it?" She canvasses my face and the area about my head. "Oh, I'd love *a go* with you," she says her eyes becoming dreamy. I'm uncertain if she's serious or putting on airs. She tosses her cigarette into the hedge below the railing and sighs aloud. "Unlikely that's going t'happen."

Stretching her tall lean body in the sunlight, she takes in the enormous garden surround before looking into my eyes, the hazel-colored irises glittering in the morning light.

"That niece o'mine is as precious to me as my own life," she states. "That's reason enough I want this devil out of the equation. We mustn't let anything happen to Morgan or the virgin child."

"What are you referring to?"

"Why, the devil that tried to do-her-in, what? Back there in the muck. We heard all about it o'er in Aberdeen, you bravely pulling her out of that hell. That *was* you lover, yes? Who stole her back from the clutches of *the dead*?"

I say nothing. She lays her hand across my shoulder and whispers in my ear, "I'd do anything to return that favor, that noble deed," and leans her lower back into the stone railing, gazing up at the mansion towering above us. "You're one of us now lad, Morgan's other half," she says mysteriously. "Ol' Vannie there is a kind soul, y'probably gathered, but not I. There's no room for kindness in the business we've now on hand."

"You're referring to the Hollowman?"

"Mark my words lover, the longer we wait around with our heads in the stars the sooner the storm'll be 'ere."

"What can be done?"

A gleam emerges from her pupils and a curve forms at the edges of her thin lips. She leans close and whispers in my ear. "Whyn't ya marry my niece love, so I can quit thinking about ya." She winks, returning to the house.

That evening Emerald arrives with Lucien and the moment is so very sad that the women sequester her and Morgan in the north study.

I sit with Lucien and Binford Grayson, sipping bourbon from shot glasses. He's informed us that Emory is now stricken with a kind of paralysis.

"He can't take it Lucien, the news. He can't come to grips with Monique's death. I'm fearin' for him. Pearl and Angeline are down there, and Talluleh's family." We sit and silently brood. "It's like the man I know'd isn't there right now. *The spirit's gone.* He's cut down by her death. She was so much more than just a daughter…a kind of spiritual guide really. Emory carries all that guilt."

"*Guilt?* About what?" I inquire and Grayson looks at me hard under salt-and-pepper furrowed brows.

"Emory was a Colonel in the army. How do you think a man goes from being a petty officer to a Colonel? His unit was in the thick of it through two wars and *a police action.* Emory's seen a helluva lot of killing…then too, there's all that business with Magenta."

"His wife? What happened?"

"This wouldn't be the proper time to discuss it," Lucien interjects, and each man is left with his own thoughts.

"I doubt Emory ever imagined he'd be alive long enough to see another daughter buried a'fore him, especially this particular one," Grayson says and his hardened gaze moistens.

"Binford, I wonder if I might have a word with you?" Lucien says suddenly breaking the quietude. "A few things in private. Excuse us Willem."

They excuse themselves to stroll the narrow concrete walkways lining the vast rear garden of the estate. I watch them walk and talk together through the glass like two gray paper cutouts. Somehow, I'm stung by this omission, being left outside of their discussion. Why? It's then I begin to realize Villa Magenta has lost its spiritual center.

The morning of the next day, in the family plot of a remote country cemetery, Monique Yvette Montaigne is laid to rest and the rain falls as if the sky were crying.

As we solemnly loiter about the family mausoleum, I look up into the trees above, surprised by a flock of ravens, four in number, huddling against the downpour as if in quiet attendance. I touch Morgan's sleeve and point.

"Yes, I know, I saw them arrive," she whispers. "I'm glad they've come." I'm unclear her meaning. I gaze at the dark solemn *murder*.

"They remind me of the ravens in the back-yard, the ones Monique used to feed by hand," I say and she looks into my eyes, through me, up to the boughs where the birds perch eerily motionless.

"It is our ravens Willem. They've come to mourn her."

Chapter *7*: Rosemary's Journal

The house is in turmoil, everything topsy-turvey. I continually keep busy, one moment I'm cleaning, the next washing dishes, driving to the store, weeding the garden, lots of weeding. I'm in awe how much work Monique contributed to the running of the house, it takes several of us to compensate.

It's during my job cleaning the children's *classroom* that I find a small tattered book in the corner behind the desk. It looks as if it had been thrown. When I smooth out the pages and return it to some semblance of a book, I realize it's Rosemary's journal. Out of curiosity I decide to read it.

Rosemary J. Enrights jurnal: no admitance.

Day one: Misses Montaignes makin us write a jurnal. She sez we gotta do it, no butts.

Day two: Bord.

Day 3: Realy realy bord. I hate this place. No video games. I hafta make my bed and wash dishs after diner. Its suposed to be Sadies job but shes pawnin it off on us smaller girls and the black lady lets her get away with it.

Day 4: Sadie thinks shes a big shot cuz shes been here the longest, big deal. I hate this place. Im goin run away first chance I get.

Day five: A new girl arrived yesterday. I thought we hafta share rooms. Magda said we hadta. When Miss Montaigne found out she said we could have our own rooms. They put Lulu in the guest room. Thank the lord. I think shes a noosense. Her names Luella but she wants to be called Lulu. What a nut. I think Luellas a pretty name but she dont. Shes kinda stupid I think just sayin.

Day six: Miss Montaignes not so creepy as I thought at first. I like her a lot better than Magda. Magda is bossy and is always tellin me what to do. Miss Moniques really smart. Im lernin a lot.

Day 7: Not sure what to write. I like Miss Morgan the best. Shes really nice and is teachin us how to paint and draw. Miss Montaigne knows how to make the crows come. Four of em there really big. They just come to her. She can pet one of em like it was a pet. They all got names and we feed em bread. The one that sits on her arms named Lila.

Day 8: I'm really sick of Sadie thinkin shes the boss of us girls. I'm skeduling a meeting with Miss Montaigne about it.

Day 9: Lulu threw up.

Day ten: We went to New Orlens today to shop and have ice creem. The old guy came along Kernel Montaigne. Hes funny. He talks a lot. I had a peach flurry. The peaches were from Georgia. Kernal Montaigne says thats somewhere next door.

Day 11: I'm sick of workin in the garden. I'm going to quit from the garden club first thing tomorow.

Day 12: Sadie did a funny thing today. We ducked a bullet today. I wish I could write it but I better not write it in case some snooper reads this. This dairy dont got no key, like I wanted, so I cant lock it. I want to get a dairy that locks against snoopers.

Day 13: I'm not sure coulda been I was dreamin but I'm pretty sure I saw Montara flyin around the garden last night. I pinched myself to double check and it hurt so pretty sure I was awake.

Day 14: Geez do I feel sorry for Ms. Montaigne. Shes got a buncha really dumb kids on her hands. Except me. I know Ms. Montaigne likes me a lot, and I like her a lot. Shes smart Ms. Montaigne and is teachin me a lot. I help her out the most. Sadies lazy and Lulus pretty much a big cry baby.

Day 15: I really like Ms. Morgan. She's really nice. She's a photografter and she's had her pitchers in magazines. I'm surprised she's wastin her time on us. I want to spend more time with her but Lulus on her all the time. Youd think she'd figure it out but Ms. Morgan is so nice she wont tell Lulu to bug off. Thats what Id do if I was her.

Day 16: I'm not too sure but I'm pretty sure aunt Monique is a witch. Sadie told us a buncha stuff last night about stuff she's seen and heard. Sadie's kind of a goof so maybe she makes stuff up but pretty sure she dint.

Day 17: I came right out and asked Ms. Montaigne if she was a witch today. I told her Sadie said she was a witch and she dint get mad or nothin. She says there's some bits of witch in all girls. I like aunt Monique a lot. But I don't like aunt Magda she's too bossy.

Day 18: Cripes I just found out Sadie gets paid for working around the house. Cripes. I've had it with Sadie not taking her turn with the dishes and aunt Magda letting her get away with it. She also is abusing privledges. Tonight I'm writing a former letter of complaint to Ms. Montaigne about it.

Day 19: We all had a sit down this morning with Ms. Montaigne. All our complainin and fightin has got us in hot water. She says someone has to go. Theres too many girls at the house. Its up to us to decide who stays and who goes.

Day 20: Cripes. Lulu and Sadie teamed up on me and voted that I have to leave Villa Magenta. Tomorrow Mrs. Richardsons coming over, so signing off. Signed Rosemary J. Enright Esq.

Day 21: We had a good day. Mrs. Richardson came to take me back to foster care and Sadie and Lulu cried. Mrs. Richardson got mad and hollered at us. And Ms. Montaigne said I could stay if there's no more fighting and one of us girls gives up there room. So I said I would. Then Lulu said she would, so I ducked a bullet. I'm glad I'm not going back to foster care. I don't like foster care as much as here. Heres a hole lot better.

Day 22: Aunt Monique said I could quit kitchen duty if I take over for her as President of the garden club. I like the garden club better especially now that I'm the President. Then Lulu quit cuz she gets hives. I think that has something to do with bees.

Day 23: Aunt Morgan took us on a photo journey in the swamp. We got bit by moskeetoes and Lulu had to go back with Mr. Willem. Mr. Willem is aunt Morgan's boyfriend I think. He's nice and he's handsome. Lulu won't never make it as a photografter cuz she's afraid to get her feet muddy. I'm not afraid to get my feet muddy at all. I like it. Aunt Morgan says I could be a really good photografter. I think cuz I like bugs and stuff. Sadie and Lulu are afraid of em. I like em.

Day 24: I love aunt Morgan. I'm going to be just like her when I grow up.

Day 25: Boy Lulu got in hot water with aunt Magda. We're not supposed to know but Sadie knows and told me but I better not write it down. Boy Lulu what a dumb kid.

Day 25 & ½ : Lulu hasta go back to foster care. Sadie said somethings up.

Day 26: Lulu left this morning with Mrs. Richardson. We said good by and hugged. Lulu was really crying. Aunt Monique started crying. Then I cried.

Day 27: Nothing to write today. Bored.

Day 27 & ½: A new girl arrived today named Sissy. She's really quiet. I think she's afraid. Aunt Monique asked me to help out. I'm going to do my best to help her along. Since Lulu left I'm second oldest girl now so us older girls got to help out the littler girls.

Day 28: Aunt Monique makes us listen to classical music. Moseart and Beattoven. She's try'n to make us play it on the piano. I don't like it. It's too hard. Sadie's pretty good at learning it and can play some stuff pretty good. She thinks that makes her smart but playing a piano don't have nothing to do with intellagents. Cornel Montaigne says Sadie's getting too big for fur britches.

Day 29: Aunt Monique gets to get some kind of medal for bravery. She's called the woman of the year by some softball team. We're supposed to wear a dress. No way am I gonna wear a dress.

Day 30: I gotta wear a dress. I told Ms. Montaigne no way am I gonna wear a dress and no one can make me. She said if I dint then none of us girls can come to the event and they got punch and cookies and stuff. Now everyone's mad at me and Sadie won't talk to me. I don't care no way am I wearing a stupid dress.

Day 31: Worst day of my life ever. Aunt Monique was kilt last night. Some man shot her with a gun. Everyone is crying and people are coming over and crying. I guess aunt Monique knew lots of people. Aunt Morgan is crying and Sadie won't quit crying, I liked Ms. Montaigne. I'm crying too.

Day 32: I don't understand why good people like Ms. Montaigne are kilt for no good reason.

Day 33: I'm not going to write in this diary no more. I only done it because Ms. Montaigne asked me.

Chapter 8: La Belle Fontaine

That night, a most peculiar meeting takes place within the sitting room at Villa Magenta. I've seen surprisingly little of Emerald since her arrival until this *meeting* on this portentous evening. It is a solemn reunion, Lucien, Emerald, the Scottish twins, Magda, Morgan and myself, all in somber attendance; everyone except Pearl and Angeline who remain in New Orleans with the Colonel.

They share tea and wine while I partake of coffee with chicory. Emerald taps on her wine goblet with a silver letter opener. "Let us begin. As you all know, Monique's death was hardly by chance. It was perpetrated. I'm convening this gathering for one purpose. *I want the entity known as Mr. Else annihilated."*

"*Mr. Else?*" Vanetta queries.

"The artificial entity that's orchestrated her murder."

"Annihilation?"

"My mind is firm on the matter Lucien, I won't be swayed. There's really to be no discussion about it. You do realize, all, Monique wasn't killed by some fanatic...she was murdered in cold blood and not by the fool manipulated into pulling the trigger. It was orchestrated by this *thing*, Mr. Else."

"Who is this, *Mr. Else* sister?"

"*Mister Else,* the person whose body was taken, *possessed*, by this creature."

"How do you know such things sister?"

"Acosta has informed me."

"Acosta? Acosta Fontaine?"

"Yes Vanetta, of course."

"You're speaking to Acosta Fontaine on this matter?"

"Not only speaking to her Lucien, she's intrinsically involved. I've made up my mind. We intend to consult *the Black Book*." A pall comes over the group.

"Mother…" Morgan whispers. I see the shock on her face.

"Is that wise?"

"To what are you referring Lucien?"

"I would be careful about involving her."

"Why?"

"Because of her…*persuasion*."

"Whether you agree with her *persuasion* or not is of secondary concern. She *will* get results."

"But at what cost?" he asks. Her gaze is not the tranquil cerulean hue I'm used to, her eyes becoming stormy, the pupils wildly dilating.

"You're next, you know," she says pointedly. "He won't rest until he's murdered you as well."

"Aye. But I'll not compromise my convictions."

"You're accusing me of doing so?"

"Certainly not, but I *am* concerned about your *emotional self*."

"I'm not hysterical Lucien, how dare you even infer it. I'm being quite responsible in my judgment. This vile, irreprehensible…*thing*…has caused enough misfortune. It should have been dealt with. Now my sister lies dead. Why don't you tell them?" she says gesturing to the group and an uncomfortable silence ensues.

"Tell us what brother?" Vanetta asks.

"Acosta has told me all about it Lucien, it's *in the know*."

He looks at Morgan and the sisters, his gaze solemn, nearly sad. "This is the...*man*, that killed Seamus, your father, your brother," turning to Emerald, "your husband...and my dearest friend." This has a marked effect on the entire group, the room becoming explicitly quiet. Vivien stamps out her cigarette.

"The dirty bastard that *done-in* Monique, murdered Seamus you say?"

"Yes, so we believe." Vivien and Vanetta exchange eye contact, Vivien's turning red, like fire.

"Then it's high bloody time somebody returns the favor," she says, the smile extinguished from her aquiline features.

"And you've always known this?" Vanetta inquires.

"I've had suspicions...that were recently confirmed."

"Well then it seems to me the bastard's carried on long enough," Vivien adds. "Do it, if *the Black Book's* the ticket, so be it," and her sister goes solemn and dark.

"Then it's true," Emerald says addressing Lucien in a most intense manner. "Everything Acosta has said is true. It's a travesty," she shouts, and all seem shocked by her sudden outburst. "It's a travesty we've let it go on."

"Em, it's not the way. Does the result justify the means?"

"He's murdered Monique!" she shouts slamming her palm upon the end table upsetting a vase of irises. The group goes numb, the silence punctuated when Vivien abruptly rises to her feet.

"Ach, it's an evil thing. He'll be the death of you brother and he's designs upon my beloved niece. Aye, do that rotter *in* I say and quickly, by any means necessary."

"Vivien..."

"The *First Cause* will accept our methods Lucien. God knows what hell that bastard's inflicted upon the living. Countless lives ruined or lost I'll wager."

"You do understand fully what you're considering?" Lucien inquires and Vanetta looks at her twin, a severe expression on her features.

"Dear me sis, what do ye think love?"

"I've said what I think love, aven't I? *Put the shears to the bastard and be done with it*."

Silence.

She goes to the sideboard to refill her wine glass when something catches her eye outside the front window. "Ach, damn it to hell, we've guests arriving, hideously bad timing. Who might that be?"

"That would be Acosta," Emerald says. You could hear a pin drop.

"Acosta?" Magdalena says slowly standing. "Acosta Fontaine? Here, now?"

"Of course. I've invited her to come and discuss what's to be done."

"Emerald, how could you invite that woman into this house, after what she's done, who she is? Lord, where are the children? We need to gather them immediately."

"Magdalena Tousseau! How dare you address one of the principle relations of this family in such a repugnant manner. As if *the Belle Fontaine* would set upon our children the moment she walked through the doors of Maison Magenta. Why, the mere suggestion of it is repulsive!" The maid stands mute, *down-dressed*, the entire host freezing from her tirade. I can scarcely believe the change in her normally tranquil demeanor.

"I-I'm sorry Emerald, forgive me," she mutters. "I don't know what came over me. May I please take the children to the east wing? They've studies and…and…" she goes mute looking to Morgan.

"Of course Magda," Emerald says collecting herself. "I've no issue with your sitting with the children."

"Yes Ma'am," she says and leaves, a profound silence cloaking the room.

Mere moments later, Morgan lets in three of the most striking persons I've ever met. *The Belle* is escorted by a thin waifish girl, either Japanese or Korean, and shadowed by an incredibly tall stout man in a black chauffeur's uniform and cap, wearing black wraparound sunglasses; returning to wait outside.

Our visitor is draped in a dark gauzy veil. When she pulls the fabric back onto her slender shoulders a most alluring face greets everyone in the room. Majo, the tough old Ridgeback, whimpers and actually leaves the room while Maud hisses and ascends the bookcase to his alcove in the topmost shelf and never removes his eyes from her all the while she remains in the room.

The Belle's complexion seems nearly white, like fine porcelain; her long lustrous hair an absolute black, like noir gauche, nearly as black as her eyes. Her fingers are thin and articulate with crimson painted nails and adorned with rings, large ornate gems. The black gossamer gown embraces her slender body like a glove.

"Emerald Montaigne," she says, nearly a whisper. "Magnificent." They embrace and Emerald turns to the group.

"Everyone, may I present Acosta, *La Belle Fontaine*." Acosta turns toward Emerald and her expression goes from delight to a mournful frown.

"Mon Dieu Emerald…Monique Montaigne…dead," she proclaims and Emerald collapses into her shoulder.

The dark stranger lovingly strokes Emerald's ebony tresses, whispering softly in her ear before addressing us. "Take heed Montaigne, the world has lost a piece of its soul, ripped away by a butcher."

"I want this thing hunted down and destroyed. I want you to release the *Black Assassins,*" Emerald hisses. Acosta's eyes seem to pulsate, a strange ephemeral luminance. She strokes Emerald's chin, whispering softly.

"Dear, dear Emerald…your veritable double, our sister…" then to the group, "shot down in the street like a vagabond. It's immoral!" I can see the rage surface in Emerald's eyes. The *Belle* strokes her with jeweled fingers. "Emerald, cousin, so very sad…*a delicate sensual nightmare.*" She stares hard at the group and no one can quite hold her gaze except Lucien. "This heinous act cannot go unanswered…a life so quiet, yet profound…taken…*like slaughtering an old goat.*"

"I want him destroyed Acosta, immediately."

"*Him? It* has no soul of its own. The succubus thirsts upon the life-pulse of the… the *unfortunate.*

"I want *it* sent from this earth, be done with it, make it so," Emerald seethes. The woman touches her cheek, the large translucent ruby on her finger reflecting the light.

"Alas…Monique Montaigne…dead," she whispers, "*as if in a dream, weak or stronger, one moment there, the next no longer.*"

Her gaze then fixates upon Morgan like a predator bird focusing on a distant quarry. She gently pulls away from Emerald, going to the daughter and they embrace. For some reason, I'm surprised that Morgan seems completely at ease with the dark mysterious person.

"Morgan MacIntyre," she breathes, "how wondrous."

"Hello aunt."

"How splendid to see you again Morgan, now a mature, lovely woman. Look everyone," she says actually presenting her to the party. "*As breath-taking as the Madonna.*" She gazes at her from the top of her head to her toes. I realize this woman holds some kind of fascination over my friends, I see it in their eyes and the subtle changes in their mannerisms. "We must travel together Morgan, you and I, those great and mysterious places. Europe, the orient...have you been to Egypt?"

"Yes aunt Acosta, I have."

"No...I'm sorry dear, you've not walked the Egypt to which I refer...I mean, *Egypte*," she says and her dark eyes pulsate anew. I'm uncertain her meaning but Morgan smiles.

"I would treasure that Belle, thank you."

"Yes, we shall, in the not too distant future...perhaps, even old Scotland," she says turning to the aunts and they both greet her, but with more reserve. "It's been much too long MacIntyre. One could fall prey to the notion you're purposely avoiding me." There's no kissing of cheeks. It's strictly handshakes and discerning looks. I sense there's history between the women.

She then addresses Lucien. "And of all people, *uncle* Lucien," she says with a peculiar emphasis on the prefix.

"And hello to you, *aunt* Acosta," he says kissing her jeweled hand in a most gentlemanly way. Her eyes gleam, a smile curving her crimson lips. She waves a long, pointed finger at him, the nails like spikes.

"Now, now uncle Lucien, you're much too much a gentleman to reveal a woman's true age," she says coyly.

"Indeed."

"And how is our *gentleman of the ages*?"

"Well. Please forward my regards to your...*father*."

She then formally addresses the entire group. "Have you all had the pleasure of meeting my debutante?" gesturing toward the frail looking girl with thin narrow eyes and a completely pale complexion, nearly bluish.

"This is Yuki. Yuki-san, you know everyone here don't you dear?" The girl softly nods exhibiting a barely discernable smile.

"Hai," she whispers in Japanese before returning to her smartphone.

"And everyone knows Bill, my chauffeur. I asked him to sit with us but…you know Bill, *forever the outsider*."

"Aunt Acosta would you care for some tea?" Morgan asks gesturing them to sit.

"I doubt you've the flavor I prefer," she says looking directly at me. Something in her look sends a shaft of energy coursing my spine. "Or perhaps you do. Who is this mortal?" she asks strangely.

"This is Willem Furey, uncle Lucien's assistant," Morgan says and Acosta smiles touching Morgan's cheek.

"I dare say he's more than that mon bijou." Acosta extends me her hand, her touch like ice. "No, not *assistant*. Correct me if I'm wrong, *uncle Lucien*, but he's very much his own man?" she inquires and Lucien nods.

"Indeed, very much his own man, and my friend," he adds and Acosta's eyes inextricably change. She embraces me in a traditional European manner. I know I'm expected to kiss her on both cheeks and the sensation is notable.

Amidst this brief exchange, she whispers quietly for my ear only: "A mortal life, so short…so sad." She then turns to Emerald. "Montara? Where is she?" and a protracted silence ensues. "Is she ill?"

"No Acosta, not at all."

"May I see her?" Another pregnant pause as mother and daughter look between each other.

"Of course," Morgan says. "I'll go get her."

When Montara enters and spies Acosta, she instantly freezes in the doorway, Acosta beaming. "Montara Montaigne," she announces in a most expressive manner and Montara shoots Morgan an odd look before re-addressing her rather formally. "Me," she says pointing at herself, *the Belle* gently closing the space between them.

"Of course it's *you* my dear, there's none other like you in all the world." She kneels before the child and they look at each other, Acosta *glowing*. "Montara Montaigne...how splendid. Look at you my dear, *now a little girl.*"

"Me," Montara says again, becoming transfixed by the large brilliant ring I had mistaken for a ruby, but now appears much more translucent; not the rich solid color of the ruby gem. Acosta's eyes widen and a strange unfathomable expression courses her alluring face.

"Look everyone, she's chosen the *blood diamond*," she says mysteriously, and Morgan takes the child's shoulders. "Of course, how could it be other? She's a Montaigne, she knows, don't you my dear?"

"Don't play with aunt Acosta's jewelry sweetheart," Morgan says but the child seems unable to relinquish her attention upon the ring.

"Oh, how glorious," Acosta whispers dramatically to Emerald. "Emerald, cousin, let me present Montara with the *blood diamond.*"

"Oh no La Belle! Surely you jest, something so, priceless? Why, the mere thought of it."

"But Emerald, she's the daughter of Monique Montaigne," she says locking her gaze upon Morgan. I can't help *feel* she's not referring to Montara at all. She then removes this incredibly lavish ring, and presents it directly to Montara, the child's eyes wide, euphoric.

"Aunt Acosta…we simply couldn't," Morgan interjects, attempting to retrieve the jewel but she refuses to let go.

"Montara…do," the child tells her, relishing the bauble as if it were a magical thing. She seems unable to remove her attention from it as Acosta takes it and slips it onto her tiny finger, the woman becoming nearly ecstatic.

"This day should be written on parchment," she proclaims. "Hold your fingers together, tightly Montara, tightly," she whispers to the child, holding her hand aloft, presenting it to the group. "Look everyone, a perfect fit. Magenta Montaigne's granddaughter, how could it be other?"

This event creates quite a stir amongst the gathering, however the excitement dims when Morgan removes the ring and gently folds it back into Acosta's pale fingers.

"Thank you aunt Acosta, but we couldn't. Something as valuable as *the blood diamond* isn't to be handed out arbitrarily." The woman holds Morgan's hand in her own gazing silently into her eyes as if suddenly frozen and the moment is profound, the two women engaged in some kind of silent commune.

"Hardly *arbitrary* Morgan, daughter of Seamus MacIntyre, the confluence of the two lines. Like two mighty rivers merging into the torrent. Morgan, the Fontaine family knows everything that goes on at Montaigne. How could you think it other?"

"Yes, but…"

"This stone belonged to Lisette, your great grandmother and Lille, her grandmother before her, now, it's returned to its rightful place within the *House of Montaigne*." The statement is so absolute, so undeniable, that all seem compelled to accept it. "This is an endowment, for you and Montara's future, your well-being. A paltry substitute for a mother…and a mentor…wouldn't you agree?"

"I hardly know what to say," Morgan whispers. Acosta kneels before Montara anew, presenting the jewel between them, her eyes strangely fixed upon the girl.

"You say the magic syllables, *the magic words* Morgan…that's what you say." Her eyes lock upon Montara staring at the jewel. "Have you learned the magic words yet Montara? Have the women of this family revealed them to you yet?"

"Montara…know."

"You do? Magnificent," the woman says, ecstatic. "What are the magic words Montara, tell us, tell everyone."

"*Please.*"

Acosta Fontaine's alluring smile instantly contorts into a very unbecoming expression. *"Please?"* she echoes like ice. "No…no, no my dear, that's not the magic words, that's not it at all." She immediately addresses the group. "Who taught her such dreck? *Please*? Outrageous!" she proclaims loudly, and Morgan is forced to take up the Belle's hand.

"Aunt Acosta, *please is* the magic word here in this house for now." I watch as Acosta glances between the two, then the room, all in attendance watching her closely.

"I simply must protest." Morgan tightens her grasp on the strange woman's ivory fingers.

"Please Aunt Acosta," she says, her eyes gesturing toward the child beside them.

"Oh, how droll…so proletariat."

"For the time being.

"How utterly disappointing. I'm in revolt, I would have it noted. Shall I put it down in blood?" she inquires dramatically, and Morgan's expression hardens. "Oh, very well...as you'll have it...*please*," she says as if the words pained her. She replaces the ring on Montara's finger and embraces the girl, her face turned to the heavens. "Monique Montaigne, you've taught your children well." All present are moved by the moment.

"Aunt Acosta, honestly though, I think you're being rather impetuous, just imagine the value of the diamond now," but the matriarch shushes her.

"Tsch-tsch Morgan, not another word about it." She then bends to the child. "Now, off to bed with you my little dear, right away, before they change our minds."

The young girl embraces her for a fleeting moment never removing her eyes from the gem. "Montara...love," she says before turning to Morgan holding the ring. "Montara...stone."

Morgan raises an eyebrow. "We'll see about that." The child decides it frugal to leave with her treasure.

"Montara...dreamtime now," she says, turning to leave the room. At the door Morgan arrests her attention.

"Montara, no *Morgan storytime* tonight?" she asks, and the child shakes her head.

"No...Montara...dreamtime now," and the collective group says goodnight as she leaves the room fixated on the jewel.

"Morgan, is that sensible, leaving such a...priceless heirloom in the hands of a child?"

"It won't be misplaced aunt Vanetta. She'll play with it for approximately an hour then it will go straight under her pillow. You can set your clock on that."

"Then what?" the aunt inquires, a most *discerning* look on her face.

"Then…I'll replace it with something less…valuable."

"Caliber, but really Acosta, *the blood diamond?*"

"Belongs to *the Montaigne daughter*," Acosta answers and looks directly at Morgan. "Magenta had no business giving it to me in the first place. I've been waiting for the right moment to…" she stops midsentence staring fixedly at Morgan, "return it to its rightful owner. It is the property of *the Montaigne daughter*."

"I don't know what to say except thank you," Morgan says, the dark woman becoming ecstatic again.

"Oh Emerald, how pleased you must be." Emerald's response is hardly effusive, and the Belle's demeanor instantly changes again. "Oh Emerald, cousin…*I know the thoughts of your heart*."

"Damn him to hell. I want *Mr. Else* annihilated," she says in a most unnerving way and the Belle's pupils explode.

"Yes. The House of Fontaine answers, yet again. The assassins await thy command, they beg for it. *Shall we commence?*" A wind picks up in the room, the kerosene lamps dancing wildly across the ancient walls, each crack vibrating.

"Acosta, we appreciate your coming," Lucien suddenly interjects. "However, we believe we've matters well in hand." It's as if she's stunned, a severe expression forming the contours of her slender face.

"Cousin? Is this so?" Emerald looks away and Acosta returns her gaze to Lucien, the look hardly becoming. "Montaigne, your house is besieged," she says wickedly, and Emerald seems to lose control.

"Yes…yes, it's murder," to Lucien, "Murder!" she screams like a knife cutting fabric. I feel the blood race within my temples. Acosta turns on the Scottish aunts.

"MacIntyre, have ye lost your voice?!"

"The bastard. By any means necessary," Vivien says and Vanetta waves these words as if to scatter them.

"Now, now. Not so fast," she looks to Lucien. "Brother?"

"You know how I stand."

"Aye Acosta, I must insist we think this through."

"Vanetta MacIntyre. First your brother, now your sister from across the great sea lies dead, in the cold, cold ground," Acosta moans staring at the floor, when a sudden unworldly look of horror inextricably creeps across her countenance, her eyes widening as if they might explode from their sockets. "*The cold, cold ground*, how hideous," she whispers, the whispering and the look, extremely unsettling.

"Viv, dear sister, whatever shall we do?"

"You know my stand as well love, do that bastard in." Vivien's words seem to shake our guest from her trance-like fixation upon the floor. She lays her slender white hand across Vanetta's forearm, the crimson painted nails clutching her sleeve like icepicks.

"Vanetta, dear, dear Vanetta, always the pragmatic one," She collects herself, her voice adopting its melodic tonality once more. "Careful, thoughtful, whilst your sister is a woman of action. However, tis neither you nor your vibrant sister who carries the day, is it?" Acosta turns and raises an eyebrow in Lucien's direction.

"Yes?"

"These, knowledgeable persons, are not the wind that keeps the sails of this mighty ship on course, are they *uncle?* That's your station is it not? *The wind,"* she says with more than a modicum of sarcasm.

"Perhaps."

"And we would never ever entertain using *the book* for such productive purposes...would we, *uncle*?"

"No," he says, and she adopts a dour expression.

"What solutions do you propose then, oh wise one, to deal with this atrocity, this declaration of war? This...affront on a principal member of this...*alliance*."

"I'm not fully sure at the moment."

"Oh? Uncertainty in the face of duress? Isn't that a stark contradiction of martial principle? The mighty field marshal, hesitant? At odds with the battle upon his doorstep?" Her fingers like knives lace her throat. "Oh dear, such a tenuous position from which to war. Master, my legion *hungers* to move upon the enemy. Devour them piecemeal...and all their confederates. No quarter will be given." She looks at Emerald. "A few small insignificant syllables...whispered in the proper cadence...nothing more cousin...say them with me."

The world seems to freeze; only the flicker of the lamp and candle light evident life exists and moves within the room; all eyes locked upon the matriarch. Her eyes are solid black and the world stands on edge. When Morgan takes her hand, it's as if she collapses inwardly.

"I wish you would refrain from such grandiose rhetoric Acosta. We've a very serious issue on hand. It requires all our best efforts of resolve." She becomes nonplussed. "What will happen once your dark force is unleashed upon this world? They'll stop with Else?" he mutters, and she adopts a coy expression, the slender black eyebrow dramatically extending toward the ceiling.

"So be it. You've no plan of action *uncle*? You're beaten?"

"Quite the contrary, my thoughts are formulating."

"And what are your *thoughts*, oh mighty one?"
"Invite him to tea."

Chapter *9*: The 'Return' of Georgiana Snipes

The following evening, we're sitting in the parlor; Morgan, Magda and the Scottish aunts, enjoying tea and wine cakes when there's a knock on the door. I think how quiet it sounds, nearly imperceptible, as if no one took notice, the solicitor would just drift away, unannounced. However, Majo howls at the top of his lungs, the delicate rap sending him into a tirade.

"Who on earth could that be at this hour?"

"I didn't hear anyone drive up."

"Quiet Majo," Magda says, disappearing from the room. In the silence that ensues we hear a soft muttering of voices from the door when the maid returns with a most astonished look on her face. "Morgan, you better come here." Morgan hesitates a moment before she rises and follows her to the front hall. I decide to join them. I'm shocked beyond words. Sitting upon the divan near the front door is Georgiana Snipes, soaked to the bone!

Morgan kneels before her, speaking softly. Magda whispers in my ear. "Who is that woman?" I tell her. "What's she doing here? At this hour?" I can only shake my head and join Morgan at her side.

"But how did you get here?" Morgan asks. Georgiana seems very far away, nearly trance-like.

"What's going on?" I inquire. The look in Morgan's eyes pricks the hair on my neck.

"She doesn't know. She doesn't know how she got here. She says she walked."

"Walked?" I look into Georgiana's eyes and a look I've never seen is etched upon her darkened features.

"Willem, look out front and tell me if there's a car outside."

I step out onto the massive front porch, framed by the tall Corinthian columns and gaze into the darkness; nothing but a soft pervasive rain falling from the shroud of mist that embraces the old manor like a cottony mantle.

"Nothing," I say when I return. We're beginning to draw attention from the parlor.

"Georgiana, tell me how you got here?" Silence. "Do you even know where you are?" She slowly scans the hallway surround.

"Yeah, I recognize this place. I've been here before."

Morgan shakes her head. "Georgiana, you've never been here before." Our nocturnal guest seems at odds with this revelation. "Did a taxicab drop you off?"

"No."

"Someone brought you, a friend?"

"No."

"How then? How did you get here?"

"I…I walked."

"You walked?" Morgan says incredulous. "From where?"

"Um…Del Rey…"

"*Del Rey?*"

"From the Ritz Carlton…in Marina Del Rey," she mutters, and Morgan's eyes dilate.

"Georgiana, that's in Los Angeles."

"I know that."

"You're saying you walked here from Los Angeles?" Confusion erupts in her expression. I take her shoulder.

"Georgiana, where do you think you are you right now? What city is this?" She looks at me with languid eyes.

"LA." We stare at her, wordless. "Are you saying I'm not in LA?"

"Georgiana, you're an hour outside New Orleans. This is Magenta, Villa Magenta."

"*Magenta*," she echoes absently, gazing about the domicile and the faces gathering around her. "*Magenta...*" she whispers like a soft wind through a vacant street. "It's so lovely...so beautiful...this was my home." Her demeanor suddenly shifts. She cups her face in her hands. "How could *this* be...? Why would it be like *this*? Magenta...it doesn't fit."

Vivien touches Morgan, gesturing, and we whisper together to one side. "Who is this woman, niece?"

"A friend of mine from New York."

Vivien looks her over. "She's not what she seems."

"What do you mean aunt Vivien?"

"Exactly what I said, *she's not what she seems*." Georgiana rises abruptly and takes Morgan by the shoulders.

"Morgan, why are you here?" she pleads and Morgan is lost for words. "You can't be here. Not you."

"Morgan lives here love. This is her home."

"No, not Morgan...not *here*...it can't be."

"Where do you think you are love?" Vivien asks engaging Georgiana directly. "Come now, out with it," and we wait for the words that convey the emotion etched across her stormy countenance.

"*Hell*." The word collectively shocks everyone into a profound silence.

As outlandish the claim is, I'm certain she's convinced of this wild idea. I see it plainly in her face.

Vivien takes Georgiana's arm. "Come, sit a moment with us dear, right over here," she says gesturing to the parlor. "Vannie, get us a glass of wine there will you love." The twin pours a crystal of the red they've been sipping. "Here you go darling, have a draft off this." Georgiana stares at the vessel like it were poison. "Come on now, have at it, it'll relax you." She reluctantly takes the glass, hesitating before closing her eyes and sipping. I'm absolutely convinced the woman is shocked, that nothing changes.

"Still here," she whispers.

"Darling, what's all this rot about Hell? Come now, let's have it."

"Because."

"*Because?*" Vivien echoes, "Because why?"

"Because…that's where you go when…" She then drops the crystal spilling it on the carpet, cradling her face in her hands.

As we mop up the spilt wine, Vivien continues to question our visitor. "What day is it Georgiana? What day of the month, or the week for that matter?" The question seems to distract her from the anguish plaguing her tormented mind.

"What day? The sixth? Yes, the sixth, we gigged *the Pond* last night," she says, referring to the arena in Anaheim California.

"What if I told you it's actually the ninth, what remains of it," Vivien says, and Georgiana narrows her eyes.

"No…no. It's the sixth. Yesterday was the fifth…we gigged *the Pond*…in Anaheim."

"Dear, how long have you been awake?" Vanetta asks. "Have you slept recently?"

"No, I can't…I can't let myself go to sleep."

"Why not?"

"Because if I go to sleep…I'll wake up in…" She scans our faces; rubs her eyes saying through her fists, "Morgan can I bum a cigarette?"

"I don't smoke anymore Georgiana, remember?"

"Wait…you said that to me once…a very long time ago."

Vivien takes up her pack of cigarettes, handing one to Georgiana. "Have one of mine love," and lights it for her, the action seeming to ground our midnight guest.

"If this is the ninth…" Georgiana mutters in a far-away voice, "then I've been awake three days…or would that be four?"

Vanetta pulls Morgan aside. "This girl needs to sleep. I know sleep depravation when I see it. This is serious."

"She's definitely on some kind of drug, an upper of some sort."

"I believe she's actually afraid to go to sleep."

"But why aunt Vivien?"

"She said herself, she's afraid if she does, she'll wake up in some horrible state."

"And she actually thought she was still in Los Angeles. Is such a thing possible?"

"Yes," I interject, and the women stare at me. "After New Orleans the tour went west, to Los Angeles, Anaheim. I remember the date on the itinerary was the fifth."

Morgan takes her aunt aside. "What's going on here?"

"Let's not get ahead of ourselves. There are still many questions to be answered. Talk to her Morgan; see if she's hungry. Find out what's happened. We'll get a bed ready upstairs."

"Georgiana, are you hungry?" She shakes her head, blankly staring into space. When she looks at us, her eyes go moist.

"Morgan, help me, it must be why you're here."

"Georgiana, what's going on?"

"Don't you get it? This isn't real…none of this. I'm going to fall asleep and wake up in…in…"

"Georgiana, listen to me," Morgan says gripping her hand tightly. "Do you feel that? Do you feel me?" The dark woman nods. "That's me Georgiana, I'm real. You're here with us, Willem and the family, you're at Villa Magenta."

"But how? How is that possible?" she says becoming frantic. "It's impossible."

"Why?" Morgan asks becoming exasperated. "Why is it impossible?"

"Because."

"Because why?!"

"Because…*I'm dead*." Silence; you could hear a moth flutter. "I did it Morgan. I finally did it. I killed myself."

Sadie enters the room escorting Montara in her pajamas, carrying her honey-colored teddy bear. The child embraces Morgan, their nightly *goodnight hug,* when she spies Georgiana and points.

"Mama!" she shouts to everyone's surprise and literally runs to the visitor. I see the gleam in her young eyes change to confusion.

"*Mama?*" Georgiana says to the girl. "You called me *Mama*?" Montara stares at her, uncertainty forming on her beautiful face.

"Montara, that's not…that's our friend, Georgiana," Morgan says, and the child seems strangely uncertain, studying her closely before turning to Morgan and pointing.

"Mama."

"*Montara*, your name is Montara, I know you!" Georgiana says falling to her knees and embracing the girl.

"Me," the child says from within Georgiana's embrace.

Magda pulls her away. "Go to bed Montara, right now."

The girl points at our nocturnal guest. "Mama," she says again and Magda scolds her fiercely.

"That's not your mother! Now go to bed, git!" Montara's eyes instantly swell with tears. "Sadie take Montara to her room. Why you lettin' her traipse about at this hour? What's in you head girl?"

"C'mon Montara," Sadie says taking her hand when Morgan embraces the child.

"Aunt Morgan will be up in a minute honey, okay?"

"Morgan…storytime?" the child says. and her sad, confused expression is heart-wrenching.

"Yes honey, *Morgan storytime* soon, go on upstairs." She does so, staring at Georgiana the entire time.

"Morgan," aunt Vanetta says from the parlor door. "We've a bed ready. Willem's room."

"Listen to me Georgiana. I don't know what's happened, but we'll figure it out tomorrow. Right now, you have to sleep you're exhausted. I think you're hallucinating."

"No. I'm not hallucinating."

"Yes, I think you are."

"No."

"Will you just trust me? You're not in Hell or any other terrible place. You're here with us, Villa Magenta, safe and sound."

"Maybe…I don't know."

"When you wake up tomorrow morning, you'll be here with us, at Villa Magenta, do you understand?" She nods. "Okay, aunt Vanetta will take you upstairs."

"Come on Georgiana, beddy-bye."

"Morgue, if I don't see you in the morning, I want you to know…that I love you, I always have, I could just never say it to you…the words. I could never say that word to anyone."

"I love you too, and I *will* see you tomorrow, bright and early."

As soon as she's gone, the conversation erupts. "Did you see that? Why did Montara do that?"

"Do what exactly?"

"Call her *Mama*. She never calls anyone by that name, except…"

"Monique."

"Yes."

"Odd."

"Very odd. What's going on here aunt Vivien?"

"Go lay down Morgan. Take your handsome young man with you and go sleep. Let Vannie and me do the thinking for now. Tomorrow will undoubtedly bring answers."

Early the next morning we're awakened from a sound sleep by a frantic pounding on the bedroom door. "Montara isn't in her room, she's missing, that woman too!" Magda shouts from the door, looking as if the devil had walked in.

We quickly change out of our pajamas and join her downstairs as she frantically scours the lower terrace calling Montara's name into the expansive garden surround.

The commotion rousts the two Scottish aunts and an impromptu search of the house and grounds ensues. As seconds tick into minutes Magda becomes more frantic. "They're not here. They're not here Morgan, she's taken her!"

"Magda please calm down."

"Good lord, that crazy woman has taken Montara! Good God in heaven, how could I have been so careless? Why didn't I see it? Lord, I'll never live with myself if something's happened."

"Magda, stop it! You'll only make matters worse."

"I'm calling the sheriff. She's kidnapped Montara! Willem go fetch Majo. If they're on foot we can track them from here. When I get my hands on that woman, I'll kill her, I'll kill her!"

There's a prevalent '*Ahem*' from the upper common above the hall. Everyone looks up to see Vivien in a crimson robe, her tawny-colored hair cascading about her shoulders and her hands poised staunchly upon her womanly hips. She stares down at us, an odd grin on her face.

"If you're finished making fools of yourselves you might want to come up here before calling in the local militia."

There's an abrupt exodus to the upper level. Vivien shushes everyone before opening the door to Monique's bedroom. We follow her inside, surprised by what we see. Nestled together like two sleeping kittens are Georgiana and Montara, their heads against each other's, slumbering away. Magda pushes through us to get a clear look.

"Why, I never," she exhales.

Morgan gently pushes past her sitting on the edge of the bed; ever so gently awakens Montara who sits up yawning, confused by all the people gathered about.

"Cornflakes," she says pensively and a couple of us laugh. Magda instantly takes the child in her arms and carries her off. This wakens Georgiana who seems genuinely shocked by all the faces staring back at her.

"What's going on?" she says. Vivien laughs aloud while Vanetta scowls.

"Ach, Viv," she says and leaves. Georgiana sits up canvassing the room.

"Where am I? You moved me?"

"Apparently you moved yourself."

"When?"

"Sometime last night." Georgiana stares at her nightshirt, then both sides of her hands.

"I'm still here?" she asks, and Morgan stands, crossing her arms.

"Yes, quite."

"I'm alive?"

"By all outward appearances."

After breakfast, we're sitting on the veranda that overlooks the great yard. Emerald has just returned from the hospital with news on Emory's condition. The women are having tea, conversing together, watching as Montara plays with Georgiana on the lawn. Majo is also cavorting with them when Emerald questions Morgan. "Does your friend Georgiana like children? She doesn't strike me as the type."

"She's never exhibited the slightest interest in children, she's even said as much, repeatedly."

"Said what?"

"That they make her uncomfortable, dogs too. She's been bitten, several times…so perhaps they don't like her."

"But look at them together. Have you ever seen Montara act this way with a complete stranger?"

"Never. Majo either. He takes after granddad, he's very wary of strangers."

"Yet, when she walked in last night, he became complacent, his tail wagged," Vanetta interjects.

"I can't understand it," Morgan says gazing across the lawn. "She's like a subtly different woman. Aunt Vivien, what did you mean when you said, *she's not what she seems*? I believe those were your exact words."

"A feeling, a momentary impulse. I know it when I feel it, so I said it."

"What do you feel now?" Morgan asks and the flaxen-haired twin gazes at the woman, child, and dog at play upon the grass.

"Fascination."

A sudden burst of laughter draws all our attentions. We watch as Georgiana goes down on her knees, embracing the child.

"I can't understand it. It's beyond strange," Morgan says and gazes at me, her lustrous green eyes reflecting the morning sun. "What do you think Willem?"

"Something has radically changed, she's different."

"Yes, but what?"

"I've no idea. What did she tell you this morning?"

"Little to nothing."

"Is she purposefully being obtuse?" Emerald queries her daughter.

"No. I know her well enough. I firmly believe she doesn't know."

"Some part of her does," Vanetta says.

"She honestly thought she was dead," Morgan says, incredulous. "She was actually afraid to go to sleep for fear of waking up in Hell."

"Hell? For heaven's sake." Emerald says, shaking her head.

"She was raised Catholic, so she carries those fears concerning the afterlife."

Emerald takes Morgan's wrist. "Did you quiet yourself about it?"

"I couldn't. I just couldn't focus."

"Well I did," Vanetta interjects arresting all our attentions.

"And what did your little angel tell you love?" her sister inquires.

"Seek the significance of the problem."

"The significance? And what is the significance?" Emerald asks and Vanetta points at the two at play within the garden. Incredibly, we watch as Montara takes Georgiana's face and twists it in both hands nearly as if she were trying to remove a mask. We hear her say *Mama* again. "Why does she keep saying that? It's unnerving."

"You're distraught Emmie, what with all that's going on, no wonder. You're too wrapped up to clear your thoughts, both of you," she says gazing at Morgan. "However, I'm not. There's something rather peculiar going on here. I think it wise to get to the bottom of it right off, we mustn't delay."

"But what? What can be done Vanetta?"

"I'd like to propose an idea, get to the bottom of this." All eyes are on her. "I want to put her under."

"Oh, that's a grand idea Van. Oh, you're wicked, in an honest and bumbling sort of way."

"*Under*?" Morgan asks.

"Hypnotize her. I've become quite good at it of late," she says, gazing at her double.

"That she has love. I'll cede that. She's got Mum's gift for sure."

"Of course, she must agree to it or it won't work. If she's agin it, we'll nary get through." We all look to Morgan who looks at her friend at play within the garden, their laughter cascading across the green lawn.

"She'll agree to it."

That afternoon there's a meeting with Georgiana. She sits with us in the parlor looking very uncomfortable.

"Ms. Snipes…" Vanetta says, addressing our guest.

"Georgiana. I hate my last name. I always meant to get rid of it."

"Alright, Georgiana…do you know everyone here?" She gazes at the family gathered around.

"I know Morgan and Willem…and I've met Emerald," she says gazing at the raven-haired matriarch, "a couple years ago."

"More recently than that Georgiana, but you were, well, *a little out of it.*"

"Yeah, probably."

"Dear, my name is Vanetta MacIntyre, Morgan's aunt. This awkward thing beside me is my sister Vivien, you spoke with her last night when you…walked in out of the rain."

"Hello," Vivien says lighting a cigarette. "Did you sleep well love?"

"Yeah, surprisingly."

"Georgiana," Vanetta continues, "we've arranged this get-together because we're confused about a few things."

"Like what?"

"We're not trying to put you on the spot dear, but we do need a few answers, if you don't object?"

"Like what?"

"First, when you walked in last night, we were all a bit confused as to how you got here exactly. Do you mind filling us in on that?"

"I don't know."

"That's what you told Morgan. Did a cab drop you off perchance?"

"No."

"An acquaintance, some other person?"

"No."

"How then? How did you manage it?"

"I walked. I remember now, walking." There's an exchange of dubious expressions amongst the group.

"That's a helluva walk, init? Seeing as Magenta's at least an hour from New Orleans?" Vivien says.

"I didn't walk from New Orleans." This admission creates a stir.

"Georgiana," Emerald interrupts, "when you arrived last night, Morgan said you thought you were in Los Angeles."

"Yeah, I guess."

"Why did you think that?"

"Because…well…I forgot about hitchhiking."

"Hitchhiking?"

"Yeah."

"From Los Angeles?"

"Yeah."

"You're saying you hitchhiked all the way from California?"

"Yeah."

"Why do you think that?" Vanetta interjects.

"Because I remember the desert."

"*The desert?*"

"Yeah…how cold it was at night…and nobody would pick me up." A silent exchange circles the room. "Hey Red, can I bum a short?" she asks Vivien, the twin in complete confusion regarding the request.

"She wants one of your cigarettes aunt Vivien."

"Oh," she says extending Georgiana the pack.

"Got to hand it to you Slim, there's not a lot of broads who smoke shorts these days," she says lighting up and exhaling a thick cloud into the room.

"Niece, what's *a short*?"

"A filter-less cigarette."

"Oh…and what's *a broad* then?"

"Slang for a woman who…knows herself."

"Caliber."

"Georgiana, I would like your permission to try a little experiment," Vanetta interrupts.

"Like what?"

"I want to put you under."

"Do what?" she asks suspiciously.

"She wants to hypnotize you," Morgan says. "We want to ask you some questions while-"

"Will it hurt?"

"Of course not."

"Okay, shoot."

Vanetta arranges her chair directly before Georgiana and extracts a small silk bag from her coat pocket. From this tiny bag she removes a long gold chain with a beautiful golden amulet, a scarab inlaid with lapis-lazuli stones.

"Are you kidding me? You're going to swing that thing in front of my face like in the cartoons?"

"This is simply a tool. I want you to focus on the amulet," Vanetta says holding it inert before Georgiana. She twists it gently in her fingers causing the jewel to rotate and sparkle. "Just gaze at it and do your best to clear your mind. Empty it of the baggage of your thoughts, the weight, be free of all thinking, your life, your body, you're becoming as light as a feather. Becoming free. Do you see the amulet clearly?"

"Yeah."

"Beautiful isn't it? Golden...radiant...it's over three thousand years old...see how it reflects the sunlight...look how it sparkles, like gazing into a beautiful sunset...just like the sun...at the end of a long serene day...a soft quiet beach...do you see the sun, glimmering over the water, reflecting the gentle waves...the golden sand?"

"Yes."

"Georgiana, you are with your friends here in this safe golden place…do you feel the soft warm sand beneath you? Feel the gentle loving breeze in your hair?"

"Yes."

"You're here with us, your friends…your family. We love and care about you. Do you believe what I'm telling you?"

"Yes."

"No one will hurt you, harm you in any way. You're safe here with us on this beautiful pristine beach, golden in the sunlight." Vanetta twists the bauble radiating gentle pulses of sunlight from the window, Georgiana becoming transfixed. "I want you to wait here for us in this place. When I snap my fingers, I want you to lie down and sleep until I come back and wake you by saying the word, *Awake*. Does that suit you?"

"Yes."

"I'll snap my fingers three times Georgiana, *First to sleep, second to speak, third and final yourself to seek.* Will you do that for us?"

"Yes."

"When I snap my fingers once, I want you to let go, just let go, release. Alright, on the count of three then. One…two…three," she snaps her fingers and amazingly Georgiana falls into a kind of instant slumber.

Vanetta, wide-eyed, gazes at us. "I did it. She's under."

"I'll say she is. You're getting rather good at this little trick," her twin whispers. "It makes me shiver."

"What now?" Morgan asks. Vanetta holds up her jeweled forefinger.

"Watch." She returns her attention to Georgiana raising her hand and snapping her fingers and a most incredible thing happens.

Slowly as if watching a sleeper emerge from a deep slumber Georgiana reawakens. However, something about her eyes and expression, seem markedly different than the woman just put under. These eyes no longer possess an opiate-like indifferent gaze. These eyes instantly fathom everyone and everything. She winces as if in pain, writhing in the chair a moment before settling down. "Mon Dieu," she whispers nearly inaudibly and studies her hands and tattooed arms.

"Are you Ms. Snipes?" Vanetta asks drawing her attention, the two women exchanging a penetrating gaze.

"Vanetta MacIntyre," *Georgiana* whispers. The voice has a familiar inflection. "I thought as much." She gazes about the group. "You're all here…even young Willem."

Emerald instantly springs from her chair, kneeling before Georgiana, looking deeply into her eyes. I watch this protracted silent exchange in awe. *Georgiana's* eyes are clearly different, no longer possessing the washed-out glaze; these eyes are now deep and intent. She reaches up with her right hand and brushes Emerald's face.

"Sister, how splendid to see you again."

"Oh my god," Emerald expounds not removing her gaze. "It's you. I'd know that look anywhere, my god," she says covering her mouth. She turns to us and I've yet to see an expression like this on another's face. "It's her, my god it's her."

"Who?" Morgan asks. A moment's pause ensues as Emerald studies her once more, a long discerning look.

"Monique."

This admission causes an intense stirring amongst the women as they immediately gather around her.

"Monique Montaigne, is that you?" Vivien asks with alacrity. When *Georgiana* looks at the cigarette still burning between the fingers of her left hand, she holds it out toward the vivacious twin who takes it from her.

"Still smoking Vivien? I'm shocked at you."

"I knew it!" the twin says boldly. "I just knew it."

We all watch with fascination–and concern–as *Georgiana* struggles anew, as if in pain. She winces before settling again. Emerald takes her face in both hands, gazing intently into her eyes.

"Monique, is it true? Is it you?"

"It is so sister."

"How? For god's sake how is it possible?" Emerald stammers. "Why?" she asks a frantic tone escalating in her voice and Vanetta takes her arm.

"Easy Emmie, calm down love, shall we?" Emerald seems to nearly collapse. "Willem, bring her chair closer, that's a lad." Everyone pulls in tighter. "Now, Monique, can you talk with us love? We've a bounty of questions." We wait with anticipation while she winces again, the strange weird writhing. "What is it dear, are you in pain?"

"This body…it's full of toxin," she says, somewhat regaining her composure. She looks at Morgan beside me and for the first time I actually see it, *Monique's gaze.*

"Aunt?"

"Morgan, contact Binford Grayson, as soon as possible. Put Georgiana under his supervision. If she's not rehabilitated soon, this body will die before the year is out."

"Rehabilitated?"

"All this drug addiction," the aunt says struggling anew. Everyone draws in even tighter, holding both hands now. "The body is screaming, it's full of toxicity. How can she endure it? Poisons abound."

"Is there anything we can do to comfort you?"

"Bin will take care of things, see to it right away."

"Monique, what on earth? Why are you here, in *this* body?" Emerald presses. You could hear a pin drop as we wait for her to answer.

"All this killing oneself, jumping off buildings and such," she mutters, "it's got to stop Emerald, right now. I'm putting an end to it once and for all."

"For god's sake, why would you re-carnate? Don't you realize what you've you done? You've trapped yourself within this body, the body of Georgiana Snipes."

"So I believe."

"For god's sake Monique, how could you? *Why* would you? Why would you do such a thing? It's unfathomable!"

"Emmie, take hold now love. We mustn't compound the situation."

"But she was free. Don't you understand? This was the last time, the last go around. Now, her karma is linked with this woman."

"She's our responsibility Emerald," her sister interjects. "All this drug and alcohol addiction…and killing one's self over and over again, unacceptable behavior for one of our clan. Something had to be done."

"No! No, you're wrong sister. Georgiana's life and her problems are of her own making and her own resolve. How could you do this to yourself? You've given up eternity!" She nearly swoons.

"She's the baby soul Emerald. We brought her up with us. We all agreed to it…you as well sister."

"Monique, that was centuries ago!" Emerald wails going to tears.

Morgan takes up *Georgiana's* hand. "It is you. You're here in Georgiana's body."

"It is so dear. Morgan, where is Lucien?" she asks wincing.

"At the hospital checking on grandfather."

"Thank the Holy Muse. With Lucien there, father should respond…yes, he should."

"Aunt Monique, what's happened?" Morgan asks and all eyes and ears are glued on her.

"I had died. It was a peaceful death. I saw you, from afar. Thereafter, I was in the interim, between this life and the next plane, the higher realm."

"You saw mother, she was there with you?" Emerald interjects.

"Alas, no sister. Grandmother, Gillian and Viola. Blanche and Tallulah."

"Where's mother, where is she?"

"We mustn't talk about that right now…a later time," she says then goes into a fit of painful writhing. When it subsides Morgan takes up her hand again.

"Aunt, what can we do to make you comfortable?"

"Once we've gotten the poison from her body, we'll begin to mend, things will become better then."

"What's wrong?"

"She's in deep pain Morgan…her youth and now what's happening to her professionally. How can people treat each other so harshly? Don't they understand when they die…*their re-living of what they inflict upon others?*" No one utters a sound. "Georgiana had such a bright future as a musician. Her mother, Myrna, was a loving soul."

"Morgan, the connection is tenuous," Vanetta whispers, "she could leave us in a heartbeat."

"Aunt Monique, what's happened? Why are you here like this?"

"I'm responsible for her, we all are. Something must be done. All this…jumping off buildings Morgan…it's unacceptable. It has to stop, within *this* lifetime. *Tomorrow will be too late for her*. Should she have killed herself again, I shudder to think where it would have lead this time."

"*Killed herself?*"

"Georgiana tried to kill herself, in Los Angeles…well, in all actuality, she did. I stopped it." This causes a profound reaction amongst the women.

"What do you mean Monique? How did you stop it?"

"Just that, I stopped it. When she stepped off the building, was falling to her death, regretting her decision most profoundly of course, I stopped it." The sound of the front door arrests our attentions and Lucien Karras steps in.

"Uncle Lucien, thank goodness you've come."

"Hello brother," Vivien says. "We've something right up your alley."

He drops his cap and positions himself squarely before Georgiana, Vivien giving up her chair. He takes her hand gazing deeply into her eyes, touching the side of her face, the left temple.

"Bless my soul. Hello Monique, are you well?"

"As well as can be expected Lucien, under the circumstances," she says, her eyes moistening with tears. "So grand to see you again."

"You mustn't remain very long. The harshness you're feeling is far too acute. You've no practical experience with the chemical nature of a body such as this one."

"So I realize. I'm having doubts to whether the decision was sound."

"What's done is done. There's no reversing it now."

"How shall we proceed?"

"We'll take care of things here on the physical plane, but you need to address matters in the ethereal. This person with whom you are now inextricably linked has little to no understanding of the higher realms. In fact, I sense she's a nihilist."

"Yes, I know. It's unfortunate."

"You've given up a century of bliss I'm sorry to say, for a time anyway. The single life you'll share could be fraught with pitfalls. It could...well, let's be honest, it *will* impact your destiny. We can only hope for the very best. If things go well, the *treasure* within could be multifold."

"Lucien, dear, dear brother, I'm dubious quite frankly. The result of *the decision* was instantaneous. One moment I was there, within the light, the next I was here, inside the body...quite remarkable."

"Obviously the body itself suffered no ills?"

"The stupid girl actually stepped off the ledge Lucien, can you believe it?"

"Yes, quite. Let's not despair, the life is most redeemable, with every likelihood of excelling, especially now, considering these recent happenings, you sharing in her...development."

"You've instilled me with hope." She then goes into convulsions.

"Vanetta, wake up Georgiana. It will release Monique from this."

"Yes brother. Monique, we'll see you again sister, very soon I'm sure."

"Of course. Lucien...Binford."

"Yes, yes, she'll be in good hands with Binford. I'll see to it."

"Bless the Goddess."

He chuckles under his breath. "I don't envy his position. Considering Georgiana's personality, it's certain to prove a challenge. But rest assured, *it will be done*."

"Bless the Holy Muse."

Emerald suddenly takes *Georgiana's* face in both her hands. "Dear sister, *whatever have you done?*" she cries. They embrace lovingly. I realize they're crying together.

"Sister, be strong for me." She goes into a painful writhing, actually crying out.

"Vanetta," Lucien says gesturing.

"*Returning to the realm above, shake the nightmare from your mane m'love. Awake!*" Vanetta snaps her fingers.

Georgiana instantly goes limp, as if waking from sleep; shocked by the sudden close proximity of everyone. She gazes at Lucien like she's seeing a ghost.

"Morgan, what the hell's going on? Get these people away from me."

"Relax Georgiana. We're all family."

"What are you guys doing to me?"

"Georgiana, relax. No one's hurting you. You were asleep, that's all."

"How long?"

"Only a few minutes."

Georgiana looks at her hand. "Who stole my smoke?" she asks, and Morgan becomes exasperated.

"No one *stole* it. You finished it."

"Well I want another one," she says and Vivien hands her the entire pack.

"Keep it love, I've others," she says, and Georgiana stalks off without another word.

"Magda's right, that woman is repulsive," Emerald says after she's gone. "I loathe the idea my sister is involved with her. Lucien, you must do something about it. It mustn't continue."

"There's nothing that can be done."

"What do you mean?"

"Exactly that, there's nothing that can be done. The process cannot be altered."

"Lucien, brother, what's it about? That woman actually committed suicide?"

"Attempted."

"And was thwarted by Monique? How was it done?"

"Gravity is a universal constant. In fact, *it's because of gravity that we know consciousness exists universally.* Composing the very substance of the gravitational force, its field and waves, involves consciousness. Through focus on this mechanism, gravity can be, momentarily altered."

"Are we were talking about suicide, or…?"

"Gravity is the weakest of the subatomic forces, yet inviolate. It permeates Universe and is a universal constant, subordinate to focused vibrational causality."

"Brother, what does this science lecture have to do with Monique?"

"Monique could affect the constant at that precise moment because her current state was beyond physical limitations, *supermundane* to the earth's gravitational *and* dimensional fields. The science is actually similar to that employed in the building of certain great monuments, Stonehenge in fact…the colossal works in the Andes."

"You're saying Georgiana didn't fall?"

"I believe that's more than extant."

"How did she get *here* exactly?"

"It would be my belief Monique directed her here, and wisely so. Magenta was the only plausible option, with the possible exception of San Francisco."

"Why not San Francisco?" Emerald asks. "Considering it closer, and my home."

"You weren't there. Monique would know this. It's uncertain how Audrey would have reacted."

"But it's so distant. How on earth…?"

"By all rights, it was universal energy that brought them here, Monique's desire to *return home* and Georgiana's resiliency in manifesting it. Extraordinary. Many persons would be incapable of this amazing feat under such conditions. It bodes well."

"It's unbelievable."

"Thank the heavens they made it or…"

"Or what?"

"Well, it's immaterial, they did make it, quite incredible. Honestly it bodes well for the union."

"Union?"

"Georgiana and Monique. Don't judge Georgiana too harshly. There's more *there* than meets the eye. Let's do our best to help her come to the realization of her situation."

"What is *her situation* uncle?"

"That she's agreed to all this. Oh yes, this would be quite impossible without her willing participation, her desire for it in fact, a deep inner calling."

"Can you explain that?"

"Apparently the instant she stepped off the building, was falling to her death, she regretted it profoundly. The material mind pushes the body to do all sorts of evils yet *cause and effect* are universal laws, irrefutable."

"I don't understand."

"There was a karmic connection between them that was active, or activated, and the phenomenon instantaneous, similar to engaging a light switch. It's usually this way to a man. Suicide is a reaction of the human, material mind and its preoccupation with pain, a very powerful amalgam. When the temporal ego gets in over its head, it is always the higher self that's left to sort things out."

Chapter *10*: *Whispering at night*

That night a difference of opinion ensues. Magda is at odds with my sleeping in Morgan's room. Having given up the guest room to Georgiana and with a profundity of visitors and young boarders, I'm relegated to sleeping on a *roll-away* in the linen closet upstairs, just off the upper bathroom. I'm more than morose about the situation having the strongest desire to be with Morgan at this delicate time. Lucien actually takes me aside about it and explains it's an unwritten rule at Magenta that unmarried couples sleep separated, the reasons not only because of the young orphan girls living at the home, but that the *rule of thumb*, as he calls it, goes back generations and has been enforce several hundreds of years.

"It has more to do with the *conservation of energy* than prudence. To assume there's never been a breach of faith, so to say, would be naïve, however, it is in everyone's best interests Willem to grin and bear it for now, please be patient with the situation." I reluctantly do so, retiring early that evening and begrudgingly taking my place on the tiny cot nestled between the fresh linen and the cleaning utensils. The mops stare at me blankly and slumber on.

However, the situation proves to be quite remarkable. As I lay in my bed, dreaming of Morgan's embrace, I become aware of whisperings through the air vent that connects to the room below.

I realize the study, a room dedicated to Colonel Montaigne and his military awards and citations, is being used as a meeting place between different parties during different nights.

Because of his absence, the room becomes an impromptu rendezvous spot for persons seeking discretion. It's difficult to make out clearly all that's being said. I press my ear closer to the old antiquated vent, designed as a passive heat exchange allowing air to rise from the lower floor; obviously a leftover from earlier days when there was no central air in the home, I assume the reason this vent had survived was due its innocuous location in the linen closet. The first night I overhear an astounding conversation between the Scottish twins.

"Can't he understand? The gorgon won't rest. That vile thing murdered Monique! Only by the will of the Divine Muse does she grace our *little island*. Incredible."

"Aye, this strange union with the woman Georgiana. Ach Vivien, no doubt there's divine intent about it. What other explanation is there than it was *ordained*, this incredible thing that's happened. This would never have happened under any natural circumstances."

"Her death is anything but natural love, in any sense of the word."

"That's what I'm saying dear, her death was a direct violation against the Goddess Herself."

"Meaning what?"

"Being wicked as you are, you weren't necessarily included in those conversations were you dearie? Didn't get the details, what?"

"Och, listen to *Penny Proper*. What *details* then? Let's have it."

"Monique Montaigne was descended of the *Vierge Noire,* one of the original seven gothics, manifest. Her death, her murder, was unholy. It's of the most serious nature."

"What do you mean, *Gothics*?"

"The Gothics, the Black Virgins, manifest."

"She's got a daughter Van."

"Montara is hardly a *traditional* birth love, as you very well know."

"This *virgin child* business again, what rot."

"You've not paid one bit of attention 'ave you? That child's a *transcendent soul*, the divine Mistress herself bequeathed it. Monique petitioned the Goddess directly. You'd know all this if you spent more time on your studies and less of it prancing about Edinburgh, carrying on as you do…poor Mum."

"Are ye sayin' Monique never had *a go* with a man?"

"Well…that…yes…ostensibly."

"Yer the one who's daft. That young Frenchman, the Creole gardener, would be the more likely methinks."

"Bullocks Vivien. Go ahead and close your ears and eyes and stay ignorant. See if I care in the least."

"Well then that's a bust. I'm certainly sorry to hear that, were it true, the poor thing."

"Poor thing?"

"If I had to go through the trials of childbirth I want the pleasures that come a'fore."

"Vivien MacIntyre, yer wicked."

"Wicked you say? I didn't invent the pains ner pleasures o' child-rearin' Van, that'd be a higher source than myself."

"My poor sister. You are lost."

"Feh!"

"*Feh,* to you, times twice. And twice reversed." An extended silence ensues.

"Van, getting back to *matters*…I'm giving over to Emmie's side on the whole bloody thing. Do that heathen bastard in but good. The thing's a devil. It should have been done long ago. Poor Seamus. God preserve his soul."

"Amen. But rest assured dear sister, we won't be poking our noses in *the Book*, Lucien won't have it, nor Acosta mixed up in this. And for obvious reasons."

"Oh, that woman gives me the shakes Vannie. Just being in the same room with her."

"And for good reason love, *her being three hundred years old.* Imagine, keeping oneself alive in such a way, how dreadful."

"I'm not casting stones Van, just saying she gives me the shudders is all."

"Well rightly so. She's behind Magenta going bad, leading her astray. Oh, she's wild and dangerous that one. You keep an eye on her, mark it."

"Van, 'ave ye noticed anything peculiar about Emmie?"

"What's that?"

"Well, she's rather a bit on edge int' she?"

"With good reason. Her sister brutally murdered, her father in his sickbed over it. I'd be a bit careworn I imagine."

"That's not what I mean."

"Out with it."

"She's not 'erself, not at all. What with her inviting Acosta Fontaine back into this house after the things that woman pulled, coming between Emory and Magenta as she done…and Emerald at peace with that? Unimaginable."

"Hardly at peace with it I'll wager m'love. Em's bent upon the annihilation of this *thing* they're calling Mr. Else. *Mister Else*, hum! As if *it* were human in the least. Bullocks."

"Sinister bastard. I'd gouge its bloody eyes out. If it bloody had any."

"I'm trusting Lucien sister. Bringing Acosta Fontaine into this is very, very dangerous business. Viv, we mustn't talk about this, best to quit it for now."

"Vannie, ye're forever ducking shadows love."

"What, with Acosta walking through walls, or being anyplace she sets her mind to? Shhh, best not discuss it until they've left, supposedly within the hour, thank the Muse."

There's a period of silence, only vague mutterings. They seem to be whispering, until Vivien's voice rises in pitch. "Well, Emmie's the *Montaigne Daughter* now. I hope she's woman enough for it."

"Hardly, I should think."

"You've dug up a few secrets have you dear?"

"Use your noggin. After what happened with Seamus thirty years ago, she's *stained*, it'll never happen."

"Who then? That *wee* little thing, Montara?"

"We've told you over and over again dear sister, Montara's a *transcendent*, an innocent being, she's not a mature soul…a blessing from the Holy Muse to be sure but nary a leader of men."

"Who then? There's always been *the Montaigne Daughter*."

"Have ye gone dumb? Morgan."

"M'sweet brogue? She's a *woman of the world*, how could she become *the Daughter*?"

"Viv, ye need to open your eyes love, it's going on right round ya."

"Oh my…Morgan…"

"Viv, it must be ordained, her coming back here to this house from her life in New York, leaving a career as she's done. It's the *Divine Hand*."

"I need a drink. Let's join them for the aperitif. We've time a'plenty to decide *who, what, where, when* and all that damnable rot."

"Agreed, just you mind the Colonel's private stocks love. You're much too fond of our homeland's native spirits."

"Och, listen to you. Off you go then. Shove off."

The following evening, while I'm dressing for dinner, is even more astounding. I listen as Morgan, Emerald and Lucien enter and quietly speak together.

"Mom, we need to talk to you about Topey. I've discussed it with uncle Lucien, and he felt, as I, that we should come to some kind of resolve."

"Topey?"

"Aunt Monique's elemental."

"I know, but what can be done? It's an elemental being Morgan. It will go the way of all of its kind. Without Monique, it will dissolve into nothingness."

"That's just it. I can't allow it mother. I can't allow Topey to just, evaporate. The creature has affinity with me, and Montara, just as any sentient being."

"Sentient? It's an elemental. It has no spirit, no soul. Lucien explain it to her."

"On the contrary Emerald. I'm disposed to give the matter further study."

"Are you mad?"

"Em, Nature is great and mysterious. It's not our place to cast opinions about other life-forms based solely upon our preconceived notions."

"*Preconceived notions*? My dear friend, you're talking about *the Mysteries*, the philosophies of old. Centuries of close analytical study...*preconceived notions?* Rubbish."

"Would *assumptions* be the better word?"

"No one's assuming anything. Morgan, I'm sorry but what you're alluding to is quite impossible."

"He loves me mother can't you see it? How more plain can it be?"

"*He?*" Long pause. "I admit the creature seeks proximity to you, but to say it *loves* you…only that which possesses the divine spark can truly love."

"Emerald, haven't you ever asked yourself why your sister was so free of Harlan Kruk after the coma? After Harlan struck her down, Topey chased him about the house, smashing things in the process. The chaotic state of the house was not what people thought, Harlan going berserk. Topey attacked him. Yes, this was revealed to me. A few months later when Harlan showed up unannounced, Topey actually tried to kill him, a human being…to grossly misuse the term in this case. Harlan barely escaped with his life. He even abandoned his car if you recall?"

"Yes. I remember…he had to have it sent for."

"This is the reason she was free of that conscienceless person, because of this so-called *mindless* creature."

"But…you call that *love*?"

"Of course. What else would you call it? What other elemental has ever acted in such a manner, of its own accord, undirected?"

"None that I know of."

"Mom, I can't explain why or how but he's acquired intelligence and free thought, free will."

"Oh, come now Morgan, *free will?* Really. I must draw the line here. That's simply impossible."

"Is it? Those occasions Montara levitates and flies over the bayou…Topey tries to follow her."

"What?"

"Yes, just like a faithful dog. He follows her until he begins to dissipate and is forced to return to Magenta."

"Unbelievable. Lucien, is such a thing possible?"

"It's possible that he's *resonating* with her and Morgan. Attaining affinity."

"*Affinity?*"

"Attaining *resonance*, thus *affinity*. An elemental, crafted from the energies of the person who brought it into existence can *resonate* so closely as to attain what's referred to within the nomenclature as *affinity*, in essence, *awareness*."

"I can scarce believe it. Does Montara *see* Topey?"

"Of course mother."

"And her reaction to him?"

"Love."

After a sustained silence, I hear Emerald ask Morgan to leave the room. "Lucien and I have a few items to discuss privately dear. We'll be along shortly."

"Alright mom. I'll see you at dinner." I hear the door close gently followed by muttering so soft I cannot discern what's being said until the escalating of voices rising through the vent removes any question regarding the conversation; Emerald speaking to him in a voice I've never heard from her before.

"How dare you interfere with my arrangements, as if I were some dilettante whose methods warrant critique."

"Interfere?"

"Sending Acosta away when I asked her for assistance."

"I certainly did not, *send her away*."

"You know perfectly well what I mean."

"Emerald, how can you seek the aid of the Belle Fontaine when you know *who* she is, *what* she is…the things she's done in the course of her existence?"

"Precisely why I seek her expertise, and for her to complete her obligations to this family."

"And in so doing, condemn it."

"That's sheer speculation Lucien. Completely unfounded. Acosta Fontaine is beyond knowledgeable in these matters. She knows how to deal with atrocities like your...your coveted *Mr. Else*."

"Emerald, you're being emotional, you're not thinking clearly. Surely you understand the gravity of proceeding under her tutelage?"

"How dare you accuse me of such base behavior. *Emotional?* This thing has killed my sister, nearly my daughter. Acosta would have surely gotten the necessary results."

"But at what cost?"

Silence.

"This is your fault you know...what's happened...my sister's blood is on your hands."

"Emerald..."

"I told you in San Francisco, to leave this alone, but no, you had to press it. And now look what's happened. I was nearly killed, and my sister was shot down like a beggar in the streets! I shall never forgive you for this Lucien, ever. Monique's death is on your conscience. I'll forever resent you for it...and now, when I make earnest, responsible strides to resolve it, you interfere."

"Em..."

"This is now entirely your responsibility and you owe it to my sister, this entire family, to finish it, once and for all!" I then hear the door close, followed by a deep encompassing silence.

Deep into the night, long after this dreadful exchange, I'm awakened by the sound of a woman crying from the room below. It's odd and strange, this quiet pitiful wailing in *the wee hours*.

As I listen to this weeping, my mind is caught between going down to the study to investigate or honoring the person's desire for privacy, having sought out this remote place in which to mourn. My concerns are weigh-laid when I hear the door open and Morgan's voice punctuate the quietude. "Sadie, whatever is the matter?" More crying. "What's happened? Why are you down here?"

"Because if I cry in my room, Magda shouts at me."

"For goodness sake, tell me what's happened? Has someone hurt you? What is it?" It takes several moments for the girl to respond. "Please Sadie, tell me."

"Aunt Monique," she finally says, her voice breaking.

"*Aunt Monique?*"

"Why? Why aunt Morgan? Why would someone kill aunt Monique? It doesn't make any sense. She never hurt anyone. All she did was good." The girl mourns from the center of her being.

"Shhh, it's all right…it's all right."

"No, no it isn't. She's gone. I miss her."

"I miss her too Sadie."

"I can't stand it aunt Morgan. My heart is breaking."

"Mine too," and they cry together.

"I'm sorry aunt Morgan."

"Don't apologize Sadie."

"Just…every time I try to sing that song…I cry."

"What song?"

"*Summertime*. She would play it for me on the guitar, on the porch, whenever I was sad. Now I can't sing it anymore, it's gone too."

"Whatever shall we do now without her?"

"When will it stop aunt Morgan? When will the pain inside me go away?" She breaks anew, a deep sorrow emanating from the girl.

"I'm sorry Sadie, but I'm afraid it won't ever go away. We just move on...doing those things she taught us. Becoming the people she hoped us to be."

Chapter *11*: The Lower Passions

The following day I join Georgiana sitting on the veranda overlooking the rear garden. I take the chair beside her, setting my coffee upon the table and breathing in the fresh morning air. All about the yard is a plethora of birds and plant fauna, the air rich and humid.

I study her. She looks tired and haggard. I know she is going into withdrawal from her drug addiction, it shows. Today however, she's not her fiery self as of late. Today she's aloof, deep in thought.

"Willem, do you think it's possible that a person can be in more than one place at a time?" she inquires without looking at me.

"What do you mean?"

"Well…like, let's say you're sitting at someone's house, there's other people there, you leave, drive straight to another place, the fastest possible route…but when you arrive, they're just sitting there already, when it's impossible they could have driven there before you. Is that possible?"

"What are you getting at Georgiana, who are you talking about?"

"Binford."

"Mr. Grayson? What did he do?"

"What I just said, twice…no wait, three times now."

"Strange," I say. She mumbles something to herself before turning toward me.

"How in hell is that possible?" she asks point blank but doesn't even wait for a response. "I mean…how could he even know?"

"Know what?"

"Where I'm going. If I never said a word to anybody, how in hell could he…?"

"You're saying you were at Mr. Grayson's and then left? Where did you go?"

"What does it matter *where*, how in hell could he be where I'm going before I get there?"

"Well, did he drive faster than you maybe?"

"How could he know where I'm going?"

"Perhaps he's following you?"

"How could he be sitting at a table drinking bourbon when I walk in?" I stare at her, trying to make sense of it all.

"How many times has this happened?"

"Three times now," she curses under her breath then grabs me. "Willem, I need you to do me a big favor."

"What sort of favor?"

"Pick up a package for me, some tubes and crap for my new amplifier." She takes a pen from the table and tears the corner off a magazine and writes. "Here's the address downtown," she says handing me the scrap of paper with an address scribbled on it.

"I don't know Georgiana, I better not."

"Why? C'mon, help a friend out."

"This is for drugs isn't it?" I ask and she shushes me.

"Shhh! Not! No, just some tubes, er, I mean resistors, for my new bass amp."

"You repair guitar amplifiers?"

"When I have to. I don't have a guitar tech anymore. How about it?" I hand the paper back, shaking my head.

"No dice Georgiana, I can't."

"Why?" she demands.

"Because, I know what'll be in there and it won't be resistors for a guitar amp."

"Goddammit Willem, it's resistors," she says pushing the paper back at me.

"No way," I say. She fumes a moment then turns on me.

"You won't do this one little favor for me?"

"Georgiana, I'd do anything for you except-"

"Listen *pal*, if you don't do this one little favor for me, me and you, we're done."

"Done?"

"*I'll make you disappear.*"

"What's *that* supposed to mean?"

"I mean it, I'll make you disappear," she says, snapping her fingers. I puzzle over this unexpected assertion.

"I don't get you. Make me disappear? How?"

"I'll never see or speak to you again, ever."

"Georgiana…"

"You think I'm kidding Willem? I mean it. I'll never talk or even look at you again, forever. You say something, I won't hear it, you walk in the room, I won't see you." She glares at me. "Don't think I don't mean what I'm saying. I've done it before, to people I don't like."

"Georgiana c'mon, don't do this, it's uncomfortable."

"You want *uncomfortable* buddy? Wait until I never speak to you again, ever. Trust me. I learned this little trick touring over the years. Every roadie knows about it. You end up on tour with people you can't stand. The only way out is to make them go away. That's exactly what I'm going to do to you Willem. Make you disappear."

"Georgiana…"

"*Yes* or *no*?"

"C'mon…"

"Done!" she shouts and waves her hand across the space between us. "You no longer exist. We're done," and like that she acts as if I'm invisible.

As crazy as it seems, I know for fact she's absolutely serious, that she'll make good her threat and the threat will go on for days, weeks, months probably. I'm certain she's done this on repeated occasions and is most likely skilled at *the art*–if the word applies. I also know it is going to negatively affect the entire household.

"Georgiana…if I do this, it'll be once, one time, that's it. Take it or leave it. I'm not going through this little game with you again," I say. She turns and extends her hand.

"Spit shake. Thanks man, you're a real pal Willem, thank god I still got at least one good friend around this lousy dump," she says. I take the note, feeling low.

"Resistors, right? That's what this is?"

"Absolutely," she says, that strange bent grin etched across her face. "Knock once on my door when you get back, *roadie code*," she says and leaves for upstairs.

The address is a dilapidated structure near the ninth ward. I park the car, double-checking that I'm at the right place. When I knock on the door a skinny edentate woman answers through the chain, looking me over suspiciously.

"Yeah?"

"I'm here for Georgiana's guitar parts."

"Who?"

"Georgiana Snipes, some resistors for her amplifier?" She looks at me as if in a daze. I recheck the piece of paper in my hand. "Is this…?"

"Oh, Georgiana, the rocker, right, I get it," she says closing the door. I hear the chain pull back. "Come on in."

I'm shown into a ragged apartment, disheveled and possessing a queer smell. There are two other people in the dimly lit room, an emaciated man and rotund woman in the corner vaguely aware of my presence.

The toothless woman points me to a chair that looks like its been extracted from a landfill and disappears into a back room. When she returns, she hands me a small glassine packet of whitish powder.

"What's this?' I ask. She looks at me blankly.

"Georgiana's stuff."

"I'm supposed to be picking up resistors for a guitar amplifier."

"Oh, shit. I forgot." She takes the envelope and disappears into the back room before returning with what is obviously the same thing inside a small brown paper bag with the opening stapled shut.

"This is the same packet," I say.

"No, it's guitar strings, or whatever," she mumbles. "Hey, she owes me ten more bucks, unless you can cover it?" I'm completely at odds with what is taking place and am preparing to return her *guitar strings* when a knock on the door distracts her. "Jesus Christ," she says and disappears out front for a moment. When she returns her expression is dramatically different. "Is your name William?"

"Close enough."

"You got some friend here looking for you."

"Georgiana?"

"Some dude," she says, and I shake my head.

"Only Georgiana knows I'm here," I say just as Binford Grayson steps into the room! He nods, scanning the place.

"Are you all right?" he asks.

"Uh, yeah, I'm fine," I stammer surprised by his sudden appearance in this place.

"Why are you here Willem? Do you know these people?"

"Not at all. I'm picking up some guitar parts for Georgiana."

"That's the equipment?" he asks pointing at the package in my hand.

"It's supposed to be but..."

"Let's have a look-see." He takes the package from my grasp and tears it open. Inside is what I feared, the glassine envelope of lemony-white powder.

"This look like music equipment to you?" he asks me pointedly.

"No, not in the least." He immediately dumps the contents of the packet across the floor.

"Hey man, what the fuck are you doing?!" the woman barks and the skinny guy is getting to his feet.

"Who is this fucking guy?" he asks *toothless*.

"Hell if I know, get rid of him, both of them," she says. Binford then procures what looks like a badge in the palm of his hand and everyone in the room freezes.

"You recognize this?" he says with intent and they nod. "What is it?"

"A badge."

"You know what it means, what it represents?" They nod. "I'll make a deal with you, *people*, just for today. I won't be as accommodating again. The next time Georgiana Snipes asks, or sends someone, for your product, you tell her you're out of business. You tell her that or I'll see to it you are, permanently. You get me loud and clear?" They nod. "I'm sorry, I didn't hear you."

"Yes sir," they both say in unison. He then turns squarely toward them. I can only see the back of his head.

"And while you're at it, send word to the rest of your, *community*, Georgiana Snipes is off limits. She belongs to me. She's under my wing. I'll not tolerate anyone interfering, is that clear?"

He hovers over them and they shrink into the couch, a look of mortal terror inexplicably crossing their faces. "Yes sir," both say again in unison.

He tips his Stetson. "Much obliged." He then gestures to me and I follow him back outside and down the street.

"What about the car?" I ask.

"Leave it, let's go have a drink."

We walk several blocks in silence before he stops abruptly, taking in a nostril full of air. "You smell that? Magnolia."

"I didn't know you were a police officer."

"I'm not, there weren't nothing in my hand except what I wanted those people to see." He studies me. "You didn't think for one moment there was wires in that dirt bag you were holding did you?"

"I had my doubts."

"You would have drove back to Magenta with that poison in your hand and given it to her?" he asks me directly, his eyes burning into mine.

"No," I say. He knows I'm being sincerely honest.

"Let's have us a drink," he says taking me by the shoulder, shoving me into the bar we're standing before.

The bar's proprietor immediately recognizes him. "Binford, long time no-see. How'ya keeping?"

"Fair Coye, my usual…leave the bottle on the bar."

"You got it."

The barkeep sets a bottle of Kentucky bourbon on the counter and Binford pours two shots, pushing one in my direction. "I know you don't like hard liquor but indulge me, shoot that son-of-a-gun," he says and downs his neat. I try to take mine in one gulp but can only manage half, the liquor biting into my esophagus.

"You feel that, the burn in your throat, the fire in your mouth? Give it a minute and you'll feel it in your gut too, like you just ate an old leather shoe." I nod. "That's your body at odds with what your mind is doing. First time I ever drank this rotgut I puked my brains out and look at me now, sitting here drinking with you. It's the same with that *scratch* you just had in your hand. First time you inject it into your body you vomit, the body rejecting it outright. You actually can feel it, *the touch of death*...not the grip of it, just *the touch*." He pours himself another drink. "So, choose your poison wisely," he says and drinks. "You understand why it's essential we all pull together and get Georgiana off *it* don't you?"

"Monique," I say taking the bottle and topping off my glass.

"Yeah...her too," he mutters, becoming reflective. "Damn Willem, a finer woman never existed. She was a wild one when she was younger, elegant, beautiful."

"*A wild one*, Monique Montaigne?"

"Rumor has it Monique changed after the coma, that that was when she started having visions." He stares at me.

"No?"

"That girl always had *the insight*, from a child. Her grandmother, Lisette Montaigne raised her to become what she became. The *Montaigne Daughter*."

"She has visions?"

"Insight. She can see through the veil that masks the sight of ordinary people."

"She's a witch?"

"A healer. She could heal a person just by looking at them, touching them. She described it to me once, like looking at a glass of lemonade. The person looks translucent, their insides sort of like ice cubes in a glass of lemonade."

"Fascinating."

"She could see what was wrong, sometimes cure them. But she has that Choctaw blood in her from her mother, and Choctaw and alcohol just don't mix. How much you know about Magenta Montaigne?"

"Almost nothing. No one seems to talk about her for some reason."

"Well, not for lack of love, that's for sure. Her girls loved her, it's just...if you got the insight and you mess around with drink, then, you got to have possession of yourself, possess control over your thoughts and emotions, your indulgences. Magenta lacked that part of the deal, control over that kind of energy."

"How do you mean?"

"Magenta Montaigne had the vision but not the control, the discipline required and she went...Monique could of gone that way. Despite what people think, she's very different than her twin."

"Honestly, I can hardly believe we're talking about the same person."

"Hell mister, she used to smoke a pack of Chesterfields a day, drank whiskey from a mason jar. Those were some great carefree days before Shel died and she off and married Harlan Kruk."

"Why? Why would she marry such a man? A man that would strike her down so brutally?"

"See, that was the karma, the *cause and effect* of her ways. Her allowing herself to become bewitched by that heartless son-of-a-bitch." He spits on the floor of the bar.

"I had no idea. I always thought of her as a mature grown woman. I never thought of her being...young."

"I still lose myself over it...see, I've been in love with Monique Montaigne since we was kids, all through school, family get-togethers, church picnics, strolls along the levee...not one day's a'gone by I haven't held that thought in my mind, her and me, together." I wait as he silently reminisces. "When we came of age, I wanted to tell her...but Shelton caught her eye, and that was a done deal. Then Shel and I come back from Vietnam...came back from war and he up and kills himself, by his own hand. She fell, fell from grace, lost her sensibilities and married a man with no conscience, no soul really, when you come right down to it, one of the *walking dead*."

"That mean what it sounds like?"

"They're out there Willem, walking around, everywhere, this world is full of them; people with no conscience...that room you was just in." He pours another shot; the jukebox playing Al Hirt, men shooting pool.

"When she come out of that coma. I was the first she seen. You can believe it. The family had gone to dinner, but I had a feeling. I sat there, like I done for days, just talking, just like you and me here now. Then, just like that princess in the storybook, she opened her eyes, well, her good eye, not the one Kruk ruined...saw me and said my name. That was the sweetest sound these old ears a'ever heard."

"What did she say?"

"I'll never forget her words, she said: '*Bin, I just had the most wonderful dream, Her Most High came to me, She took me. I saw Saint Angela Merici, she asked me to join her work. So glorious Bin, I've agreed to it. I've agreed to be one of the Goddess' virgins. I've given myself to Her Bin, given my word.*'"

"Incredible."

He stares at the drink in his hand. "And that's a'how it's been for thirty-five years. Thirty-five years of loving a woman from afar. Knowing you'll never have her like a married man has a wife, embracing under the moonlight. All that in exchange for *that look*," he says and studies me.

"*Look?*"

"The look in her eyes each and every time we see'd each other, that special look *in her eyes only*…knowing how she feels but knowing too that when we take a vow to those things greater than ourselves, that vow means something, more than life itself."

"I had no idea. It sounds like what I'm going through with Morgan."

"You're a young man, and young men are taught by the fools and idiots of this world that the mark of a man is getting a woman in the sack. But you're no idiot, are you? You know the mark of a true man is earning the love and respect of a woman, everyone around him in fact. *Death sorts it all out in the end*."

"Death?"

"I've seen a lot of it…death. When you die Willem, will they call you *a good man*, or make excuses over your grave?" We drink in silence. "Willem, if you don't understand what I'm telling you boy, then you're going to learn it the hard way."

"The hard way?"

"You're in love with a Montaigne daughter. Morgan, like Monique, is cut from the same cloth, *a being in the know*. Morgan's been wandering in a fog most of her adult life, but you see it in her eyes now don't you boy? *That look*."

"Yes."

"That's the real deal. You're a blessed man...or bound for hell in a handcart like that fool Harlan Kruk, with his pin-up god, and mean empty heart." He pounds his fist on the bar. "I'm sick to death of these fools spitting salvation from the pulpit like it was there for anybody willing to say *I do*. Salvation isn't a once-a-week operation. It's a helluva lot of work and endless. It's up to you mister, choose your poison wisely." He downs his shot, tosses a fifty-dollar bill on the bar and leaves without another word.

When I walk back through the front door of Villa Magenta, I'm shocked by a plate of food cascading down the mahogany staircase, the sound of Georgiana screaming.

"Get out! Get out and leave me alone you freak! I'm done with you, you get it?! I don't want your help. Stay away from me!" I rush up the stairs passing an irate Magda on her way down and join Morgan and Binford at the door of the guest bedroom.

"Please Georgiana, control yourself. Binford's trying to help you. It has to happen, you know why, it's been foretold." Georgiana grabs her own hair as if she would pull it out, the skull rings reflecting the sunlight from the windows in the upper hallway.

"I can't stand it! Get him away from me, I hate your lousy guts!" she screams, and Morgan grabs her.

"Stop it! Stop talking to him this way when he's saving your life!" She takes Morgan's face in her hands.

"It isn't fair Morgan, it isn't fair. I'm a goddamn rock star. I've played in front of twenty thousand people, gigged all over the world. Now, I'm being shoved around by this fucking hick!" she shouts then drops her head into Morgan's shoulder. "It's not fair, it's not fair," she chants, Morgan consoling her while Binford wipes food from his beard.

"Hang in there babe," Morgan says stroking her, "we'll get through this…we can do it, we'll get through it…and when we do, your life will begin again, brand new."

The next few days prove trying as Georgiana goes through withdrawal from prolonged chemical dependency. It's extremely taxing and she becomes upsetting to everyone. Magda and Emerald refuse to have anything to do with her while the Scottish twins do their best to help. Morgan and Binford do most of the *heavy-lifting,* Binford becoming the repository of most of her mental and verbal abuse.

The man astounds me, his ability to retain his composure and toward the end of the week, she's in remission. Eventually, she's able to spend time with Montara again who has been kept secluded from her during this stressful time.

I'm shocked how a substance can take hold of a person. Binford informs me that she's been in this state for so long, the withdrawal was particularly strenuous.

"It don't help that *something inside* doesn't agree with what we're doing for her, fighting us every step despite us saving her life. The drug's become *more important than the person.* It's always that way."

"How many people have you cured?"

"Of addiction? I never counted…mostly veterans. Things will change as she comes back to life."

"*Comes back to life?*"

"Waking from the stupor she's been in."

"Stupor?"

"When a person becomes addicted to an artificial substance, some part of the triumvirate will pay the bill, usually the body but sometimes the soul."

"*The soul?* You mean the spirit?"

"The spirit is undeniable but make no bones about it, if the temple, its keeper, becomes diseased beyond redemption...*the spirit will up and flee*. When that happens...well, just make damn sure it never does. I've seen those people walking around; dead men walking the earth."

"Is Georgiana...?"

"Damn Willem, I hope not. I don't think so. Despite the long use, she never stepped over that edge, the point of no return. That's tough to do over such a long period of time, not stepping into *the abyss of eternal night*."

"That sounds ominous."

"Some people walk right in, never to be seen again. I don't think it of her. The girl has spirit. We'll be all right. But she'll want that stuff for a long time, the very poison killing her, *the craving of this thing that's inside her*." I think deeply about his choice of words, wonder about them.

"I'm in it for the long haul at this point Willem. I'm happy to take on this particular responsibility. Hell, to be with Monique again after losing her like that...it's like a miracle. I've asked that red-haired woman to put me through to her tonight. I need to know if she's all right. That was pretty much hell, the last few days, anything could have happened."

That night we're seated together in a circle of chairs in the parlor when Georgiana is brought in wearing a mauve-colored robe, looking frazzled but more *herself* than the previous few days.

"How are you feeling Georgiana?"

"Just peachy," she says, glowering at Binford in the chair beside her. "Being kept prisoner by your hick jailer has been a real load of laughs."

"Georgiana, no one has ever locked the door of your room or posted a guard at the door of this house."

"Oh yeah Morgan? Old buddy, old pal. Just your heavy here."

"What are you talking about?"

"Him! I couldn't step outside the door without you ratting me out."

"I've never phoned Mr. Grayson about your coming and going."

"Oh really? How come he showed up every time I went downtown? Every frickin' time Morgan. There he was, scaring my friends and screwing with *my thing*."

"No one in this house needs to tell me what you're doing downtown sweetheart," he says.

"And don't call me *sweetheart!*" she shouts, giving him *the finger*.

"Georgiana, do you know why we've asked you down?" Lucien interjects.

"Morgan's uncle Lucien…"

"Indeed, it's good to see you up and around."

"Yeah, yeah, cut the crap. You wanna hypnotize me again."

"Georgiana, I want to put you under just as we did a few days back," Vanetta says pulling her chair closer.

"You gonna make me strut around like a chicken this time? Cackle like a bird? Hang upside down from the chandelier like an ape?"

"Georgiana, really," Morgan exhales. "You could be a little more appreciative of what everyone's trying to do on your behalf."

"I didn't ask for this bullshit Morgan."

"No? I dare say the opposite, as you damn well know," Morgan says, exasperated. "You came here for help, well, we're helping, despite your best attempts to the contrary." Georgiana rubs her forehead and runs her fingers through her hair tossing it back and looks at Vivien.

"Hey Slim, you holding?"

"Am I what?"

"She wants another one of your cigarettes," Morgan mumbles and the aunt extends her pack.

"Amazing, it's like a completely different form of English," she says, lighting it for her. "That's what I like about you sweetie, you keep it interesting."

"Yeah? Back atcha Red. You and your *photo double* have been a real gas."

"Gas? That would be Vannie dear, not I."

"Vivien! You really are vulgar."

"Vulgar am I? Well, I could *cast a few aspersions* about you that might turn some heads in this room dear sister."

"Oh really? Like what?"

"Miss Prim and Proper, I doubt you'd appreciate my sharing it with the group, although they'd all love hearing it I'm certain."

"Bollocks. You really are awful. I'm certain I could do you one better love."

"Is that so love? Let's have it then."

"Aunt Vanetta, can we please get on with it?"

"Right you are Morgan. Georgiana, we can't do this unless you're with us in whole. It only works if the person is in full agreement. You don't sound very agreeable dear, not at all." Georgiana exhales a large volume of smoke between them.

"What do I got to lose?"

The entire process repeats as it did the prior week, Vanetta using her amulet; we all watch in amazement as she methodically puts Georgiana under. When she counts to three and snaps her fingers Georgiana falls into a silence as if asleep. When she repeats the counting and finger snapping, we sit mesmerized as an amazing transformation takes place. Gone is the narrow vindictive look in Georgiana's face to be replaced by a deep empathic expression.

The eyes slowly canvass the group until they rest upon Binford and in the softest of voices she reaches out and touches him. "Bin…"

"Hello Moni, is it you?" She caresses his cheek. "Yeah, it's you…I'da know that look anywhere. Are you a'right? It's been a rough road."

"Yes Bin, we're feeling much better now, things are better."

"That's good darling, that's real good." She then gazes about, at each and every one of us.

"Hello everyone," she says and we all answer. Her gaze comes to rest on Lucien and her eyes glow like two jewels in sunlight.

"Hello Lucien."

"Hello Monique, how are you? Are you well?" She nods not removing her steadfast gaze. I wonder about that look. She speaks so softly, she's nearly inaudible.

"I know who you are," she says with great emotion. "Forgive me for not divining it during my lifetime, being more appreciative."

"You are a true friend Monique. I'll forever value our time together," he says. Her face glows then turns toward the Scottish aunts.

"Hello sisters." The aunts both smile.

"Well, you certainly have become more civil I must say," Vivien says taking the cigarette from her fingers.

"Georgiana?"

"She's rather trying love. It'd be a boon if you could give her a little *kick*, from that side of things," Vanetta adds. She smiles genuinely before she looks upon Morgan with deep emotional eyes.

"Morgan…" she whispers, and they embrace. "How can I thank you for what you've accomplished." I see tears welling in both of their eyes.

"We wanted to know that you were all right, that you hadn't been hurt…by…everything." She begins to weep covering her mouth and Monique takes up her hand.

"Dear, you mustn't cry, it pains me."

"I know," Morgan stammers, "I can't help it."

"Morgan, things are getting better daily, be strong."

A soft sound from the door arrests our attention and we see Magda holding Montara by the hand.

"Montara. Come here dearest one," she gestures. The mysterious girl goes to her, touching her cheek with the very tip of her index finger.

"Mama," she says, and they embrace.

"Yes Montara, mother is here, inside." They look at each other lovingly as she strokes the child's long dark tresses.

"Mama…sick?"

"Yes dear, but I'm getting better, every day."

"Mama…storytime?"

Magda takes her shoulders. "Montara, go back upstairs sugar."

"No," the child declares siding closer to *Georgiana* who reaches her hand out to the maid, the Creole woman turning and exiting the room.

"Magda is having a hard time accepting this," Morgan says.

"She disagrees with my decision," *Monique* says, looking about. "Emerald, where is she?"

"At the hospital in New Orleans with aunt Pearl and aunt Angeline."

"Father?"

"Your death struck Grandpa deeply. He still can't come to grips with it. We're very worried."

"I was afraid it would be like this. Once his anger turned to despair. I better go to him."

"Monique," Lucien interjects, "you mustn't over-extend yourself. Emerald has things in hand."

"Yes, I suppose," she says looking at Binford. "Bin, are you well?"

"Yes. What about you? What do you need right now Moni?" She looks at Morgan.

"I need our teeth fixed. Morgan, arrange an appointment with Doctor Jenner, immediately."

"Of course, anything else?"

"She needs to eat better. The body is suffering from a prolonged lack of nutrition."

"I'll see to it," Morgan says and *Monique* smiles looking at everyone. When her gaze rests upon Lucien again there's a knowing look.

"Monique, what can you tell us about Mr. Else?"

"Mr. Else?" she echoes.

"The...*man,* behind your murder, and Morgan's near death."

"Yes...yes I'm aware." She winces.

"Are you in pain?"

"No Lucien, not really."

"The concept of Mr. Else pains you?"

"Of course. It's base, most foul. The entity keeps itself alive artificially."

"It's an artificial entity?"

"Far worse…he was human…once. Now he-" She checks herself, looking at Montara but Vivien presses on.

"Something must be done sister. This has gone on long enough. Did the thing murder Seamus?"

"Yes."

"How do we get at him, *the Black Book,* aye?"

"Sister…to do so, would be to align yourself with the very *essence* of which you do battle."

"What about Acosta dear?" Vanetta interjects. "Is it wise to consult with her? We seem torn."

"Acosta Fontaine is one of our oldest familial relations, *forever beloved.* Yet you know as I, she is *hopelessly wicked.* What nectar can come of such fruit? I love her dearly, but I fear for her soul…what's left of it."

"Monique, do you have anything for us? How do we set about this path?" Lucien inquires and she radiates *a warmth* toward him that is very apparent.

"Dearest mentor, you've walked within *the Light,* the higher realms. You need not fear that which hides within the shadows, shuns and disdains its very source. It knows *that* from which it hides. Yet beware, tis a delicate process. Fathom your spiritual mind Lucien, the answer is within you."

"Indeed."

After a brief silence she looks directly at me. I can't hold her penetrating gaze. "Young Willem, come here, take my hand." I do so, a warmth I've never felt from Georgiana's touch radiating her being.

"Hello Aunt Monique."

"Willem, you're weighted with regret. Don't lay my death upon your conscience. It's a lie Willem, not based on any reality. This voice in your head, that you've somehow caused this, or could have prevented what happened, dispel it immediately. There was nothing you could have done. I treasure you." She releases my hand and addresses the group. "All of you, how I treasure you all, such fine people, so very precious," and everyone takes a moment to reflect upon these words. She then looks at Binford.

"Binford Grayson, my dear, dear friend…thank you. Thank you for what you've done. I apologize for the harsh berating you've endured. It's inappropriate you had to bear it. Georgiana is spirited, but quarrelsome and headstrong."

"Don't worry over it Moni. I've been through worse."

"Somehow I doubt that," Vanetta interjects.

"Bin, what happened to our life together? I've *seen* it, in the Realm of Light, our life together, what could have been."

"You did what you had to. Your vow to the saint."

"Binford, the vow, while in the coma…after Harlan struck me down…I walked *the bush of ghosts*. I was afraid Bin, that dreadful place I was forced into because of the trauma, Harlan striking me. *Her Majesty Most High*, she came and took me from that horrid world, but she asked nothing of me. I chose *that* path, my longing for Her. But you and I Binford, we could have been together, not apart as it were, I've *seen* it."

"You've touched lives. Children bound for earthly hells, all given hope, a new start," he says and a tear courses her cheek. She smiles, gently caresses his face.

"I love you Binford Grayson. I *reckon* I always will." Her smile is like the sun and they gently kiss.

Suddenly, her eyes widen with a look of shock and she slaps Binford sharply across the face so hard it leaves welts above his beard-line.

"What the hell are you people doing?!" she shouts. We clearly see that Georgiana has *returned*. She actually spits on the carpet. "Morgan, how could you?" Morgan is wide-mouthed, incredulous.

"What?"

"You hypnotize me and make me kiss a man? That's what you sick bastards do for kicks?!" she screams and all of us begin to chuckle, then laugh. "Screw you people!" she rails giving us all *the finger* and storms off upstairs, slamming the bedroom door and Montara points.

"Mama," the child says lovingly, and the laughter renews, Morgan taking the child in her arms and tickling her, the girl's laughter instantly dispelling the tension in the air. Binford is the only one not laughing. He carefully moves his jaw back and forth, Lucien taking him by the elbow.

"Binford, are you all right?"

"Damn, I think that woman broke my jaw."

That night I'm awakened from sleep by a buzzing in my ear. When I focus my eyes, I'm startled to discover Montara staring at me from the darkness. "Montara? What is it?" I ask, more than surprised by this unexpected nocturnal visit.

"Willem...no moon," she mutters hugging her beaten honey-colored teddy bear.

"Moon?" I ask and she nods. "What about the moon?" I ask and she seems confused.

"Willem...no moon, come." I sit on the edge of the cot. She then takes me by the hand and leads me out into the darkened silence of the great house.

A thin veil of moonlight cuts through the windows casting the old manor in an ephemeral silver glow. The old house seems to watch as we pass quietly through the vacant hallway to her room. She takes me into the darkness and points at the floor beside her bed. "Willem…moon," she says again.

"I'm sorry Montara, I don't understand. Maybe we should go get Morgan, okay?" I ask but she shakes her head and–amazingly-gets down on her tummy and points at something under the desk.

"Willem…come," she beckons. At a loss, I do as she instructs, getting down on my stomach, gazing into the darkness beneath the desk to where she points. "Moon…" she whispers. I then realize she's pointing at a tiny nightlight plugged into the outlet. The bulb has evidently burned out. When I begin to wrestle with it, it ignites, apparently a bad connection between the apparatus and the antiquated wall outlet.

The two of us just lie there staring into its soft amber light. Her large dark eyes reflect the glow of the lamp and she giggles, hugging her bear. "Moon," she says again, pointing.

"No Montara, not *moon*, nightlight," I say but she shakes her head.

"No Willem…moon," she says pointing at it. Seeing the confusion on my face she takes me by the hand and leads me to the large bank of bay windows overlooking the garden. She points up at the bright silver orb that illuminates the midnight sky. "Moon," she states firmly. I sit with her on the divan and smile.

"Right Montara, *moon*," I laugh softly, never having made this innocent connection before.

We sit together staring at it for several minutes the moonlight coating the landscape in a dream-like ethereal glow. She suddenly excites and opens the window and takes my hand. "Willem…fly…" she says pointing into the vast night sky.

"Fly?" I ask and the girl actually mounts the sill. "Come Willem…fly." I quickly take her down.

"No Montara. That's dangerous." Her face clouds with confusion under the gentle embrace of moonlight. She points into the sky.

"Fly Willem…there…" I take her thin shoulders and shake my head.

"No Montara. Willem no fly…I'm sorry." She looks at the moon then me, a strangely sad look. "Bedtime Montara, okay?" I put her back in bed, tucking the blankets snuggly about her.

"Willem…" she whispers from behind her bear.

"Yes Montara?" She pulls my neck down and whispers into my ear.

"Montara…love," she says. I kiss the top of her head.

"Willem love too," I say. She curls into the blankets. I close the door and return to my cot.

There's a small window above the sink perpetually covered with an old cloth curtain. I pull back the fabric and the moon enters the room coating it entirely in silver. When I lay my head upon my pillow, *it* is there, framed in the tiny window smiling down at me.

The following morning, we say good-bye to the Scottish twins. Morgan and I see them off at the airport. They discuss Montara's future over coffee and as we hug them one last time at the gate, Vivien whispers in my ear.

"Don't forget what I told you in the garden handsome," she says pinching me on the derriere.

"I won't aunt Vivien," I say trying not to rub the spot despite the pain. She winks before turning and we watch as these two incredible women are swallowed within the maelstrom of passengers and airline personnel.

Deep into the evening, being restless and unable to sleep, I take the winding back-stairs down to the kitchen and steal outside into the heavy humid night of the great southern swampland, the scent of Magnolia hanging thick in the air like perfume. Frogs and night insects create a cacophony of sounds. The moon, pregnant and full, gazes down placidly from her berth within the vast ocean of space.

I'm breathing in the night's rich splendor when a voice nearly rocks me from my shoes. I discover Lucien sitting on one of the stone benches beneath the moon-shadow of the magnolia trees.

"Lucien, you startled me."

"My sincerest apologies."

"What are you doing out here this late?"

"Enjoying the evening. I depart in a few hours."

"You're leaving?"

"I need to do some research back in Boston. Have a seat." I take the space beside him and try to delve what he's looking at so intently. "Trouble sleeping?" he asks withdrawing his meerschaum from a waistcoat pocket and tamping it.

"Yes."

"What is it?" he asks in response to my stare.

"This *is* you right? Or are you in your *Shade* form?" I inquire, actually touching his sleeve. He laughs softly.

"This is very much me in the full," he says. "It would have been inappropriate for me to send my *Shade* to such a serious, and solemn, occasion. What's on your mind Willem? You seem deep in thought this evening."

"I've been wondering. What is the soul Lucien? I mean, what is it exactly?"

"That question has been bantered about for thousands of years. Would you appreciate the long or short form?"

"What is it Lucien? Does it really exist, or is it just a convenient phrase for something unknowable?"

"Now we're getting somewhere." He takes a moment to light his pipe, the smoke forming strange patterns under the moonlight. "*Man*, is a material construct, an aggregation of physical forces yet also distinctly comprised of more diaphanous, spiritual qualities. These *qualities* emanate from a primordial *First Cause*. The body itself is inert material, for lack of more time to explain it, impenetrable were it not for the *spirit,* which suffers no boundaries, here on this plane nor the myriad of dimensional realities that abound this one."

"Then we're, in actuality, spirit not substance?"

"Both. Without spirit the body would be an inert mass. Nor would spirit have substance, as it were, if not for the body, thus the inexplicable union that is *Man*."

"But I mean the soul. Is the spirit and the soul the same?"

"The spirit is an invisible thing Willem. It never appears *without a mask*. That mask, is the soul of which you enquire." He relights his pipe, the wisps of smoke vaguely forming a human shape in the near mystical twilight of the garden. "What brings on this line of questioning? I'm not at odds with it, merely curious."

"Binford, he was speaking recently about what he termed *the triumvirate*, the body, the spirit and the soul."

"Indeed, and no better a practitioner of it." He quietly puffs on his pipe, the coals glowing in the darkness. "What's troubling you Willem?"

"Nothing's troubling me Lucien, exactly, but, Mr. Grayson, well, we've been talking about some pretty intense things."

"Go on."

"Something about him puts me on edge. Yet, I admire and appreciate him, what he's doing for the benefit of the family. It's strange. The other day for instance, he just showed up out of nowhere in a place he would otherwise never be. It can't be coincidence."

"There really is no such thing as *coincidence* per-se. It's a convenient tool of the ego but technically speaking, groundless. You need to develop the analytical ability to look at life subjectively as well as objectively."

"What do you mean?"

"When you look at reality without blinders, or pre-conceived notions regarding *the nature of things*, the concept of *coincidence*, as we use it, begins to dissolve rapidly." I consider this deeply, staring at the moonlight upon the grass, the look, and feeling, timeless. "Can you elaborate on what it is that's concerning you about Binford?"

"No, I don't think so. Sometimes he seems like a pleasant man, then other times..."

"I believe I get the gist of your quandary. The great *First Cause* is the parent source of all, what we term *good* as well as what we think, *evil*. When you fully understand this fact, it becomes necessary to understand exactly why we refrain from judging those things not within our immediate sphere of knowledge."

"*Sphere of knowledge?*"

"The sum total of who you are, what you've become. The *collation of your complete awareness and understanding.*"

"Forgive me Lucien, I'm not sure I understand what you're saying."

"Binford puts you on edge because he's a warrior, in the very truest sense of the word."

"Warrior?"

"I'm not referring to the fact he's half Choctaw Indian, a medicine-man…or to the time he's spent at war, physically engaged in the *hunting and killing of other men.* I'm referring to his specific spiritual nature. Some men do good deeds out of a sense of love for their fellow man, Monique for instance…others do it out of necessity."

"*Necessity?*" I say and he looks at me squarely.

"Yes, the necessity to dig oneself out of the muck and mire of physical bondage." The glint of moonlight in the pupils of his eyes freezes any further questions I may have harbored about Mr. Grayson. As I sit pondering, I sense his scrutinizing me closely. "There's more on your mind than Binford Grayson my friend."

"I don't understand what's happening with Georgiana, what's happening with Monique, it's too fantastic."

"Willem, when a man is born with psychic powers it's usually the result of his efforts in his previous incarnations. I believe you're coming to this realization?"

"About what?"

"That you possess psychic ability. You do fully realize?" Long pause. "Well, an aspect of yourself does. You need to put more effort into accessing this part of your being. This is, in reality, *who you actually are.*"

"I'm sorry Lucien, I know I'm a great disappointment to you…and to Morgan and the family."

"Again Willem, don't allow your mind to speculate ideas regarding the thoughts of other people. This is a flaw in human nature, quite frankly a mistake, a trap in fact."

"But, is it her? Is it truly Monique coming through? It's too fantastic."

"Don't use your temporal, rational mind, use your inner mind, your intuition and answer your own question for me." His gaze is relentless.

"The change in Georgiana is beyond doubt. It *is* her Lucien, it's Monique…but then, why do I feel so sad about it? I feel a deep…sadness, not joy at all."

His eyes seem as if to glow, the cornea's reflecting the moonlight. "You're connected with Monique Montaigne in ways that would defy your current understanding, but I will say this…disembodied human spirits, of a pure nature which Monique most certainly is, under remarkable circumstances, some incredible occurrence, something vastly important, can manifest their presence by various means."

"You mean ghosts?"

"I will say this Willem…it must be a profound attraction to draw a pure disembodied spirit from its radiant home into what the great poet called *the Twilight Kingdom*, this dense heavier world from which it has escaped upon leaving its earthly body."

"But Lucien, I was taught that possession, soul possession…was an evil thing."

"Willem, here's a bit a knowledge for you. Who distinguishes good from evil?"

"God?"

"The great First Cause is the parent source of good and evil alike. All these things you see and feel. It is boundless and eternal yet infinitely small, *forever hidden from the narrow senses of man*."

"What is it?"

"It is the vastness of the cosmos, so too, empty and non-existent. Even in the smallest point it is endless since great and small are both contained within it."

"How can it be everything and yet nothing?"

"It is all these things, everything within and without, yet too, nothingness. It is this nothingness that permeates all things, everything."

"Then, what is the answer to your question? Who distinguishes good from evil?"

"*You*."

"Me?"

"*Man. Man* distinguishes them from his own nature. If the First Cause is infinite and eternal, then it must contain the qualities of nothingness. Within nothingness, *thinking* and *being,* as we understand these terms, cease because these qualities are distinctions and infinity and nothingness bare no distinctions. There are no structures or walls, no *fabrications* known that can hold or withhold spirit. It is boundless but, in essence, *substance less*."

"But there *is* evil, Mr. Else for instance."

"You're referring to the individual personality, the practitioner of black magic, the black sorcerer, who summons back the dead by use of the incantations of necromancy. He surrounds himself with entities, *persons* that have lived selfish, fruitless lives and thusly suffer the *cause and effect* of their ways and actions. This...*evil* behavior, originates from *Man* himself."

"Who are they, these persons of which you speak?"

"Denizens of the iniquitous lower plane, whose hatred and contempt for their fellow man have cast them into utter ruin. They aid the black magician—or are coerced in adding him-in these negative, morbid pursuits."

He smokes quietly while I try to take in this amazing concept. "Do you understand the difference here…regarding Monique?"

"Yes. I think so."

"Monique Montaigne is a divine, had become so at the termination of that lifetime. She had mastered her nature, given of her time selflessly; alleviated misery and human suffering to the fullest extent of her abilities."

"I know. She was a truly incredible person."

"Did you know she died penniless? She had given everything of her inheritance and earthly possessions to the less fortunate."

"Emory mentioned it…several times."

"Even more importantly Willem, she gave of herself, the light of her spirit, and unfortunately, as so many who attain enlightenment on this particular planet, her life."

"Lucien, why am I here? Why did you hire me?"

"Certainly not your ability to manage things."

"So you've said…on occasion."

"The real reason Willem? The stars."

"*The stars*?" He points the stem of his pipe toward the firmament above us.

"The network of light that stretches from star to star, from star to planet, planet to man…and through the mechanism of man's spiritual nature, back again, hopefully."

Late into the night, well after seeing Lucien to the airport, I'm awakened by a commotion in the hallway outside my room. Upon investigation I'm surprised to discover the children are being gathered under the guise of a hurricane drill.

The sleepy-eyed girls all voice their discontent as Magda and Morgan drape their shoulders with blankets and commence to escort them downstairs, directing them to the hurricane-bunker in the rear of the property.

"Is a storm coming?" I hear Rosemary ask Sadie.

"No stupid, it's a drill," the older girl says.

"I'm not stupid, you're stupid."

"You're stupider than stupid, you're an ignoramus."

"Girls, hush," Morgan says and sends them downstairs with Magda and the kerosene lantern.

"What's going on?" I ask from the darkness and she takes my hand.

"Come Will and be very quiet."

We tiptoe past Georgiana's room, down the grand stairway and enter the study where I'm shocked to find nearly every adult in the house present including Jerome, the Creole cousin.

Amidst the circle is Binford Grayson with an eagle feather tied into his salt and pepper hair and a bowie knife strapped to his leg. "Is she awake?" he asks Morgan.

"No, the children didn't wake her."

"Are they all out of the house?"

"Yes, Magda has them in the storm shelter by now."

"Okay, go get Georgiana," he says and Morgan exits for the upstairs.

"What's going on?" I whisper to Binford, his eyes dilated.

"I'm a'gonna cut the devil outta that girl once and for all. That damn thing won't never leave her be, so I'm taking it out right here and now. Tonight."

"You're going to cut her with that knife?" I ask incredulous, staring at the formidable blade on his hip. He glares at me.

"Are you insinuating I'd hurt that girl? You'd think it of me?"

"No, I wouldn't."

"Then do exactly what I say. When she comes down, you and Jerome hold her by the arms, tightly Willem, don't let her break your grip. She's stronger than you think. I'll have enough on my hands dealing with the demon than her busting my other jawbone."

"*The demon?*"

"The devil that's been in her since she was eighteen. I thought you knew all this?"

"I'm not sure."

"Monique said her *guardian* reached out, the thing's gotta go, it's him or me. If the devil wins this fight, I'll carry it inside me the rest of my borne days, but hell or high-water Willem, the girl will be free of it tonight."

"I don't understand?"

His steel-gray eyes burn into mine. "I ain't no damn priest, I'm a soldier, this here's the only way I know how to do this sort of thing."

"Do what?"

"Hit the devil with all I got, when it ain't ready, put this here knife into it. Kill it." He extends the long silver blade that glints under the kerosene lamplight. It's razor-sharp and carries strange meandering inscriptions forged into the metal.

"Kill…the demon?"

"*Pure-Silver* is this knife's name in Choctaw, it's a demon killer. It belonged to my pap and his pap a'fore him and its a'gonna kill this devil that's haunted this woman since she was a girl."

Our conversation comes to an abrupt halt when we hear Morgan and Georgiana approaching. "Quiet now, take the other side of Jerome." I'm at complete odds as to whether I'm about to take part in an exorcism or a murder.

When they enter, Georgiana looks half-asleep. Morgan maneuvers her to the center of the room between the men. Around the periphery sit the women, the blind and rotund aunt Pearl and thin frail Angeline. To the north sits Emerald, strangely silent and when Morgan joins them, they loosely form a circle about us. When Georgiana realizes she's *surrounded*, the sleepy expression on her face changes.

"What the hell's going on?" she asks as Binford removes his shirt, his arms wiry and strong, salt and pepper hair upon his chest. In the light cast by the kerosene lamps, I can see several large scars on his chest and back.

He pulls an object seemingly out of thin air and holds it before her. I can see plainly that it's a small ornate hand mirror composed of the same luminescent metal as the knife. It seems to give off a thin diaphanous mist or glow.

"Georgiana, do you know what this is?" he asks showing her the finely crafted object.

"A mirror?" she says scathingly.

"Not just *a mirror*, this is a *magic mirror*. Passed down my family, half a dozen generations."

"No shit, a magic mirror huh? What's magic about it? Wait, don't tell me, it talks."

"This mirror shows the face of a person's inner demon, every time, without fail," he says and her eyes narrow.

"No kidding?"

"Are you prepared to see what's been living inside you all these years, eating away at your insides?"

"Are you nuts? Morgue, is this some kind of a joke?" Morgan, in fact all the women, remain motionless engaged in an eerie silent concentration. "I don't think this is funny."

"We're not being funny. You need to open your eyes and see yourself. You got the guts to do it?" The tension, like lightning, ignites the air between them.

"Okay big-shot, show me your *magic mirror*," she says and without the slightest hesitation he raises the glass before her. From over her shoulder I see, within the reflection of the glass, a most hideous face gazing back! She gasps and instantly slaps the mirror from his hand shattering it upon the floor. "Quit playing games with me. I don't dig your sense of humor," she seethes through clenched teeth.

Grayson takes a small hemp rope, looped around the back of his belt, and begins winding the length around his left hand like a boxer taping-off his fist before a fight. He then withdraws the blade from its sheath, clenching it firmly between his teeth.

When Georgiana sees the knife, she tries to bolt but Jerome grabs her. "Allez, allez Bonaparte," he shouts to me, my body reacting, and we have her firmly in our grasp.

"Morgan, what are you doing?!" Georgiana screams but the women remain completely silent.

When Grayson squares before her, she kicks him in the gut. Jerome holds her leg down with his, shouting for me to do the same. She struggles fiercely, like a cat gone mad and it's as if a wind erupts in the room, things bounding from their place on the table and shelves. Binford leans into her and like a surgeon commencing to operate, I actually witness his right hand penetrate Georgiana's chest as if it had lost its material properties. Georgiana watches this, screaming wildly.

Then a most incredible thing happens. We watch in horror as Grayson slowly *extracts*, with his bare hands, a most hideous and foul thing, materializing as he pulls it from her body. It's a dull ruddy-brown color, like old blood, and writhes voraciously, wrapping itself about his arms and torso causing him to fall backwards, caught in what looks to be a death struggle, the man and this unworldly beast. When I go to assist him, Morgan screams. "Willem don't touch it! It'll entwine you!"

All we can do is watch as Binford struggles to gain the advantage. They roll over and over several times smashing one of the chairs and toppling the reading lamp.

"My God, someone help him!" I shout and feel Jerome grip my arm like a vice.

"Parlay Bonaparte," he shouts, his eyes reflecting the horror of the situation.

Binford finally manages to get atop the devil, freeing his left hand when the thing slashes his cheek. Blood gushes from three large incisions coursing his beard, running the length of his neck and chest.

He returns his grip upon it and forces both of its appendages into his right hand, freeing the left again. He then ties the creature's *wrists* with the rope wrapped around his left hand like a bronco-buster roping a calf, the caustic thing hissing and spitting at him all the while.

When he's gotten the thing's *arms* tied, it tries to toss him aside with an enormous heave of its viscous body but he digs his boot heels into the legs of the sturdy oak desk and leverages his weight fully atop the creature.

"Good lord," someone says.

Slowly, deliberately, he takes the knife from between his teeth with his free hand and drives it into its hideous body and a horrendous unearthly wail portends the termination of this vile creature from the face of the earth as it disintegrates into thin air.

I'm first to help him to stand. He has suffered lacerations on both arms and the gashes across his face are bleeding profusely, blood dripping from his beard

The women hurry to stop the bleeding. He stands before Georgiana breathing heavily, his chest heaving. I see the disappointment in his face when she turns and rushes out of the room.

"Shall I go to her?" Morgan questions Emerald.

"Leave her be! Attend to Binford."

They clean the wounds and bathe the cuts with the same lemony salve Magda used upon the bite I had suffered from the Coyoteman; the salve–amazingly-arresting the bleeding.

We exchange a deep intense look. He says nothing, Lucien's words from the garden repeating over and over again within my mind. When he's fully bandaged, Emerald takes Binford in a long deep embrace. When they part I see the tears in her eyes.

"God bless you Binford Grayson, how can we ever repay this noble sacrifice?" she says as he wipes the sweat from his brow and returns his shirt over the newly placed bandages. He takes up his Stetson from the floor and tipping it to the women, without a word, disappears into the night.

After he's gone, Angeline carefully picks up every shard of the shattered mirror, piece by piece, placing them into a black silk cloth and takes it from the room.

Chapter *12*: *In the still of the night*

A number of days later I wander into the back garden and look up into a timeless indigo sky. The waning moon is brilliant, its light coating everything in blue. I spy a dark shape sitting at the very end of the fruit trees. Upon inspection I find Majo and Georgiana, staring into the night.

"Hello," I say taking the bench next to hers. I breathe in the night's rich atmosphere. "How are you feeling?" I ask pensively, having become sensitive to her reactive nature.

"My teeth hurt. I was at the dentist again. That frickin' old guy gets a lift outta digging into my gums. I know he's doing it on purpose."

"Why not take the painkillers from your root-canal?"

"I did. Grayson won't let me refill it."

"Why?" I ask and she seems reluctant to answer.

"I took the whole week's prescription in two days. He won't let me refill it, Morgan either."

"Oh."

"Screw it, I'm getting used to the pain."

"You seem rather quiet today, what's on your mind?"

She stares at me blankly. "Nothing."

"Nothing on your mind?"

"Right. Know what Willem? I realize I'm the kind of person who always has something rattling around in her brain. Last couple days, I've kinda…I don't know…been thinking without working at it too hard."

"Have you been playing music again? Thought I heard you playing in the parlor yesterday."

"Oh, that. I was showing Freckles some bass patterns on Monique's guitar."

"Rosemary?"

"Freckles, I call her that to rile her up, she hates it. It's so easy to get under that kid's skin, it's hilarious," she says cracking a grin. "I like her, she reminds me of someone I used to know."

"Oh yeah? Who?"

She gives me a strange look. "Me," she says quietly, becoming serious. "Which is worse Willem? Your father beating on you…or your mom?"

"Either," I say, and she actually seems to mull this over. "Are you going back to New York?"

"I was planning to. I mean like, I was going to…but…think I'm going to hang around awhile. Morgan and Binford are pushing me to stay…and Montara," she says wistfully before exhaling loudly. "Besides, I can't go back to my place in Manhattan, *someone else lives there.*"

"What about your music? Won't you miss playing?"

"Didn't you hear? I'm gigging with Cristobal and Jerome's band starting this weekend. They've never had someone on bass, go figure. We loosened up a little and it was good. I like Creole music, and folk. It's got pathos yet…optimism. Maybe the word is *honesty*. We're gigging at some event in New Orleans on Saturday."

"That's great." We become silent under the moonlight, her blue iris reflecting the light of the moon.

"Willem…do I seem different, to you?"

"Different?"

"Yeah…" she shrugs, "…different."

"How? In what way?" I ask. She considers this question a moment before standing.

"Never mind," she says softly and returns to the house, Majo shadowing her steps.

That night I'm awakened by soft music playing through the vent from the lower study. I listen and realize I'm hearing the song, *In the Still of the Night* by the Five Satins, playing over and over again.

Thinking someone has left a CD on repeat I don my robe and carefully make my way through the silent empty house. I enter the study and startle Georgiana sitting in the dark playing a 45rpm record on the old Sears turntable next to Emory's desk. "Willem, what the hell!" she exhorts pulling the needle across the disc and instantly turning off the machine. "Why are you sneaking up on me in the dark?"

"I thought I heard music," I say uncertain how to respond to this odd situation. She straightens her robe and seems at odds with what to say.

"I…I couldn't sleep. I was just checking out some of the old man's collection," she mutters before slamming the top down on the turntable. "Christ, can't a person have some peace and quiet around here?" She pushes past me. I can hear her return to her room upstairs.

The following morning I'm having breakfast with Morgan and the children. The discussion is about music and the girl's collective disdain for the on-going French lessons when I question Morgan to one side.

"Morgan, speaking of music, do you know the song, *In the Still of the Night*?"

"An old fifties tune?" she asks looking at me strangely. "Of course, it's on the top twenty in this house."

"Oh?"

"It was one of aunt Monique's favorites…think it had something to do with mister Grayson, I'm not sure."

"That's interesting."

"Anyway, she adored that particular song, the Flamingos, the Starlighters, the Moonglows…aunt Monique grew up during those times, that kind of music." Suddenly a row interrupts our conversation and Sadie slams her silverware upon the table and storms out of the room.

"Rosemary, what is it now?" Morgan asks the freckle-faced youth.

"I'm sick of being a second-class citizen in this place."

"Rosemary, how on earth are you a *second-class citizen*?"

"Sadie."

"What?"

"Magda gives Sadie all the privileges and dumps all the chores on me and Sissy."

"Rosemary, that's completely untrue."

"Miss Morgan, you don't know what it's like, what goes on around here behind your back when you ain't looking," the eleven-year-old confides.

"Rosemary," I interject, "would things be better if I take you on another photo journey?" and the girl beams.

"Gosh Mr. Willem, that'd be great."

"Okay, if you do the morning's dishes I'll take you and Sissy and we'll not tell Sadie." Her reaction to this is hardly effusive.

"I'm sick of doing the dishes. Miss Montaigne said I din't hafta do 'em no more."

"*Any longer*," Morgan corrects her. "Rosemary, Sadie is twenty-one years old, you're only eleven. Doesn't age account for something?"

"It accounts for her being a big fat cheatin' crummy squelcher," she says. Morgan touches her temple and looks at me, her lustrous green eyes becoming moist.

"How did aunt Monique manage?" I see the tears forming in her eyes and embrace her.

"Rosemary, no!" Montara scolds the girl. "Morgan, no cry!" and breakfast takes on a somber tone.

Two days later, Rosemary Enright's tenure at Villa Magenta comes to an end when Mrs. Richardson informs us her aunt has decided to adopt the child.

We line up in the front hall of the house as Rosemary descends the curving stairs with a pink suitcase in her hand and–amazingly-wearing a polka-dot dress.

"Why Rosemary Enright, if you're not the image of a true southern belle," Mrs. Richardson says and Rosemary gives me a dubious look, wrinkling her freckles. "Thank Miss MacIntyre for all she's done for you and we'll be on our way." The girl gazes up at Morgan, a questionable expression on her face.

"Are you ready?" Morgan asks.

"Yeah, guess so."

"We'll miss you."

"Yep." They embrace. I see moisture rimming Morgan's eyes.

"Please write me, you will write me, won't you?"

"Yeah." She rubs her nose. "Thanks Miss Morgan for what you done for me."

"*Did*…yes, it was my privilege Rosemary," and Morgan is incapable of containing her tears.

"Ain't Miss Georgiana gonna say good-bye?"

Morgan flashes me a look. "She's…indisposed dear."

"*In* where?" the child asks. Morgan looks at me.

"I think she's busy with something Rosemary," I say and see the child's confusion.

"I liked Miss Georgiana. I liked the way she teached me music better than Miss Montaigne. Miss Monique was always try'n to teach me chords and stuff that hurt my fingers, but Miss Georgiana showed me how to play music just like whistling." She actually demonstrates by whistling a snippet of *You are my Sunshine*. "Well, tell her I said good-bye."

"We will, take care of yourself. We'll see you again soon, I'm sure of it," Morgan says, and Mrs. Richardson taps the child's shoulder.

"Come now Rosemary, your aunt has travelled all the way from Biloxi." Rosemary gives us a rather long look.

"Thanks Miss Morgan, for taking good care of me, and teaching me stuff...see ya." It's a heartfelt moment.

When the child is at the door there's a sudden commotion from the common above the hallway and we all watch as Georgiana suddenly descends the stairs and kneels before the girl.

"So, you're taking off huh?"

"Yeah...guess so."

"Wow, wearing a dress too huh?"

"Mrs. Richardson made me do it."

"You look nice," she says taking her in her arms. "Take care Freckles, okay?"

"Okay." Georgiana points a boney finger at her.

"And you better not quit playing music or I won't ever talk to you again. Got it?"

"Yep," she says bravely, her eyes filling with water.

She brushes the hair from the child's face. "Try to be nice to your new parents Freckles, okay? You're lucky," and Rosemary's cheeks go wet. "Geez, you're not gonna start bawling are you? C'mon. What did I say about being tough?"

"I'll write you my address, maybe you can come visit, maybe sleep over," Rosemary says wiping her eyes with her sleeve.

"Really? You'd put me up for a night? No kidding?"

"Yeah, you can stay over...we can make popcorn and cocoa and stuff." Georgiana sticks out her hand and they shake.

"It's a deal." She hugs the girl again then abruptly turns the child's shoulders, nudging her toward the waiting parents. "Now scram kid, get lost." Rosemary gives her one last look over her shoulder.

"See ya."

"Yeah, yeah," and like that, Rosemary Enright walks off into the morning sunlight.

Georgiana continues to stare at them through the window until they drive away. It's only when Morgan gazes over her shoulder that she realizes. "Are you crying?"

Georgiana turns away from her. "Not..." Morgan is relentless, trying to see her face.

"You're crying."

"Knock it off Morgue, I don't cry." Morgan forces her shoulders and it's very obvious she has indeed become teary.

"I don't believe it, you're crying over a little girl." Georgiana wipes her eyes smearing her mascara then wraps her arm tightly around Morgan's neck. "Ouch, Georgiana you're pinching me."

"Make me a cup of your coffee, please? I can't get that damn French-press thing down right," and she *drags* Morgan in the direction of the kitchen.

The next evening, Binford Grayson asks Georgiana Snipes for her hand in marriage. No one seems more shocked than Georgiana and she spends the following day stewing over it. That night near midnight I hear Morgan and her enter the study below and their conversation through the vent.

"Just calm down, should I make tea?"

"I don't want any tea, I just…need to talk."

"Okay, what's on your mind?"

"C'mon Morgan, work with me here willya?"

"Georgiana, what's to get all worked up about…just say *yes*."

"Say *yes*? That's your advice to me?"

"Yes."

"Come on man, you know I can't."

"For god's sake why not?"

"Come off it Morgue, you know *why*. Nothing's changed in that department."

"Binford knows that."

"Jesus frickin' kriminy…what kind of man asks a woman like me to marry him?"

"Binford Grayson. He's one of a kind."

"He's freakin' crazy."

"What's crazy about it? He's fallen in love with you, it's obvious to everyone but you."

"He doesn't love *me*."

"How can you say that, after what he's done for you? My god Georgiana, he risked his mortal soul to free you from-"

"I know all that! That's not what I said."

"*What you said?* What are you talking about?"

"Just that…he doesn't love *me*. He's in love with someone else."

"Someone else? Who?"

"Are purposely rubbing my nose in it?"

"What?!"

"He's in love with Monique Montaigne, who do you think!" and the door slams.

The next two days are strained as Georgiana sinks into a funk and there's tension between her and Morgan. It comes to a head at ten o'clock when a knock on the front door brings Binford into the parlor where Emerald, Morgan and I are playing a game of cribbage.

"Binford, what brings you here at such an hour? Morgan get Binford a drink," Emerald says but he holds up his hand.

"Don't bother over it, I didn't feel it proper to up and leave without stopping by to say farewell." The women sink back into their seats, concern emerging on their faces.

"Farewell? Whatever do you mean Bin? Please, sit down with us." He places his Stetson on the end table and stands beside the chair nearest the lamp. He wears, what looks to be, a well-oiled leather weatherproof.

"I can't stay long, it's already a quarter of ten and I was aiming to pick up the midnight runner."

"Binford, you're not alluding to a train?"

"Em, there's no reason to stay on right now. It's been awhile since I rambled. I've got the itch."

"Binford Grayson, you sit down here and relax a moment. Willem please pour Binford a scotch or-" He cuts her short with another gesture of his hand.

"I really need to be getting on, just…wanted to say, so-long for now."

"Mister Grayson, does this have anything to do with Georgiana?" Morgan asks and it's clear to everyone the answer need not be said.

"You know I can't sit still too long. It ain't in my make up."

"Binford, I stood right here two years ago when you told my father and my sister your rambling around was over for good."

"A man can make a mistake about these things."

"You're a terrible liar Bin, you always were. This is about Georgiana and you know it. Let's discuss it. Willem, pour him a bourbon."

"Willem sit. Emerald, there's a tension over this whole thing. Hell, it's there the minute I walk in the room…I shouldn't of ever asked her. It was stupid."

"Why? Why was it *stupid*?"

"She don't love me…an old man."

"Binford, you're a handsome man, brave and honorable. What woman with any sense would reject you? …that damn fool upstairs!"

"No. She's right. I ain't right for her, we're cut from different cloth."

"Mr. Grayson, I've known Georgiana for over twenty years, nearly as long as I've known you. You are both very much alike, especially now that she's healing, coming back to life." He stares at Morgan, wonder etched upon his face, his gray eyes searching hers. "She's just confused. Can't you give her a little more time?"

"She said *no* Morgan. I respect a woman who knows her mind."

"She always says *no* when she means *maybe*. It's a defense mechanism. What she's actually saying is, '*Can I think about it?*'"

"I appreciate what you're trying to do Morgan but truth be known, I'm stirring up old dust. She's on the mend...now here I go putting this sort of pressure on her and the family. It's not right. It's best I'm on down the road someplace so you all can get settled."

"Binford, please," Emerald says, a most concerned expression forming on her face. "Don't leave us, you are a treasured friend."

"Likewise Emerald, those words are as sweet as honey." He retrieves his hat, Morgan and I rising from our seats.

"Mr. Grayson, I mean what I'm saying."

"I know'd that Morgan, you cain't lie about a thing like that...you've a pure soul." He extends his hand to me and his shake is solid and firm. "Keep an eye on things," he says quietly.

"Binford," Emerald says embracing him. "Don't do this. Don't go a'wandering again...the last time almost killed you. You are family to us, you belong here, with your friends, not out there amongst strangers." He tips his hat to Morgan and like that, Binford Grayson walks out of our lives.

Emerald seems to collapse inwardly, covering her eyes with her hand and doesn't move an inch for the better part of an hour. Morgan and I just sit, watching the flame of the kerosene lamp flutter as if swaying to some silent rhythm.

The next morning at breakfast, Sadie is talking to Georgiana about another upcoming event in New Orleans.

"You're not going to play with uncle Cristobal anymore?"

"Wrong again. I'm still playing with them, but this is a chance to perform some of the new music I've been writing, with professional musicians, established players."

"What's the name of your new band?" the sandy-headed girl asks. Georgiana looks at Morgan and I.

"Well, it kinda came up suddenly…and you gotta get the word out, right? So…"

"So, what is it then?"

"*So*, I'm calling us the Georgiana Snipes band."

"Cool," Sadie says nodding. "I like it."

"You do?"

"Yeah. It sort of has appeal."

"Whaddya mean?"

"It's different."

"How?"

"Well…no one else has a name like that…so, it's kinda new…but old."

"Old? How's it *old*?"

"*Georgiana Snipes* sounds like an old black lady's name," Sadie says and Magda points at her.

"Watch it." Morgan and I exchange a smile.

"No Magda," Montara interjects, "Sadie…love," she says to the elder.

"Sadie Montara love," the honey-haired girl says gesturing back from her heart. Montara kicks at the leg of the table.

"Montara, no kicking," Magda barks and everyone returns to eating.

"Sadie, what do you mean my name sounds *old*?"

"You don't think it sounds old?"

"I never thought about it. I always wanted to change my name."

"Why?"

"Never mind. So, you want to come?"

"Yeah, that'd be cool. I've never been to a nightclub."

"I'll put you on the guest list, you can hang with us backstage. Bring a pal along if you want."

"Backstage? Really? Can I bring Deirdre?"

"Are you joking? Can't ya dig up someone else?"

"What's wrong with Deirdre?"

"Fine, bring Deirdre."

"Awesome, thanks Georgiana. Magda, can I be excused? I've got history lessons."

"*History lessons* is code for daydreaming in her room...go on," and Sadie leaves, depositing her plate and silverware in the sink.

"Old? Is she kidding?" Georgiana asks Morgan, who's busy with the morning paper, her bifocals on the end of her nose. "Speaking of *old*, when did you start wearing glasses?" Morgan ignores her. "Hey Morgue, think I should invite Binford, just for laughs?" Morgan lowers the paper.

"Binford left." Georgiana's expression flips.

"What do you mean?"

"He left...last night."

"*Left?* For where?"

"I don't know," Morgan says picking the paper back up. Georgiana presses the paper to the table.

"Morgan, look at me, left for where?"

"We don't know. He said something about taking the midnight train." She looks at me. "Where Willem?"

"He didn't say where." This causes an amazing reaction as Georgiana first stares blankly into space then abruptly exits the room.

That night, through the vent, I over-hear Morgan and Georgiana talking downstairs in the study.

"I searched all over. His place is locked up and they haven't seen him at *the Albatross*. His horses are being quartered at Cowen's."

"Calm down. I told you, he left."

"But where?"

"How should I know? He drifts sometimes…it's been like that since he came back from Vietnam years ago."

"You let him just walk off and you say nothing?"

"Georgiana…what am I supposed to say? What do you expect from me?"

"I expect you to tell me if he up and splits!"

"Georgiana, I don't get you, not at all. It's like you're blaming *me* for his leaving."

"No, I just want to know where he went."

"Why?"

"*Why?* Are you serious?"

"Quite!"

"My god, what's happening? Morgan, what's going on with me? Why am I…why should I give a rat's ass where he goes?"

"Say it. You're in love with Binford Grayson."

"What's happening to me?"

"What's happened to countless millions of people you dope, you've opened your heart, you've fallen in love."

Late that night I'm awakened by a soft sound, nearly indistinguishable through the vent. I get down on the floor and press my ear to the grate. There's no mistaking it, the music well known to me, *I Only Have Eyes for You,* by the Flamingos, playing over and over again.

The very next evening I'm wandering the confines of the great back yard of the estate. I've grown fond of wandering it under the moonlight with Colonel Montaigne's 1873 Colt revolver strapped to my hip like a gentleman cowboy.

I've also become fond of his collection of fine cigars and my evening sojourn under the great Southern moonlight has become nearly routine, smoking, strolling, thinking; I actually begin to feel I'm reconnecting with the history of the place, something about the nature of the light upon the trees and marble statues. The grass itself possesses a hue that seems to become more fluorescent under the Goddess' radiant orb.

This evening I'm alone, everyone having departed for home. The Scottish twins back to Aberdeen, Emerald has left for San Francisco and Lucien for Boston.

I'm sitting on one of the stone benches along a length of palms when I'm startled by strange sounds issuing from a stand of willow trees near the property-line.

At first, I think it the effects of the wind but soon I begin to realize the movement within the fauna is not of the wind's making and an odd feeling begins to creep into my mind. It's strange, the boughs swaying unabated in the moonlight then abruptly stopping.

I watch this weird display in the thin diaphanous twilight when a series of bizarre sounds emanating from the bush sends a spike of energy up my back. Sometimes it's the hoot of a whippoorwill or mourning dove then a high-pitched whistle nearly like a lark, which I'm certain doesn't sound at night. "Who's there?" I call out and the sounds instantly stop. I feel my heart beating.

At the point I decide to return to the house I'm grabbed forcefully from behind. I feel a cold steel blade lay across my throat; see the glint of it under the moonlight and my life flashes before my eyes.

There can be no other explanation than it's the Hollowman come and my days upon the planet will vanish now in a heartbeat when I'm abruptly released. I spin around and witness Binford Grayson sheathing a buck knife into his belt. "What the hell are you doing?" I shout and he shushes me.

"Quiet down, you want to wake the house?" I have to control my earnest desire to punch him in the mouth, or just pull the pistol and shoot him.

"You scared the living hell out of me."

"Yeah, well that's your own damn fault," he states and I'm beyond furious.

"How's it my goddamn fault? You sneaking up behind me, pulling a knife on me?"

"Exactly Willem. How in hell could you let me, or anyone else for that matter, just walk up behind you and put a blade to your throat? You better work on that son."

"But the bushes," I mutter looking back at the now still trees. "How could you…?" I try to fathom how he could be in both places when he squeezes my shoulder.

"How are things here?"

"Until this moment pretty much routine."

He studies the darkened windows of the house and nods. "Good. That's good."

"What the hell Binford, you always go sneaking around at night?"

"When I have to."

"What are you doing?"

"Cutting through Magenta back to my place. I forgot something."

"You've been gone two days. What did you forget?"

"Never mind what. I saw you sitting here in the dark like a target on a stump. You honestly didn't hear me walk up behind you?"

"Not at all."

"You best work on that boy."

"Yeah, so you told me."

He touches my shoulder. "Well, see you around Willem."

"Hey, wait a minute, where are you going?"

"I already told you."

"Come on inside for a minute." He studies the house like a wallflower on a prom date.

"Naw, I better be moving on, but thanks." He goes to leave.

"Wait, wait dammit, just hold on. Come in and we'll catch up quietly over a drink, then you can-"

"I ain't stepping foot in that house, forget it."

"What, you're afraid?" I say and his eyes fire.

"What'd you say?"

"You heard me, you're afraid…afraid Georgiana's going to see you." These words seem to freeze him to the spot.

"I ain't a'fear'd of no woman."

"Then come inside and say hello."

"I ain't got time for this chitter-chatter," he says and goes to leave again.

"Binford," I call out and he looks back. "How many favors have you asked of me, over the past couple weeks? Couple dozen?"

"I reckon."

"So, I'm asking you to do me one for a change. I want you to come in and have a drink with me…one drink, then you can go wherever is so damn important." He stews silently over the request. "One damn little favor…" Same stoic stare. "You'd just walk away?"

"You're a real sonofabitch, you know that?"

"I've been called worse."

He gestures toward the house. "After you." When I turn, he's got me by the throat again, cutting off my air with his forearm across my windpipe. "Willem, don't ever turn your back on a man with a knife," he says in my ear then releases his vise-like grip.

"Bastard." I rub my throat and gesture. "*After you*."

When we enter the parlor and I pour him a shot of bourbon something catches his ear, the soft faint sounds of music. I follow him to the study when he enters and surprises Georgiana at the turntable playing a 45rpm of *I Only Have Eyes for You*. The moment she sees him she startles, pulling the armature back to the off position, scratching the disc.

"Put that record back on," he says, and her eyes turn to fire.

"Don't tell me what to do!" It's a stare-down.

"Georgiana, put that record back on, right now." At first she's at odds, then slowly she places the needle back on the platter, the soft tones of the song filling the dark void of the room, the singers singing a'capella over the dulcet strokes of the piano. He sits in one of the leather chairs and closes his eyes. She quietly takes his side.

"What are you doing here?"

"I forgot something."

"Yeah? Like what?" she presses, and he glares at her.

"Something."

"*Something…*" she echoes a grin turning just the corners of her mouth. "Like your head for instance?"

"Luckily that's attached," he says. She crosses her arms, the tattoos on her forearms like a Gauguin painting in the dull ochre lamplight.

"I don't believe you. I think you're making it up."

"Oh yeah?" He goes to the desk, picks up a glass paperweight, a Vietnam war-era military insignia suspended within its crystalline center and drops it in her hands. She cocks her head, that bent grin of hers forming on her face.

"No kidding? All the way back for this huh?"

"I lent it to Emory awhile ago…so I want it back. Okay with you?"

She studies it, tosses it a couple turns. "That's a damn nice paperweight."

"Like you, sort of…one of a kind."

"*One of a kind?*" she asks waiting for his gaze.

"I pulled a Colonel out of the bush, bunch of years back. His ride went down fifteen *klicks* behind the Vietcong line. Carried him out with two broken legs. I took a few frags, a few bullets doing it, but we made it."

"So…he gave you this?"

"Not then, twenty years later when I…helped him through a personal problem. Got him back on his legs again…so to say." Silence.

"I can see why you want it back," she says caressing its surface, studying the small black and yellow shield suspended within the crystal.

"I reckon." She places it back into his hand, stroking his fist, then–incredibly-lays her head into his shoulder. Something touches my hand. Morgan has heard the commotion.

We watch the couple as they begin to gently sway together to the music, her eyes *smiling* when she looks into mine. When the disc finishes and the record ejects, the silence in the room is deafening. Binford looks deeply into her eyes.

"Georgiana, I've fallen for you. Don't ask me *how* or *why*, just so happens. I say'd it a'fore and I'm saying it once more…I want you to come away, be with me." Her soft expression hardens.

"And I *say'd* it to you Binford. I can't *love* you like a woman to a man, I can't. I can't ever be with a man that way…I'm being truthful."

"Georgiana, I don't care about any of that. I want to be with you."

"Me? Is it *me,* Mr. Grayson?"

"What do you mean by that?"

"You think you want me…but it isn't *me* you love Binford, you're in love with someone else." I see the pain in her eyes, the pain I saw the very first night on the roof of Morgan's apartment.

"Someone else?" he asks wonderingly.

"Yes."

"Who might that be?" he inquires genuinely and Georgiana scowls.

"Monique you square-head. You're still in love with Monique Montaigne, and that's the woman you see when you think you see me." Her voice cracks and her eyes tear.

"Georgiana, I ain't never asked Monique Montaigne to marry me, never once in all those years. She was an enlightened person, too proper for a man like me."

"You're saying I'm not?"

"You? You talk too much and too loud."

"Because you're quiet and quiet people make me nervous."

"You smoke and drink and cuss like a sailor in front of the children."

"You're backwater, crude *and* rude."

"You're so self-absorbed you can't see past the end of your own nose."

"Okay tough guy, two can play this game. You're the classic example of the all-American hick. You smell like chain-oil and your hands are always dirty. I bet you got no chin under that sagebrush you call a beard."

"You say you hate men, but you dress and talk like one. You're surrounded by intelligent, enlightened people like Morgan who love you, for whatever reasons, yet you blaze away, firing your guns like Custer at Little Bighorn just before he got hisself scalped."

"You're…you're so… errr!"

"Georgiana, Mr. Grayson…now that you've aired out the negatives, perhaps you might like to say a few positives; the things you do like about each other?"

"That's a mighty tall order Morgan."

"Mr. Grayson, please…"

"Well…I like that tattoo, the tiger that laces up over her shoulder and down her back…sort of suits her personality."

"Mr. Grayson…"

"Okay, what the hell, let's roll the dice. I like the way she plays music, that's for real, a person in their element. I like the words…the songs she writes. They affect me in strange ways…ways I used to feel, long time ago. Not always pleasant, but good." Silence. "Uh…I like the way the girls *act* around her, comfortable, happy, despite her tongue…that Montara's taken to calling her *aunt*…that's good…shows character."

Silence.

"Georgiana?"

"You gotta give me something to work with Morgue. I'd rather tell you what I like about a horse's ass."

"Georgiana…"

"Alright, alright…um…I like that he's, for some crazy reason, sorta *rock and roll* somehow, yet he doesn't even listen to it…go figure. Oh, that he owns that baby-blue '59 Harley panhead, exactly just like mine…that's weird, huh Morgue? Except his is in mint condition and purrs while mine looks like shit and hasn't run in two years." Her eyes soften as she looks into his. "I like that he's gentle with women, a gentleman, but men get nervous around him…I like that." Long stare. "Somehow, I know, he'll never hurt me…never break my heart…strike me or throw me out of the house in the middle of the night. I like that he's not afraid of anything…except women."

"I ain't a'feared of no woman."

"Yes, you are…numbskull."

"You're hallucinating again."

"Hey, whose turn is it?! Um…I don't know…he's a hick…but he's a gentleman hick…and I…I…"

"You what?" They stare into each other's eyes.

"I know you…have known you, somehow…for a very long, long, long time." A lone tear cuts her cheek.

"I'm a'gonna say this once more…if it's *yes* then, I figure I'm about the *contentest* man this side of Metairie…if it's *no*, I'll walk out that door and never bother you again. Georgiana, will you take my hand?" No one breathes.

"I don't know, you're kinda *scroungey*…who knows, maybe a little spit, little polish…" She smiles.

"That's a *yes* then?"

"Whaddya think it is?"

"About the worse *yes* I'da ever heard."

"In response to the worst marriage proposal *Ida* ever heard," she says growing fiery.

For some inexplicable reason the turntable clicks to life again and the machine starts the record over. We all stare at it a moment before she lays her head on his shoulder, wrapping her arms around his neck and the couple returns to swaying to the music. I look at Morgan, her eyes glimmering in the darkness. She takes my hand and leads me into the quietude of the great back garden of the estate.

A day later we're cutting green beans for the freezer, laughing and joking together when Georgiana's beaten, nearly forgotten, cell phone suddenly rumbles to life where she's left it on the sideboard. When she answers it, the expression on her face changes and she immediately leaves for the veranda. We watch as she paces back and forth. When she returns, I sense an odd feeling.

"You'll never guess who that was," she says, and Morgan doesn't remove her eyes from the work on the table.

"Victoria."

"How did you know?"

"By the way you left the room."

"You'll never believe where they are."

"New Orleans," she says and Georgiana stares at her.

"Yeah, they're in town. They saw the posters for my band. They're coming to the show tomorrow." Morgan stops cutting and looks at her. "All of them are coming, Bambi, Tiny…Victoria."

"What's happened?" I ask, in the ensuing silence.

"They crashed and burned in LA after I…left. They got rid of Nyle. They're on their way back. They want to…" she stops and is suddenly very far away.

"They want what Georgiana?" Morgan asks. "What do they want?"

"They want to get back together, just as we were…get back on tour again. She was really, really sorry Morgan, about everything that went down. She wants to…" She never finishes her sentence and Morgan quietly leaves for upstairs. After a few minutes, I follow her. When I enter the bedroom, she's lying on her side facing the wall.

"Are you all right?"

"Yes."

"Do you want to talk?"

"There's nothing to talk about Willem."

"You don't think she would actually leave with them, do you?"

"She's completely capable of it." I'm shocked by this admission.

"But that would be a mistake, wouldn't it?"

"The end of her life as we know it."

"Let's talk to her Morgan, let's set this right, right now," I say. When I go to leave, she takes my hand.

"It would be wrong for us to interfere."

"How can you say that? After what everyone's been through? You'd just let her walk off with those people?"

"Yes."

"Morgan, I don't understand you."

She sits up and looks into my eyes. "It's something uncle Lucien taught me about energy and consciousness. Energy is cyclic, like sound waves. Sound travels by one molecule pushing against another, this creates the crest of the wave…but, there's always a reciprocal movement backwards, called *rarefaction*, this creates the trough. This is how wavelengths are created, therefore, propagation."

"What are you getting at?"

"This principle is a universal principle, permeating life, matter and energy...consciousness. When we force our *will* upon others, we create the potential for *rarefaction*. Often, we cause the very thing we wish to avoid. This is the explanation for that phenomenon."

"I don't understand."

She takes both my hands. "Willem, I know Georgiana nearly as well as I know myself, which isn't much really. But I can tell you this, whatever happens tomorrow night, was meant to be, painful or not, and there's really nothing we can, or should, do about it."

"But what if she leaves? What about Binford?"

"This is her test, whether she's finally become a *human being*...or just another *person* walking around out there."

The following morning is filled with a quiet tension. Georgiana leaves early to rehearse, driving separately, while Binford, Sadie and her odd friend Deirdre Steck, wearing horn-rimmed glasses and a knit sweater, ride with us.

When we arrive at the nightclub, Georgiana is at their table, talking and laughing; Victoria, Bambi, Tiny and '*a few friends from Nola.*' A heavy viscous feeling fills my stomach.

At the table, Binford sips bourbon and Sadie and Deirdre talk on and on about Anime and Manga. Georgiana joins us. I'm surprised, for some reason, she's not drinking.

"You two wanna see backstage or what?" The girls become giddy. "C'mon, I'll introduce you to the band." Georgiana leads them through a door behind the stage.

After a few minutes Bambi joins us at our table. I'm not surprised in the least she's already inebriated. She wears a white body suit beneath a white leather jacket.

"So, you hear the good news?" she says slurring her words. "We're getting the band back together. No shit. Freakin' awesome us finding her again. Man, that asshole Nyle, screwed us royally, trying to change who we were." She then goes into a kind of incoherent rambling. "G was right about all that shit, shoulda listened but, you know how it goes, I was in love," she says, and drinks arrive from her table. Morgan gazes at me. I know she's thinking the same thing. I look at Binford. I can't tell if he's fuming or just listening.

"Hey, thanks for keeping an eye on her Morgan, that's pretty cool what you done, about getting her clean. She told us all about it...that's...fucking amazing man...G, clean," she says and–for whatever reason-laughs about it. "You guys must have used whips."

"Nothing quite that extreme," Morgan says gazing at Binford who merely sips his bourbon.

She stares at me. I try not to, but I feel a kind of sorrow for her. "Hey, didn't you tour with us dude?" she asks. I remind her of my brief tenure with them. "Right, right, Dave bailed, I remember that. But then, you jumped too...here, you bailed here in New Orleans." She then looks at Morgan and grins. I see the mischief in her eyes. "Ah, right, look who's here, hanging around New Orleans. I getcha man, right on." She canvasses the crowd slowly filling the bar before she readdresses Morgan. "So, you like it down here, in the swamp? Don't you miss New York Morgan, all the fun?"

"I'm having fun Bambi," she says and Bambi laughs.

"Yeah right. So, when you coming back?"

"I don't know. I need to look after my place in Tribeca. Perhaps we'll come up for a few days before I put it on the market."

"You mean sell your place? In New York?"

"Perhaps."

"What the fuck Morgan, are you going nuts or something?" Morgan studies her silently. "You can't sell your place. When G moves back in with VD, well...we're going to have some ass-kickin' parties babe, just like old times. Right?"

Morgan smiles. "We did have fun."

"Damn straight girl. Besides, who's gonna shoot our publicity photos and shit like that? You, natch." The emcee announces the show is about to start. Bambi whispers near Morgan's ear. "Well, anyway, you always got a place to crash with me gorgeous, anytime day or night." She clicks her tongue and winks. When she goes to leave Morgan takes her by the wrist.

"Us too Barb. Our door is always open." She looks into Morgan's eyes and smiles, gently nodding, before returning to her table and entourage, becoming quite loud.

"What do you make of that?" Morgan queries Binford.

"I'd say that woman is drunk...or insane...or both."

Sadie and Deirdre rejoin us, talking nonstop about their foray into the vaunted backstage realm and meeting the band, in particular the '*handsome young drummer.*'

Soon the band enters. The club's emcee takes up the microphone. "Thanks for coming out tonight everybody, without further adieu, from New Orleans, Louisiana, the Georgiana Snipes band!"

The music is eclectic, filled with poetic imagery and quality musicianship. Georgiana plays bass, solid and full, while Danny, the guitar player, seems to have an extra finger.

Snow, a stunning albino woman with solid white hair and red eyes–nearly the visual opposite of Georgiana-sings the lead vocals, her voice waifish and timeless. Jon, the drummer, is incredibly talented for how young he looks.

They work through a series of tunes, some rock, some bluesy, and nothing in Georgiana's new music reminds me of the wild acid-rock of her *Concrete & Steel* days. This music strikes me as being well-crafted, the music and words creating a world of thought and reflection, unlike the *C&S* tunes which were incredibly loud, simpler and oft-times shocking.

I look over at their table. Was Bambi for real, what she said about reforming their band, Georgiana moving back to NYC? The answer comes at the very end of the show when they are preparing to say goodnight. As the band begins to quietly play behind her–Snow taking up Babe and playing the bass part-Georgiana takes the center microphone, the lights focusing on her alone, the rest of the band falling into shadow.

"Thank you all for being here tonight for our premiere. We deeply appreciate your presence. I wanted to close the night with a song I just wrote. In fact, I wrote this last night, about two…three in the morning, for some special folks in the audience. It's called *The Sucker Punch Lover*. Hope you like it."

Morgan takes my hand as they start this soft melodic song, somewhat bluesy yet nearly a love song about a time in her life when she was down; a song about taking someone, a lover, into her home, her life, eventually into her heart.

The second verse is similar, the growth of the relationship despite constant betrayal and hurt. As the song progresses getting incrementally louder, I realize she's singing not to her friends, but to herself.

At the end of the song she asks, *the lover,* for release from three simple words, *'I love you,'* because these words are lies and the hurting these words create, unbearable.

The song ends, as it began, quietly returning unto itself and the feeling this tune leaves in me is memorable. Then, like the passing of a soft rain, the concert is over. When the band leaves the stage, her friends exit the bar en-mass. Apparently, there are no further words necessary to be said and a quiet joy emerges within me. I look into Morgan's eyes, see it there plainly, feel it in my chest, in the way Sadie and Deirdre go on about their exciting evening; the subtle look in Binford's eyes as he waits for her.

When Georgiana joins us, she glances at the now empty table where her friends are no longer waiting for her. She smiles at Morgan, that same odd bent grin.

"Guess they couldn't hang around."

"I guess not."

Georgiana turns toward Sadie. "Well, whaddya think kid?"

"Totally awesome, you guys are great," she says and Georgiana stares at Deirdre who squints back at her through her rhinestone studded glasses.

"Well?"

She shrugs. "Not *too* bad," she says in an annoying way and Georgiana laughs, a laugh I've not heard from her since the very first time we met.

Snow and Danny stop by to say goodbye and Georgiana introduces us. Snow is a remarkable woman, striking and elegant. I compliment Danny on the quality of his guitar-work, some of the best I've ever heard and when we return to the conversation Snow has become quite animated.

"So, *you're* the photographer from New York? You live here now?" and Morgan confirms this. "Cool to meet you in person. I love your work. It was *so beyond* what they were doing back then, last year. Talk about breaking the mold. You're an artist man, not a *fashion photographer*. I mean it, I've been reading Vogue, Cosmo, all that *vamp* for years. My mom's crazy over it. She's got subscriptions to all the magazines, piled in stacks in my old room."

"Did she work in the industry, modeling I mean?"

"She got me into it as a kid, that whole scene. I think she was trying to relive her youth precariously through mine...the auditions, the photo shoots."

"Mommy dearest," Danny interjects.

"I love my crazy mom-bomb, she's crazy but I love her. Of course, being the *freak of nature* that I am, it was all very traumatic. They used to call me *El Blanco*," Snow quips looking at Morgan. "Wow, cool, you're living here now. Big *like* on that. Hey, I actually still model from time to time."

"I didn't know that," Georgiana says.

"Keeps me in shape," she says stroking her lithe figure. "Hey, how about it, want to make some art sometime?" she inquires, striking an exaggerated pose, and Morgan smiles.

"Sure. I'd love to."

Eventually the conversation shifts to their next gig in a week. Everyone shakes hands before they leave, the barkeep taking up the empties. "Last call, drink up," he says and Georgiana takes Binford's glass and finishes it.

"Good lord, how can you drink that stuff?" she says.

"Why? What do you drink?" Sadie queries and Georgiana ruffles the girl's hair.

"What's it to ya? Punk kid." She then looks at Binford. "Well, are you going to just sit there all night or drive me home?"

Binford calls for the check and pays for everyone's food and drinks, refusing to take the money we offer him. As they begin to leave, Georgiana returns and embraces Morgan, looking deeply into her eyes; they catch the light, the blue iris shining. "Thanks," is all she says then takes Binford's hand and they exit into the night.

I drive us home, Morgan silently holding my hand while Sadie and Deirdre carry on and on about Anime, Manga and the *handsome young drummer*.

The following morning, Georgiana moves out of Magenta and in with Binford Grayson at his farm a quarter mile up the road. A few days later they're married in the backyard of Magenta in a festive ceremony and I realize she gets her wish, a new name; she's now Georgiana Grayson. When Morgan refers to her as *Aunt Gigi*, it sticks like glue and everybody begins using this misnomer. Everyone from the area is there. I finally meet some of Talluleh's family, several *aunts* and a bevy of cousins, all speaking Cajun.

Georgiana tosses the bouquet over her shoulder to the girls dressed in bows and lace and its hardly missed upon anyone how and why Montara ends up with it, the child exhibiting '*a remarkable ability to get off the ground*' as the old reverend Piper puts it.

Binford, looking dapper in his tuxedo, and Colonel Montaigne, the best man, just turning ninety-five that morning share a toast, Binford congratulating his friend on *another year*.

"I insist upon a half day's grace before I'm ready to be another year older," he states formally, slipping bourbon into his sweet tea.

The two cousins, Cristobal and Jerome, play the accordion and fiddle, respectively, singing Cajun ditties accompanied by the two older black men, Robert Anthony on the guitar and his sleepy-eyed brother Carter scratching on the washboard and snare drum.

The men sing and play all afternoon with barely a break, their voices ringing out into the clear afternoon sunlight, the children going round and round together hand in hand while the billowy white clouds seem to loiter, as if listening from above.

I converse with Morgan's aunts, the blind Pearl and silent Angeline who seems to say more with her eyes than most people with their tongues and the entire day is filled with music, joy and laughter right into the night, several of the children falling asleep where they lay.

It's with a profound sense of amusement I watch as a sleeping Rosemary Enright, the flower girl, in a soiled blue gown, is lifted from the large wooden swing by her stepfather. The parents say good-bye to Morgan and Georgiana–before they leave for Biloxi. Rosemary just dozes away, despite Georgiana kissing her heartily on the forehead.

"*Geez*," Georgiana says to Morgan.

"Yeah, *cripes,*" she responds, and they laugh together.

Chapter *13*: *The End*

A week later, Lucien arrives in the middle of a stormy night. He shakes the rain from his weatherproof dispensing his cap on the rack. Morgan makes him comfortable before turning in. I sit with him for several hours, watching the rain. When we awaken in the morning, he is already having coffee and reading a book, entirely in Latin. I wonder if he's even slept.

Montara converses with him for nearly an hour and shows him her cache of treasures, bits of tin and broken jewelry, glass beads and silver coins; *treasures* she keeps hidden under her pillow. I notice the blood diamond is no longer amongst the baubles and question Morgan about it.

"The ring is in a quiet place," she informs me, "*where it won't cause any mischief*," she adds oddly. "That jewel is literally priceless, a red-tinted diamond, exceedingly rare. It's been in the family for over three hundred years but the stone's history dates back to the eleventh century. You could write a book about it Willem," she says, her eyes dilating.

"*Mischief?*"

"Its history is tainted. *We shan't be wearing it anytime soon.*" The look in her gaze piques my curiosity. However, she's oddly reticent about answering my questions regarding it, or as to why Acosta ended up with it in her possession. "Honestly, I'm amazed Acosta returned it. It shows a great deal of accomplishment, her doing so."

"Who is she Morgan…Acosta Fontaine?"

"That question deserves volumes Willem. It would take me a week to answer it. A conversation for another time." She senses my disappointment. "What's the matter?"

"I'm just curious about her. She's so, different."

"I'll say. To answer your question, she's my second cousin on my mother's side. Well, and my aunt, in a weird sort of way, its rather complicated."

After lunch, Lucien reveals the reason for his sudden unannounced visit. "Mr. Else is on his way here as we speak. Emory will go to Pearl's home. Morgan, take Magda and the children to Binford's. Spend the night with them there, you too Willem."

"No Lucien. I'll stay here with you." I see the smile beneath his beard.

"Willem, I appreciate that more than you know, but it's too dangerous. I've asked Mr. Else to cease and desist in his...*enterprises*. If he fails to heed my advice, and I'm dubious that he will...I intend to do it for him."

"What does that mean uncle?" Morgan asks, a deep concern forming within her eyes.

"That you'll no longer need to fear this...*person*. You, Montara, this stately home and those sheltered beneath its eves, by tomorrow morning, will be free of him, forever." Incredibly, I watch as Morgan quietly goes to tears, a slow penetrating sorrow, and I'm shocked into silence.

That evening, as we're beginning to leave for the Grayson home, just as we're walking out the entrée principal, I stop, drop my bag and look into her eyes.

"Willem?"

"I can't Morgan. I can't go with you."

"Willem..." she whispers, and her eyes instantly tear.

"Someone has to second him, am I right?"

"Sadie, take Montara and your bags to the car," she says, and the girls disappear into the mist. We stare into each other's eyes. I feel her delving my thoughts.

"I can't just leave him to face that devil alone, it would be unconscionable." She embraces me tightly as if she would never let me go. "Don't worry, everything will be all right," I say and pray she doesn't fathom my true feelings. As if in response to this fear she gazes deeply into me, her eyes suddenly radiating a glow I've seen before, sunlight on sea-green waves.

"Willem, you who hold my heart…I'll wait for you. *If it takes forever Willem, I'll wait.*" I kiss her, deeply, then let go, watch as the twilight envelops her, then the car, then only the lights are there, fading down the old two-track, through the iron gates and into the night.

At a quarter past midnight a knocking–more of a rapping with a stick-echoes through the quiet old manor. I answer the door. He's there, the same loathsome man I remember from my flat in London. He's dressed in a fine silk suit and–despite the late hour-wears dark wrap-around sunglasses disguising his *eyes*. He stands mute a moment, staring at me.

"Well, well, well…Mr. Furey…how enchanting. And *here* no less, this worm-eaten relic." I hold wide the door and he casually enters, as if taking a leisurely stroll. The man actually extends me his hat and cane as if I were the butler.

He enters directly into the sitting room where Lucien calmly awaits his arrival, still engrossed in the book he had started that morning.

"Come in Else, can we get you something to drink?" he says gesturing to a chair but Else meanders, taking in the surrounds.

"Lucien Karras, yet again. Yes, but not tea, as per the invitation. I'd prefer wine, dark red wine, like blood, the bloodier the better."

"Willem, do you mind? There's a Bordeaux in the sideboard."

"I don't want your damn Bordeaux. I came for blood Karras…yours."

"Willem…" Lucien nods. I pour a large goblet full placing it upon the table near where Else sits. He looks at me with contempt as I take my seat, the extreme opposite his.

Else raises the glass of wine. "Since you don't have my *vintage*, salut." He raises the glass and–incredibly-drains the entire crystal in one draught.

"Impressive," Lucien says. "You know why I've invited you here, to Villa Magenta?"

"You've become lonely? Eternity *is* a very long time," he says mockingly.

"You shall never know."

"Is that actually a threat? A veiled threat from the *gentleman of gentlemen*?"

"No, rather I'm informing you of a decision."

Else rises to his feet, silently pacing the room as if in thought. He stops at my station and glares down at me like looking at an insect. "You managed to save your little neophyte. That's a cute bit of tomfoolery. How did you manage it?"

"*I* didn't," Lucien says, and the man actually hisses, expelling an odor quite unbecoming. The man's paste-like complexion nearly turns red.

"Filthy liar," he snarls. "Come now, tell me how you did it Karras. I'd be very interested in knowing. Cat got your tongue? Of course. We can't give away any secrets now, can we? *Mums the word* and all that rot!"

He glares at me. I feel his rage seeping through the air molecules that separate us; I actually hear the *man's* teeth clatter. "I don't like anyone meddling in my affairs. When I pull the trigger, you stay dead!" he shouts at me as if the words themselves could render me lifeless.

"Else, this isn't a social visit. I've come to deliver an ultimatum," Lucien interjects. The man seems incredulous.

"A what?"

"A dictate, requesting your immediate abdication."

"My *abdication*?" he echoes as if lost of understanding.

"Yes, time to go home."

Absolute silence.

"Is this some form of comedic levity Karras? Your slanted attempt at mirth?"

"Come Else, time to go," Lucien says rising from his chair, extending his hand. "It's time."

"You swarmy bastard! How dare you think yourself above me you rot! I'll deliver your hand to you, in a box!"

He lashes out with a gesture the length of his arm that I perceive as some kind of invisible energy, which Lucien brushes aside as one might wave aside a curtain. This, surprises Else I chance to notice. He then procures the pistol I *experienced* in London and fires the damnable thing several times directly into Lucien but without the slightest effect. This shocks our nocturnal guest; sweat instantly beading on his brow.

"Willem get behind me," Lucien says. I do so, expediently.

"That's very cute," Else mutters. "I should have expected it. No matter." He instantly throws the pistol at Lucien's head but again he merely waves the thing aside, sending it careening across the floor.

"I'm going to kill you Karras!" Else screams and his voice, his rage, goes through me like an icepick. However, Lucien remains unfazed, he actually welcomes his advance and Else falters, suddenly unsure of himself.

After a moment of indecision, the man commences to make a circle, counter-clockwise, with broad strokes of his arm, slowly at first then gaining momentum. He jabs at the center of the circumference with his free hand like one might thrust a sword and the circle takes on the form of a gaping orifice that spills forth a profundity of ugly writhing creatures! They instantly swarm, the creatures vaguely resembling the likes of their earthly counterparts, insects and rodents, but contorted and disease ridden. This myriad of creatures spills out into the room like roaches evacuating an old refrigerator. They scurry helter-skelter filling the room with a hideous miasma.

Within the midst of this chaos emerges the form of a great mastiff, its body covered with welts and sores, some of the pustules sporting wormlike parasites. The '*dog*' emits an unearthly howl that penetrates the core of my being.

"Willem," Lucien shouts over the clattering din of the horde, "you mustn't engage with it! It's illusion. They're only phantoms," he says before Else swallows his attention with a renewed attack. I'm left staring into the *animal's* gaping jaws, its yellow teeth dripping a viscous reddish liquid and the moment, the visage, is beyond horrific.

The demon, or whatever it is, locks its attention directly upon me and begins stalking me. I back into the adjoining room, the thing growling fiercely, gnashing its pitted teeth and a mortal dread permeates my being.

"Willem don't believe it. See through it, it's not real!" No matter how earnestly I try to absorb Lucien's words, the thing is monstrously *real* to me as it backs me against the fireplace. I topple the table near the reading nook when I extract the poker. With this in hand, I thrash at the horrid creature, smashing various things, lamps and sculpture, in my panic.

I'm nearly out of my head for the thing's eyes are languid pus-laden pools of phlegm, the odor from its gaping maw pestiferous and overwhelming. It stalks me relentlessly, always pressing me further from Lucien. Why doesn't it attack? Why this cat-and-mouse game? Is it possible it's actually powerless as Lucien said? Something inside me knows its behavior is premeditated. It is purposefully attempting to break my will, fill me to the skull with fear, and that same *something* also knows it is *fear* that will be my ultimate undoing.

However, I'm slowly succumbing to a dread, seeping through my mind like the tendrils of some viral affliction. The realization that I'm going to be psychically devoured by this horrid creature comes to a head when it backs me into a corner in the kitchen and prepares for an attack that I'm certain will go badly for me. I feel the thing sucking my life energy, the vitality of my inner will, and slowly *hope* dissolves.

Then the devil emits a howl into my face, the stench and ferocity dousing what little fire still burns. I collapse inwardly, fear consuming my reason; the end of a long arduous road. They're going to steal my soul, ending my life and I'm letting them do it. Remorse, a profound regret, permeates the moment.

The moment it attacks, a most incredible thing happens. An enormous black shadow in the form of a great wolf with eyes the color of burning coal intercedes, blocking the mastiff's advance. A horrendous fight ensues, the mystical creatures engaging in a vicious series of attacks and counter-attacks, smashing dishes and upturning furniture.

As I slowly come to my senses, I realize Monique's *shadow wolf*, the elemental that protects Villa Magenta, has stepped between the hellhound and I.

"Topey," I mutter, barely above a whisper. The great black wolf gazes at me, its glowing eyes a burning fire in an absolute night. I *feel* its thoughts. A *knowing*, floods through the liquid-fire of its unfathomable gaze before the hell-dog lunges for me. However, the wolf is too fast, too keen, and in a flash, has the larger brutish animal by the nape of its neck.

The hound rages in a fit of frenzy, the two unworldly beasts engaging in a dreadful fight smashing the table to splinters and scattering its chairs about the room. Even the appliances are uprooted from their places and nearly every dish within the room is shattered.

An incredible fight ensues, my body incapable of movement; the cupboards, even the baseboards, torn and ripped asunder. When the beasts part, the hellhound has suffered severe wounds and not blood but the same oozing pus that drains from its myriad of sores, drips from the gashes lacing its neck.

The mastiff is in a fit of uncontrolled rage. When it attempts to attack me by flanking him, Topey has its throat in a death-clench. The creature howls horribly until Topey releases his bite and the vile thing cowers back in the direction from whence it came, mortally wounded.

There is nothing left now except the shattered remains of the room, silence, and the great black *creature* with glowing eyes. It looks at me, the fire in its crimson gaze, dimmer. It has not been spared injury from such a taxing ordeal. When I reach out, the creature lets me touch it. I stroke its forehead, the *feel,* similar to touching an actual animal except the pelt is more like touching an energy field, or something with a static charge.

"Topey."

It narrows its eyes and begins to purr. I stroke its ebony coat; the sound it makes, a low throaty rumble, nearly melodic. When I run my hand over the entirety of its head, it closes its eyes like shutting the doors to a furnace. We sit this way together, this mighty *animal* in humble submission before me; a deep compassion saturates my being.

"You are conscious, aren't you? What Morgan said through the vent is true, you think and feel," I whisper. He rubs his head along my shoulder, purring loudly. I know it to be anything but mindless. I sense its intelligence; the way it has come to my aid and its superlative ability in battle.

Then, as abruptly as it appeared, it turns as if in answer to some silent calling and slips away, disappearing down the back stairs that lead to the garden; and is gone.

Returning to the parlor, the mastiff is nowhere to be seen. The plethora of horrid creatures has diminished to a trickle seeking the shadows. There is only Lucien confronting a nervous and perspiring enemy. It is plain to see Else is faltering badly, Lucien having exhausted the *man's* barrage of assaults.

"Dammit Else, quit this game. Let us be done with it. Let's move together to seek your abdication before it's too late for you."

"I'll never bow to you or your swarmy horde, to hell with you and the lot!"

"Don't you realize what's at stake Else? The very *fabric* of the man you once were. It's not too late."

"I'm above that now Karras. Your vaunted *Brotherhood?* Go to hell! I'm my own god and maker. They've no authority over me or what I choose to do. You know as fact your *God* or *Gods* are nothing more than stories, fables…written long ago by a dead people. Join *me!* Think of it. I could use a man like you Karras. We could accomplish great things amongst these primates."

"Else, you're wasting valuable time."

"Think Karras, minister…regent! You want to be president of some ignorant country? All it takes is fear, a bit of strategic lying, perhaps a murder or two, a bit of subterfuge, someone's head on the end of a pike. Divide and conquer Karras, simple dealings amongst these primitive fools. Divide and conquer my friend."

"Else…"

"They're ignorant and fearful putty Lucien, easily manipulated. They dither away in useless frivolous pursuits incapable of higher thought. You know as fact they're stupid beyond measure. You'll be rich beyond your wildest dreams I assure you. Gold? Women? Luxury? Name it…if not material riches then political intrigue and upheaval. You'll relish in it."

"*Relish* in it?"

"Wielding *power* upon this primitive, useless planet is the greatest, the grandest of games. Murder, torture, it's sheer ecstasy…these are our tools, our means to accomplishing our ends."

"And what are your ends pray tell?"

"Power, power and glory, those noble riches, ours for the taking because we can. You don't give a dog or an ape power, you take it and show them the whip, cross their backs with it when they step out of line."

"You're not talking about *power* Else, or anything noble, you're talking about misery, nothing more than misery; centuries of it."

"*Misery?* That's what you think? I'm talking about evil Lucien, true evil. *True evil* holds the power and the pleasure. Get them believing evil is some old woman bent over a pot of mushrooms and you're half way there. True evil runs this planet make no mistake about it my old friend. True evil, masked however loosely as power and riches, flaunted before them and they line up for it, clamber over each other for it, kill for it. Join me Lucien, all of it can be yours as well. Think! The ecstasy."

"Else, you know your words are hollow. To turn my back on these *ignorant savages* as you delight in calling them would be in contradiction of all I hold honorable; the collective soul of Man, the sacredness of Nature, honor and loyalty."

"*Honor and Loyalty?* Don't be a fool Karras. Do you think for one moment any of these damn apes wouldn't sell you down the river in a heartbeat, given the chance? They would sell you to the devil himself for thirty pieces of silver. Don't be foolish. Join us. Think of it Karras, the power, the riches."

"Else, you leave me no choice. I can't allow you to walk away of your own accord, not again. If you've not the sense to surrender to your higher source, then so be it," and Lucien moves upon him.

"Stay away!" Else bellows but too late, Lucien has him by the shoulders and the two men become locked together in a kind of electrical field, the air snapping and popping, crystal shattering throughout the room. I watch in horror as smoke begins to rise between them; wonder if they're slowly electrocuting themselves. Else seems in terror. I can't see Lucien's expression from behind, however, something inside me knows that this is killing him.

At that point I decide I might possibly turn the balance in favor of my friend, if I can only leverage myself accordingly. When I decide to do it, I pounce like a panther, for Else's throat. I'm going to crush his windpipe similar to the way Binford cut off my air in the garden. As my fingers make contact, the last thing I hear is Lucien shouting: "Willem don't!" and everything goes black, like turning off a light switch.

Fini

The Wicker Woman copyright 2017
by M. E. Nyberg. All rights reserved.
1st Edition

~

No part of this book either text or illustration,
may be used or reproduced in any form without
written permission from the author and publisher.

~

All names are fictitious. Any resemblance
to persons living or dead is purely coincidental.
)(

Book designed by Don Mangione

~

Cover photography by M. E. Nyberg

~

ISBN 13: 978-0-9970986-2-4
eISBN 13: 978-0-9970986-3-1

~

Library of Congress registration
Copyright #TXu 2-076-182
Nov. 16, 2017

www.menyberg.com

www.ingramcontent.com/pod-product-compliance
Lightning Source LLC
Chambersburg PA
CBHW020253200626
46816CB00001BA/275